Also by Susan Gabriel

Fiction

The Secret Sense of Wildflower
(a Kirkus Reviews Best Book of 2012)

Temple Secrets

Trueluck Summer

Grace, Grits & Ghosts: Southern Short Stories

Seeking Sara Summers

Circle of the Ancestors

Quentin & the Cave Boy

Nonfiction

Fearless Writing for Women:
Extreme Encouragement & Writing Inspiration

Available at all booksellers
in print, ebook and audio formats.

Lily's Song

Susan Gabriel

Wild Lily Arts

Lily's Song

ISBN 978-0-9835882-9-0

Wild Lily Arts

Printed in the United States of America

CHAPTER ONE

Lily McAllister

At the kitchen door, I try not to light too long or Granny will give me something to do. Granny doesn't believe in lingering. Lingering makes a soul lazy, she's told me more than once. But it turns out that lingering is what I am especially good at, and my soul doesn't feel lazy at all.

"Where's Mama?" I ask, giving her a quick hug.

"Wildflower's up at the cemetery already," Granny says. "You know how she gets on the anniversary."

Granny takes a baking sheet lined with biscuits out of the oven. My mouth waters from the yeasty smell and the sight of the golden tops. Mama says that Granny's biscuits can make a believer out of anybody. That's because if you add fresh churned butter and a healthy dollop of homemade strawberry preserves, the first words out of your mouth are *Oh, God*. Or *Oh, Lord*, depending on whether you're leaning that day toward the Father or the Son.

"Take those scraps out back for Pumpkin and the others," Granny says.

The biscuits have caused me to linger, and I've been caught doing nothing again. The plate of scraps from breakfast sits next to the sink, and I grab them to do as I'm told. The cats have already gathered, as though possessing secret knowledge that I've been asked to feed them. Pumpkin sits at the center while the others weave around him like kite tails on a windy day.

Pumpkin is a year older than me. Fifteen is old for a cat here in the Tennessee mountains. Most cats are lucky to make it past year one, given hoot owls consider them biscuits right out of the oven. Not to mention the foxes and bobcats who hunt morning and night for their next meal. Pumpkin is good at surviving and has scars to prove it. Half an ear is missing, as well as the tip of his tail, and one paw points to the right like he's hitching a ride into town.

The kite tails mew and stand on their back legs as I lower the plate. Yet they wait until Pumpkin takes the biggest piece of scrambled egg before digging in themselves, as if to show respect to their elder. At least half of the cats assembled are orange tabbies like Pumpkin. He's been a daddy and a granddaddy many times over.

As for me, I've had neither. The mountains are my kin, just as much as the people, my Great Aunt Sadie tells me. So any time I linger on a soft piece of earth, I imagine sitting on my Granddaddy McAllister's lap. I've heard stories about him my entire life. About how he knew all the names for things here in the mountains, read books and played banjo better than anybody in Katy's Ridge. He used to sing, too, and Mama says that's where I got my singing talent.

Every year on the anniversary of the saw mill accident that took his life, Mama spends the day at the cemetery. Today marks fifteen years since it happened, and I think she still misses him.

The longing I feel for a daddy goes beyond missing and is the dull pain that comes from total absence. Sometimes in the middle of the night I can feel the loss at the center of my chest, like old Pumpkin has fallen asleep there, pressing on my heart. The grief feels as old as he is.

Just this morning I dreamt about a man standing in the shadows of my bedroom watching me. I've had this dream several times in my life, and I can never see his face, but I can hear him breathing and feel his presence. When I wake, I am full of yearning. Mama refuses to tell me who my daddy is, no matter how many times I ask. I know she has her reasons for not telling me, but that doesn't make me not need to know.

"Can I take Mama a biscuit?" I ask, when I come back inside. "She'll be getting hungry about now."

"I reckon," Granny says, tucking a sigh at the end of her words. She and Mama have been tearing down and fixing the same fence their entire lives. Love resides in the center of all the mending. Of this I am certain. But I can't imagine the two of them living together without ending up looking like Pumpkin.

Granny gets a small basket from the cupboard and wraps up two biscuits with melted butter and jam already on them. They ooze their sweetness onto the worn cloth wrapped around them. Granny puts a ball jar full of water in there, too, in case our mouths get gooey.

Before I leave, Granny kisses me on the forehead and says, "Give a kiss to your mama, too."

I tell her I will.

Granny is fond of saying I'm just like Mama, and she smiles when she says it like that's just what she deserves. I'd rather hear how much I am like myself. Or how much I am like my daddy. That would be something different at least. But nobody ever mentions him and me in the same breath. Nobody mentions him at all.

I've lived in Granny's house since the day I was born, so I've had time to figure out ways to stay on Granny's good side, which doesn't have a whole lot of room. Mama says she wasn't always irritable. She says she changed after Granddaddy died. Sometimes I wish I had known her before.

The anniversary of Granddaddy McAllister's death is treated sacred like Christmas or Easter. If it falls on a weekday, I get to stay out of school so I can go to the cemetery with Mama. Then later this afternoon, all my aunts, uncles and cousins will come over for a special supper and I'll be asked to sing. Usually I sing *Down in the Valley* or *Amazing Grace*, the songs my granddaddy loved most. My family is sometimes my only audience, except for the times I sing at the small Baptist church. At this rate, I'll never reach my dreams.

The first chance I get I'm leaving Katy's Ridge. Although I'm pretty sure it would break Mama's heart if I did. In some ways, I'm all she's got. Yet a voice tells me from somewhere deep inside, I am meant for bigger things. I want to sing in each of the 48 states and then go around the world and sing in every place I've ever read about in books. Cathedrals. Palaces. Concert halls. Nobody knows my dream of becoming a world renowned singer. It is a secret I keep even from Mama.

After leaving the house, I take off down the path that leads to the road. It is 1956 and most of the roads in Katy's Ridge are now paved and a few folks even have paved driveways, but not us. Mama said we didn't have indoor plumbing until after I was born, so I won't be holding my breath for a paved driveway. Unlike me, Granny has never made a friend of change and is fine with her world staying small.

Katy's Ridge is about as small as the world can get. If it were a puppy or a kitten it would be the runt of the litter and in danger of not surviving. Most kids I know have no intention of staying in this area after they graduate high school, and many don't even keep it a secret.

Mama's old Ford truck that she drives to work every day sits at the bottom of the hill, but on the anniversary she walks to the cemetery. I run my fingers along the truck's passenger side. Although I learned to drive as soon as I was tall enough to reach the brakes, Mama says I can get my driver's license in a year to make it official. Mama's not a big stickler for rules. Never has been, to hear her tell it.

I toss a wave to the four Red Bud sisters, trees that Grand-daddy McAllister named back when Mama was a girl: Susie, Samantha, Sally and Shirley Red Bud. More than once I've wished for sisters, at least one, instead of being an only child. It would make it so much easier to leave Katy's Ridge if Mama had someone else to fret over.

After walking down the road a few hundred yards, I take the shortcut beside the old dogwood and follow the path Mama took earlier that morning to the cemetery. Because of my earlier dream, the shadows look thick enough to hide a person and the breeze through the trees sounds like breathing. To take my mind off the creepy things, I pretend I'm Judy Garland walking the yellow brick road. Except I'm actually walking a leaf-covered path that I've taken a million times. I hum *Somewhere Over the Rainbow* and take note of the blue skies, wondering if dreams really do come true.

The Wizard of Oz finally came to the movie theater in Rocky Bluff two summers ago, when I turned twelve. A movie has to be a hundred years old before it makes it to the back-woods of Tennessee. Most Saturday nights the theater runs Gene Autry films and other cowboy westerns that are as dull as old kitchen knives. The women in those pictures work in saloons and are always in need of rescuing. Mama doesn't rely on men for anything, except maybe Uncle Daniel, who keeps the books at the sawmill.

I think of Crow Sector, who I've had a crush on forever. With his black hair and blue eyes, he can ride up on his white horse and rescue me any time he wants. I'll just throw up my arm like in one of those cowboy westerns and let him pull me up in the saddle.

Meanwhile, it is mid-October here in Katy's Ridge and the tree leaves race each other to the ground. They crunch underneath my feet releasing the perfume of fall. On the path in front of me I find a perfect red maple leaf, its color bold in the afternoon sun. I put it in the front pocket of my overalls to give to Mama.

Gusts of wind race over the mountain and my long hair flies wild behind me. I never think to bring a rubber band, and I stop long enough to tuck my hair into the back of my shirt. A whirlwind of leaves dances up the hillside, gathering others to join in. It's the most playful time of year here in the mountains. The leaves and the wind have a last bit of fun before the seasons change. A hint of winter floats on the breeze, a ribbon of cold air mixed in with the warm.

At the footbridge I repeat the ritual Mama taught me when I was younger. A rabbit's foot keychain hangs from a small nail under the top railing of the bridge. I take it off and rub it between my hands before returning it to the nail. Three months ago, on my fourteenth birthday, Mama gave me a necklace that she'd had since she was a girl, a Madonna and

Child that my great grandmother gave to her. I kiss the Madonna and ask for her blessing and protection. Then I ask Granddaddy McAllister, and any angels he knows, to help with the crossing, too.

A much older bridge crossed this ravine years ago, but my uncles Daniel and Nathan built a new one the year I was born. It doesn't look so new anymore, but it's as sturdy a footbridge as you'll ever cross. At least that's what my Uncle Daniel says. This doesn't change the fact that I get an uneasy feeling every time I cross it.

At the center of the bridge, the whispers start. I tell myself it's just how the wind sounds when it blows through the trees. But it sounds more like a human voice than the wind. It's like this part of the mountain has a secret story, and it can't help saying: *Once upon a time....* I want to know the rest of the story.

Granny says I'm too curious for my own good, and I should remember what curiosity did to the cat. But this has nothing to do with a cat, I simply want to know things.

The old wood of the bridge creaks when I stop and gaze into the ravine. Goose bumps raise on my arms and the hair prickles at the back of my neck. People say when this happens that you've just walked on top of somebody's grave. I've walked on plenty of dead people in my lifetime, having visited my kinfolk in the graveyard since I was a baby. Something about this old bridge feels just like a graveyard.

Pushed by a sudden gust of wind, I grab my necklace and run the rest of the way across. The whispers call me to come back. They aren't ready for me to leave. Sometimes I wonder if Katy's Ridge will actually let me go when I finally figure out how to leave this place. It's like it has its reasons to keep me here. Reasons I don't begin to understand, but that yank at me whenever I dream of escaping.

At the backside of the cemetery, Mama sits under the biggest weeping willow tree. The sunlight dances off the green and gold almond-shaped leaves. Mama turns and waves to me. On account of her secret sense, it is impossible to sneak up on her. She pats the ground next to where Granddaddy is resting, and I join her. Mama is the one who taught me to linger.

"Granny sent biscuits right out of the oven," I say.

Mama caresses the side of my face like she always does.

I unwrap our treasure and spread out the strawberry stained napkin like it's a fancy tablecloth for our picnic. We each take a bite of biscuit. In a way, it's like we're taking Holy Communion and the biscuits are the wafers. Mama takes a bite and then looks up at the sky like she is seeing a bit of heaven.

"How's Granddaddy today?" I ask.

"He loves getting caught up on how we're all doing," she says, between bites. "I told him how well you're doing in school, and how you're just like him when it comes to reading big books."

"Did you tell him about my singing?"

"I did. I told him you're the best singer in the Cumberland Mountains."

And someday the world? I want to add. But no one in our family speaks their dreams out loud, as far as I know.

I read the sadness in Mama's eyes that visits her on anniversaries and other days throughout the year. She's even sad on my birthdays sometimes, though she is an expert at hiding it. Once we finish our biscuits, she looks out over the river as though something this beautiful requires witnessing.

"This is the prettiest spot in all of Katy's Ridge," I say, repeating one of Mama's favorite things to say.

"You know, it really is." She smiles, like she's just now noticing.

The wind kicks up and an empty paint can from recent upkeep at the church rattles through the cemetery. Mama sits up with a jolt. Something about the sound turns her eyes dark and narrow, as though she's looking through a portal into the past.

"You okay?" I ask.

She doesn't answer.

Sometimes Mama seems haunted. Haunted by something she never talks about. I wait for her return, pressing bread crumbs into my finger and eating the remains of our host. I begin to hum *Over the Rainbow* again. Sometimes I wish a cyclone would transport me to a world outside of Katy's Ridge. I click my heels together three times, wishing I was anywhere but home.

Before long, the spell Mama has fallen under is broken. She smiles at me again.

"Did I ever tell you how Daddy could make us all laugh until our stomachs hurt?" she asks.

Even though I've heard Mama's stories multiple times, I ask her to tell me again.

"Your Aunt Amy was all grumpy because she'd had a tooth pulled. Doc Lester did the pulling, which is a story I'll save for another time."

A quick grimace turns into a grin.

"Amy's mouth was full of cotton," she begins again, "and we could barely understand her when she talked. When Daddy tried to tease the bad mood out of her she said, 'addy, op it.' 'Who's Addy?' he said. 'I don't know any Addy.' Then he asked every single one of us, including your granny, who this Addy was. He wanted to talk to this Addy, he said, so Amy would feel better. Well, by the time he did that for a while, even Amy had tears in her eyes from laughing."

Mama and I laugh with the telling of the story.

"That was his nickname for Amy. He called her Addy," Mama concludes.

"And he called you Wildflower, right?" Sometimes I ask to hear the story of how she got her nickname just to see Mama's face turn bright.

"Yes, he called me Wildflower," she says. "He said I'd sprung up here in the mountains like a wild trillium, and that trilliums take your breath away if you see a patch of them. I was ten when he gave me that nickname. As you know, some people still call me that. Mostly family."

Mama gets another one of her faraway looks. Sometimes she'll visit the past and stay gone for an entire afternoon. I hope this isn't one of those times. The world gets lonely without Mama in it. Despite my plans to shed Katy's Ridge like a snakeskin, I'm not sure how I'll live without Mama.

Nobody in Katy's Ridge will talk about who my daddy was. I've been told that he died before I was born. But when I ask for his name and what he was like, people tell me to ask Mama. Then when I ask her, she says some things are better left unsaid.

My best friend Pearl thinks my daddy must have been someone Mama met in Rocky Bluff. Maybe a soldier passing through or a traveling salesman. But Mama isn't the type to take up with someone for just a day or two. She's slow to warm to strangers, although I've heard from her sisters this wasn't always the case. Maybe Granny isn't the only one who changed after Granddaddy McAllister died.

The breeze rattles the leaves on the weeping willow behind us. The branches sway over our heads. The sound reminds me of the electric fan on Mama's dresser that lulls me to sleep on hot nights. I recall the dream again from the night before and wonder if the man in the shadows is my daddy. If I were living in a fairy tale and was granted three wishes, my first wish would be to know who my daddy was. The second wish would be to understand why Mama refuses to tell me. And my third wish would be to live anywhere but Katy's Ridge.

CHAPTER TWO

Wildflower McAllister

Aunt Sadie says Lily's singing talent is repayment for the way she entered this world. She possesses a voice that can make people drop to their knees. I tend to agree that God's hand might be in on it, though God and I have barely spoken for decades now. I also wonder if Daddy might be in on it, too. It would be just like him to make sure things go well for us.

Lily lowers her head into my lap, something she doesn't do that often anymore now that she's fourteen, the age I was when I had her. Her hair is darker than mine, the color of chestnuts. Brown eyes, too, while mine are blue. At times, her features remind me of the one person I most want to forget. Not only in her height—she's taller than me—but also in the way she stands. Like she's waiting at a crossroads for something to happen.

After Daddy died, I sometimes fell asleep on his grave. My sister Jo would come looking for me. Now it is my daughter who sleeps here. Maybe we all sleep on the bones of our ancestors in one way or another. Each one of us a descendant who eventually becomes the one who came before.

I rest an arm on Lily's shoulder. I've spent fourteen years working to keep her safe. Trying not to hold on so tight that she can feel my grasp. Determined she will never go through what I went through. Determined to keep the secret of how she came into this world. Knowing, too, that the biggest secret I carry has nothing to do with her.

Seconds later, Lily startles awake and looks up at me. Her face flushes, as though caught doing something childlike. More and more I feel her distance, her letting go of me so she can grow up and grab hold of herself. Do daughters ever get fully free from our mamas? It doesn't help that I still live in my mama's house, but I could never afford to live and raise Lily on my own.

Lily sits up, pulls back her long hair and then lets it fall like the tail flick of a chestnut mare. I miss the warmth of her head against my thighs—the closeness that has become rare in the last year.

"I can't tell you how many times I've done the same thing," I say, to soften her embarrassment. "That first year after Daddy died, Mama was sending your Aunt Jo up here to get me all the time." I stare out at the river. A scene that's changed very little since those days.

Over the years, I've grown impatient with cemeteries. More and more I feel the need to have community with the living. I'm twenty-eight-years-old. Daddy was only thirty-eight when he died. Ten years older than I am now. A lump of emotion catches in my throat, the grief revisiting like an unwelcomed guest.

"We'd best head back to help your granny," I say. "Everybody's coming to supper in a couple of hours."

Lily stands first and then offers me a hand. We brush the dirt and leaves off our pants and walk back toward the back gate. At first, we walk hand-in-hand like we used to when Lily was a girl. Perhaps since this is the anniversary and nobody's looking, she is allowing me this pleasure from her childhood.

"Mama, how old were you when you had your first kiss?" she asks.

Like me as a girl, Lily asks lots of questions. Her curiosity is like her appetite; she's always hungry. I pause, wondering how to answer. For most females, the answer is clear, but does a forced kiss count?

"My first real kiss was with Victor Sweeney," I say, deciding it doesn't. "He was the brother of my best friend, Mary Jane."

"What happened to him?" Lily asks.

"Victor moved away a long time ago," I say.

"Why?"

This was Lily's primary question since the age of three, nearly driving me crazy with its repetition. Mama always thought it humorous.

What goes around, comes around, she'd say, often with a smile.

"A lot of people move away from Katy's Ridge to get better work," I answer.

In truth, this wasn't why Victor left. After Mary Jane moved to Little Rock to go to college and live with her grandmother, Victor took over running his family's store in Katy's Ridge. We had several dates back then—going into Rocky Bluff to see a movie and summer picnics at Sutter's Lake. Lily was only one-year-old. As much as I tried to convince myself that Victor would make a good father for Lily, he felt more like a brother than a potential husband.

It didn't help that people here in Katy's Ridge were slow to let me forget how Lily came into this world. Not that they said a word. It was their looks that spoke their condemnation, as if I was to blame. Victor began to lose business just by dating me. In the end, it was no surprise he closed the store and moved away. Last I heard, he's married now with three small children, and sells insurance in Memphis. How would life be different if I was the wife of an insurance salesman?

Mary Jane and I stopped being friends that summer after Lily was born. Sometimes I still miss her. Aunt Sadie says my life simply took a different road than Mary Jane's did, leaving us nothing left to do except wish each other a safe journey.

"What are you thinking about?" Lily asks, as we continue to walk.

"Victor," I say.

"You've told me about him," she says. "He's the one you swear isn't my daddy."

"Still true," I say, wishing Lily would drop it. I don't want to deal with all her questions today.

We take the path down the mountain that has grown over in places and lift our clasped hands to avoid the briars and vines that take over the trail and grab at our ankles.

"Have you ever thought of leaving Katy's Ridge?" she asks, letting go of my hand.

We stop on the path. A flicker of fear passes through me. I wonder briefly if her question about kissing was simply a warmup to this one. "I did think of leaving right after you were born," I say, surprising myself with my candor.

"Why didn't you?" she asks.

"It's a long story," I say.

"I like long stories," she says.

Lily can be relentless when searching out the truth of things.

"The McAllisters have been here since the 1840s," I say, as if this is reason enough to stay. "Besides, I run the saw mill that your granddaddy used to run. If I left, it would probably shut down."

A woman in backwoods Tennessee running a sawmill is unusual, but I needed to make money doing something. Not to mention, Mr. Blackstone—the owner of the mill—had sufficient guilt over what happened to Daddy to agree to take me on.

Lily eyes me like I'm a puzzle she's trying to solve, and it reminds me of how I used to look at Mama.

"In case you're wondering, I haven't kissed any boys yet," she tells me.

I hide my relief.

"Do you think there's something wrong with me?" she asks. "That I haven't been kissed?"

I put a hand on her shoulder, pretending I have the wisdom of Aunt Sadie.

"Lily, coming to love someone is a long, slow process. It'll happen, but you're still young."

"I'm not that young," she says, as if I've insulted her.

"Makes no sense to push the river," I say.

My own love life is more complicated than anyone can imagine, not that Lily knows a thing about it.

"Have you ever been in love?" she asks.

Her question gets me walking again, and she has to run a bit to catch up.

"My love life is none of your business, Lily McAllister."

"So you did have one at some point?" she asks, hiding a grin.

I stop long enough to point a finger at her. "Where did you learn to be so sneaky?" I say with a smile. "You're like a fox stealing eggs from Mama's hen house."

"I know you don't have anybody now," she says with conviction.

You'd be surprised, I want to say, but tighten my lips instead. *Loose lips sink ships,* Daniel likes to say, ever since he came back from World War II.

We approach the section of the path where my life changed forever. Somber now, I slow my gait. It is the anniversary of another death that feels just as real. In a way, it is the death of my childhood, or at the very least my innocence.

"It's so beautiful here," Lily says, not knowing the history of this place. She doesn't ask why we always linger here. Beauty gives us reason enough.

Over a decade ago, I planted thousands of seeds of wildflowers in this spot. Today the last of the autumn flowers are in bloom. Several river rocks tower among them like monuments built to honor past wars. Fourteen years ago, I could have easily died here. In the early spring the tiger lilies I planted remind me of the gold Mary, the vision that visited me that day.

Nobody knows what really happened here. I told parts of it to Daniel and Mama and the sheriff from Rocky Bluff who came to the house that day. I told them just enough to quiet them. My heartbeat quickens, and I take a deep breath to calm the nerves that want to come. I've done what I can to make peace with this place, and most days I'm fine. But something about today has awakened my secret sense. However, what I am to be watchful about is still unclear.

Aunt Sadie says the secret sense is the wisest part of us. It knows when something's not right and steers us clear of what's bad for us. It also guides us toward what is right, and sometimes it's hard to tell which is which. That day, fourteen years ago, I didn't listen when it told me not to go to the cemetery. But, over the years, I've become better at listening. At least I hope I have.

Opening Daddy's pocket watch, I check the time. It is nearly 3 o'clock and the sun sits atop the tallest ridge. Supper is at 4:30.

"We'd best get home," I say.

We continue walking, kicking leaves as we go. I didn't anticipate staying at the cemetery this long, or the length of Lily's nap. I didn't anticipate what happened fourteen years ago, either. A lot of what happens to us is unexpected.

"Tell me a story you've never told me before," Lily says. "Like if you could only tell me one more story in my entire life, what would it be?"

"It would be about the gold Mary," I say, before I have time to talk myself out of it.

"The gold Mary?" she repeats.

I pause, wondering what compelled me to talk about this now. But it is a good story. At least it is if I leave all the bad parts out.

"I saw her right about here," I begin. "The sun had already dropped low behind the mountain and it was getting dark."

A shiver comes, and I shake it away like a chill. I leave out why she came to me. Details I hope Lily never knows.

"She was like a vision except she seemed real as anything," I continue. "Just like you and me. But I could see through her to the trees behind."

Lily is as quiet as I've ever known her. The fallen leaves are so dry under our feet they sound like short bouts of applause.

"Do you think the gold Mary has anything to do with the whispers?" Lily asks.

"The whispers?"

"You know, the whispers that happen at the footbridge."

I stop and look at her. "I don't hear whispers when I cross the footbridge."

"You don't?"

Lily looks surprised. I am about to ask her more questions when she insists that I continue the story. She promises to tell me about the whispers another time.

"When did you see the gold Mary? Was it on the anniversary?" She looks around as if hopeful we might see her again.

"Yes it was," I say, "and Daddy was with her. He had died the year before. He seemed real, too. I remember thinking at the time that he had brought the gold Mary to me."

Her eyes widen. "How come you've never told me about this?" she asks, all serious.

I wonder why she hasn't told me about the whispers.

"I haven't told anyone about her," I say. "Only you."

Despite her seriousness, she looks pleased.

"But why did the gold Mary come to you? What happened?"

I tell her I don't know, all the while hoping a lightning bolt doesn't get tossed at me for the lie I just told. I'm not sure why I am telling Lily about the gold Mary at all, except that whenever we pass this place I think of her.

Lily stares at the gold medallion around her neck that I gave her for her last birthday, as if all of a sudden realizing its meaning.

"I only saw her that once, but what's strange is I have moments when I miss her terribly," I begin again. "Plenty of times I've wondered if I just imagined her."

Lily's gaze shifts from the necklace to me. I didn't plan to tell Lily this much, and wonder if I've overdone it.

"I wish you'd just tell me who my daddy is," Lily says, as if taking advantage of a small opening. "I don't understand why it has to be such a big secret."

My attention darts down the path like an animal looking for a place to hide. I do not deny my daughter anything, except this.

"Just tell me, Mama. I don't understand why you won't."

I know she deserves to know, but as many times as I've thought of different ways to tell her, I never have the courage to say the words. What if she blames me for what happened?

"Lily, I can't do this right now." I feel more sad than angry. The anniversary always weakens me.

The McAllister women are known for being strong. Sometimes, too strong. Strong enough to scare away tears that are better off shed. My face warms with a familiar shame. Does Lily not see the way the old women at the church look at me? Or how they look at her when they think nobody else is watching? In those moments, my sisters literally surround Lily, to protect her from the judgment. Christians can be some of the worst people there are for judgment.

Why can't I just tell her? I ask myself.

Aunt Sadie and I have talked numerous times about this. But the truth always lodges in my throat, making me mute. If I tell Lily, she will never see herself the same way again. I can't risk that.

We continue walking, this time faster. Anger sweeps down the mountain with the shame. Lily offers an apology, as if she knows she's caused me to flee.

"Why can't you leave well enough alone?" I ask, although I know if our positions were reversed I'd be asking the same questions.

The only sound is the thundering water in the deepest part of the ravine.

"I have no one to visit in the cemetery, Mama," Lily begins, her words soft. "You've told me he's dead, but I don't know where he's buried. I don't even know how he died. Can you at least tell me that much?"

"Not now, Lily," I say. "Not now."

Chased by the past, I approach the footbridge. Fourteen years ago today, I was too injured to cross this bridge. Today, I barely slow down and walk straight across without doing any of the rituals I've practiced since I was a girl.

Without meaning to, I have fallen into the depths of my history. The history that lies at the bottom of the ravine. I think of Lily hearing whispers here and wonder if she's inherited an aspect of the secret sense after all.

A nagging from somewhere deep inside informs me that this story isn't over yet, and that what's coming may be just as dangerous as what came before.

CHAPTER THREE

Lily

The rest of the way home, Mama is quiet, as though carrying something weighty up the hill to our house. I wonder if Mama's secrets are heavy like a ten-pound bag of flour or sugar that make your arms ache. I'm glad she told me about the gold Mary, though. It makes me not feel so strange about the whispers that seemed louder than ever as we crossed the footbridge.

Mama and I go into the kitchen where Granny is basting a chicken in the oven. She's made cornbread stuffing, too, like she does at Thanksgiving. Green beans cook on the top of the stove, and I give them a stir anticipating what will be asked of me. A piece of lard the size of a hen's egg bubbles on the top with the beans. Baked sweet potatoes, their skins puckered and dark, rest in between the stove eyes to keep them warm. The smells make my mouth water.

Mama tells me to go ahead and set the table, and Granny hands me her grandmother's tablecloth from the top shelf of the cabinet. Brought over from the old country by Granny, this tablecloth marks every special occasion that involves a meal, and she has promised to pass it on to me after she dies. Will this change when I move away?

"How is he?" Granny asks Mama, and I know she's talking about Granddaddy.

"He sends his regards," Mama says.

Granny scoffs at Mama's silliness, but her eyes get misty.

"Be sure and use the good dishes," Granny tells me, and grins from behind the mist. There are no 'good' dishes, only the dishes we use every day. The extra leaf is already in the table and the smaller card table is set up in the living room just like on other holidays that have a big meal that go with them. While the younger cousins are doomed to sit in the living room, the grownups gather around the big kitchen table.

Since I turned fourteen last summer, this is my first time at the grownups table.

With anticipation, I set ten places in the kitchen and five at the card table, all the while imagining the secrets I might hear while in the company of adults. Maybe Mama or one of the others will let a clue slip about the mystery I am intent on solving.

"Stop daydreaming," Granny tells me, giving a soft nudge with her elbow. "This meal won't get on the table by itself."

"Yes, Granny," I say and lower my eyes to show my remorse. Granny loves repentance as much as Preacher Evans.

"You and your mama are the most daydreaming bunch I've ever seen," Granny says, more to herself than to me.

Mama gives Granny a look that says *go easy on her.* She is protective, even when I don't want her to be.

"Lily, you need to change your clothes to get ready," she says.

"Why do we have to get dressed up for a meal in the kitchen?" I ask.

Mama answers with a look she inherited from Granny.

In the bedroom Mama and I share, I change into a skirt and blouse and shine my saddle shoes with spit and a tissue. With the help of the mirror over the dresser, I run a quick brush through my hair and gather it in a rubber band.

A rap at the window causes me to jump, and my best friend Pearl laughs at me through the glass. Pearl is part Cherokee and part white, which makes her a shade or two darker than me. She motions for me to come outside. When I do, Pearl is all grins and giggles, to the point that it's irritating.

"What is it?" I ask. "We're about to have supper."

"Crow's home," she says.

"Crow?" My knees hint at weakness until I pull myself tall again. Crow looks like Elvis Presley, who is new to the radio this year. My Aunt Meg showed me Elvis' picture in one of her movie magazines. Crow is four years older than me and has been away for a solid year, stationed in Korea with the

Army. It took me a long time to find Korea on the map. The war ended three years ago, but they still have troops there to keep the peace.

Pearl is all grins again. "Mama wants to know if you can have supper at our house."

Pearl's mama, June Sector, is one of my mama's best friends. She gets messages from dead people, and I've been after her for years to get a message to my daddy that I want him to contact me. But June says it doesn't always work out the way we hope. I wonder if anything works out the way we want it to.

"What's wrong with you?" Pearl asks. "Your face just went all white."

"I'm getting that feeling again, Pearl, like I'm a mermaid living in a tiny pond. I want to swim in bigger seas."

"What brought this on?" she asks.

"It's the anniversary, remember?" I say to Pearl. "That's why I wasn't at school today."

Pearl goes from goofy grin to frown in record time.

"How long is your brother staying?" I ask.

"Just through the weekend," Pearl says. "Then he gets shipped back to Korea."

"Ask your mama if I can come tomorrow instead," I say. "Or any night except this one. Mama would never forgive me if I missed the anniversary."

"Are you going to come back every year, even after we move away?" she whispers.

"If people are still talking to me," I whisper back. "That's a secret, remember?"

Pearl slouches. Everybody in Katy's Ridge knows she can't keep a secret to save her life. Perhaps I was foolish to confide in her how much I want to leave.

Neither of us has ever traveled any further than Rocky Bluff. In our fantasies, I marry Crow so Pearl can be an aunt to all the kids Crow and I have. Since I am an only child, I want bunches of babies, at least four, maybe seven. But what Pearl doesn't know is that I also want to travel the world singing, so I'm not sure how that will work if I have babies hanging all over me.

"Tell Crow I said 'hello,' okay? Tell him I'll come visit as soon as I can."

She agrees and we say our goodbyes. When I go back into the kitchen it's time to crimp the edges of Granny's apple pie that's about to go into the oven now that the chicken is out.

"Where you been?" Granny asks, wiping the sweat from her forehead with a dishtowel. She gives me a look like she's caught me lingering again.

"Pearl came over," I say.

With the oven on and all the burners going, the kitchen feels like a summer heat wave. We're lucky that it's still warm enough to keep the house open to let the heat disperse. But that will change soon enough.

Mama comes in from outside with a worried look.

"You okay?" I ask.

"Why does everybody keep asking me that?" She sounds irritated.

"Because you've got that pale look you get when you're about to get sick," Granny says to Mama.

"I feel fine," she says. "Maybe it's just my secret sense."

Granny gives Mama a look that says, *don't start with that nonsense.*

Minutes later, I hear my cousins racing up the hill to see who can touch the porch first and go outside to see who wins. If I'm racing, I usually win. Otherwise, it's a tie between Bolt and Danny. Bolt is Jo and Daniel's oldest son and Danny is the youngest. They are a year apart but look almost like twins. Bolt's real name is Joseph, after Granddaddy. He got the nickname when he was four years old and swallowed a small tractor bolt. Luckily, it didn't cause any damage. Bolt is a few months older than me. He sat at the grownups table for the first time last Easter and has rubbed it in for months.

Aunt Amy and Uncle Nathan's kids come in third and fourth. Lizzy, ten, is a total brat and Nat, twelve, is the opposite. They're wearing new outfits that Aunt Amy sewed for them. Aunt Amy owns a seamstress shop in Rocky Bluff where she makes dresses and also does alterations. Out front she also sells threads and fabrics. Uncle Nathan died in World War II. A photograph of him hangs on the living room wall. He is in uniform and has a hand on his hip like he's hitching up his pants. Another photograph sits on Mama's bureau of him holding me as a baby.

Uncle Daniel comes into view walking with his usual limp. He was in the same Army troop as Nathan and got injured in the same battle that cost Uncle Nathan his life. Aunt Jo and Aunt Amy walk next to him carrying casserole dishes propped on thick potholders. When she gets to the yard, my cousin Lizzy snarls at me like she's already bored and it's my fault. I have to resist pulling one of her pigtails.

"I'm starving," she says, as though she might swoon on the spot.

"Ask Granny for something," I say.

Lizzy runs into the house.

"Thanks for getting rid of her," Nat says.

"Anytime," I say, and we exchange a grin. Nat and I have spent entire summers making it a sport to avoid Lizzy.

A copy of *Robinson Crusoe* is tucked under his arm. Mama says Nat prefers books to people, and it's true that he spends most of his time reading. But I think it's because he doesn't have a daddy, either. It does something to a person.

"Aunt Meg called Mama and said that she and Cecil are running late," Nat says.

With all the *Mama's* in the house at the same time, it can get confusing. At more than one family get-together, I've yelled 'Mama?' and had four women answer back.

Uncle Daniel greets me in the front yard with a hug. After he looks around to make sure nobody is looking, he passes me a roll of cherry Lifesavers like we're passing secrets to the allies. I know he does this with all the cousins, pretending each of us is his favorite, but I play along.

"Where's your mama?" he asks.

"In the kitchen with Granny," I say.

It takes effort for Uncle Daniel to get up the porch steps on account of the shrapnel that's still in his leg. He never complains, though. The cane he uses has the etchings of an oak tree on the side. He's the best whittler in Katy's Ridge.

Mama must hear him coming because she opens the screen door for him to enter.

"Good to see you, Wildflower," he says to Mama.

"Are you ever going to stop calling me that?" she asks, but she smiles at him like she counts on him not to forget.

"Can I get your help inside?" Mama says to me. "Granny wants you to put everything into serving bowls," she says. "She trusts you with her food more than me."

When I come into the kitchen, Granny tosses me her spare apron. Without saying a word, she hands me several large bowls. I know what to do. It is no secret that Mama never learned to cook. She swears good cooks skip generations in a family. She can make oatmeal and toast and that's about it. Granny has taught me everything she knows, even how to make a meringue for her lemon pies. I get busy, trying not to think of how much I'll miss these gatherings once I become a world-renowned singer.

A baked chicken fits onto her white platter that has a chip on one of the handles. I carry it to the table, surprised by how heavy it is. I place the chicken at the center of the lace table-cloth. Green beans fill the second smaller bowl, and Granny's cornbread dressing fills the third. I take the bowl of churned butter from the refrigerator and put it next to a plate of plain cornbread. Aunt Jo places her sweet potato pudding on the table, too, and Aunt Amy's macaroni and cheese.

Upon seeing the spread, my dreams of leaving Katy's Ridge dim. The kitchen hums with the voices of my family as they gather at their places. When I think of living someplace different, I can't imagine what it will be like without my family around. At moments like this, it's as though Katy's Ridge pulls me back just as I'm about to get away.

Sweat dots Daniel's brow, as well as Bolt's. So far, the adult table isn't that much different from the kids, except the adult table is hotter. But maybe all those family secrets will come to a boil, and the truth will burst open.

My cousin Lizzy weaves in and out of the adults, picking up bits of macaroni and cheese with her fingers. Aunt Amy tells her to stop, but Lizzy never listens. We'd be eating already if we weren't waiting for Aunt Meg and Uncle Cecil to arrive. As if on cue, the screen door slams announcing their arrival, and they make their way through the house full of apologies. Uncle Cecil's daughter, Janie, age 10—a whisper of a girl—skulks at their heels.

Aunt Meg used to ride to Rocky Bluff with Uncle Cecil when she worked at the Woolworths, a job she quit after they got married last year. Now she stays home and takes care of Janie who is Uncle Cecil's child by his first wife. She died ten years ago giving birth to Janie at the small hospital in Rocky Bluff. Janie almost didn't make it either, on account of she didn't breathe right away after she was born, so she always looks like she's gasping for air.

Pearl says Janie's not the sharpest crayon in the box. Truth is, if she were a crayon—sharp or not—she'd probably be the color beige. Aunt Amy makes Janie colorful clothes so people won't notice how bland she is, but it's hard to miss.

Uncle Cecil has the opposite problem. A strawberry birthmark takes up the entire right side of his face. A birthmark I've spent a great deal of time trying not to stare at. Shaped like a map of Russia, the birthmark has a mole right where Moscow would be.

Until Aunt Meg and Uncle Cecil got married, she was the oldest old maid in Katy's Ridge. Now it's Miss Blackstone who teaches at the school. Mama would be next in line for old maid status, but I'm not sure it counts if you've never been married but have a daughter. There may be another name for that.

The back door is open, as well as the window, to help the kitchen cool down. Pumpkin and two of his offspring look in through the screen door, as though plotting a way to overtake the chicken platter while nobody's looking. Granny calls for everyone to take their seats. My feelings act like a yo-yo going around the world. One second I'm ready to leave, the next I'm ready to stay. It's no wonder I feel a little nauseous.

Great Aunt Sadie comes in from the back porch and puts a hand on my shoulder and kisses me on the cheek. Her eyes are gray/blue and her white hair is pulled up in a bun on the top of her head. When she smiles it looks like her wrinkles smile, too. Great Aunt Sadie attends all family functions, but she also keeps to herself more and more these days. A fact that worries Mama.

"You set a beautiful table," she tells me, leaning in so I can hear over everybody talking. "You're going to join us at the big table, right?"

I tell her I'm looking forward to it.

"It's a rite of passage in the McAllister family," she says, squeezing my shoulder like she's proud of me. "After today, you will never again be exiled to the living room."

She touches a finger to the tip of my nose like she did when I was younger, and then embraces Mama before sitting at the table. I wonder which spot will be mine until Mama pats the chair next to hers. I sit between her and Great Aunt Sadie, with Uncle Daniel on the other side of Mama, then Aunt Jo, Bolt, Aunt Amy, Uncle Cecil and Aunt Meg. Bolt looks over and gives me a wink, as though to welcome me to the grownup table. I'm not sure what we'll do when the other kids get old enough to join us because we already sit elbow to elbow. I imagine it may be good that I plan to leave Katy's Ridge after all.

Lizzy's obnoxiousness can be heard from the next room, the others complaining that she's drinking out of their cups. I imagine my other cousin, Janie, blending in with the beige walls, and Danny and Nat talking about cars. I sit straighter with the knowledge that the kids' table isn't where I belong anymore. This is my next step to being free.

Mama wears pants and a flowered blouse, the closest she gets to dressing up. She glances at Granddaddy's watch like she has somewhere to go, and I wonder if she and Miss Blackstone have a Scrabble game planned for later.

When Granny takes off her apron and sits at the table, the room grows quiet enough for pins to drop while angels dance on the heads. But it is Mama who speaks instead of Granny.

"We're here to remember Daddy today," Mama says, a slight quiver in her voice. "We need to remember Nathan, too, who we lost in the war. These were two great men who we sorely miss."

Aunt Amy's lips tighten with the emotion she rarely shows.

Nobody in our family is real big on feelings, except maybe Great Aunt Sadie. Granny will tell anyone who'll listen, that feelings should be saved for death beds, so it isn't surprising when she announces that the food is getting cold.

We've come to expect Granny's interruptions, and everyone laughs.

Uncle Daniel says a quick grace before passing the green beans. My aunts fill plates for the younger kids and take them into the living room before filling their own. Meanwhile, a flurry of serving dishes are passed at the big table and plates are filled. I wait to feel different, yet it's like everything has changed and nothing at all.

"So what's it like to sit at the grownups' table?" Aunt Jo asks, passing me the gravy.

When I look at her, I realize again how beautiful my Aunt Jo is. She's as pretty as Sandra Dee, who appears in the Hollywood magazines, and is about the same age.

Several people turn to look, expecting me to say something thoughtful. Instead, I shrug, something Mama has asked me to never do again.

Everyone eats. Uncle Daniel and Bolt fill their plates twice, while Mama and Uncle Daniel talk about the mill. At the same time, Granny complains to no one in particular about the price of electricity and that it is President Eisenhower's fault. Every now and again I hear talking and laughing from the kids' table and wonder if being a grownup isn't all it's cracked up to be.

Every now and again, Mama squeezes my hand to let me know she hasn't forgotten me, but mainly I am left to my own thoughts. Thoughts that even when I'm full of good food, challenge me about where I fit in the world. My last name is

McAllister, just like my Mama's. She didn't take my daddy's name, which means they weren't married. In the third grade, Davy Jenkins called me a *bastard*. I didn't even know what it meant back then, but I do now.

My father's side of the family is totally unknown. I wonder what it would be like to have supper with them, but it's like a blank slate in my imagination. My insides feel jumpy. Is this the secret sense Mama keeps talking about? Until now, I thought that skipped generations like cooking talents.

Bolt looks at me. He knows I am quieter than usual. In the past, at the kids' table, I challenged Lizzy to count her green beans as she ate them, or umpired Nat and Danny's thumb-wrestling contests, or tried to get Janie to say even a few words. For years, I thought I must be missing the best part of family gatherings by being stuck in the living room. I never dreamed that sitting at the grownups' table was more than a little boring. No secrets. No confessions. No big deal.

Why do I always I crave a bigger life than the one I have? I wonder.

Pearl and I have spent entire afternoons imagining glamorous lives where we live in big cities, far away from tiny Katy's Ridge. Cities where we go to parties and I sing while she works at a swanky job.

Near the end of the meal, Mama rests her hand on mine. "You're awfully quiet," she says. The worry from earlier hasn't left her. "Something you want to tell me?"

I shrug again, and then try to erase it, but it's hard to take back a shrug. How do I tell her that every day I wish I was anywhere but here?

"Please answer with words, Lily," she says.

"She doesn't have to tell you everything," Granny says to Mama. For someone who is hard of hearing, she often chimes in like she's heard every word. "Lily, why don't you get the apple pie ready," Granny adds.

Mama gives me a look that says *we'll talk later.*

When I fetch the pie, Pumpkin stretches against the back screen door as though to remind me he's waiting for his special holiday scraps. His old claws get stuck in the screen, and I hope Granny doesn't see him or he'll get a swift slap with her broom. Two pies sit on the kitchen counter. I slice enough pieces so that everyone has a slice, and then pass them around. Once everybody has dessert, the room gets quiet again except for the occasional noise of pure satisfaction. It occurs to me that the world could avoid wars if there was enough pie to go around.

Meanwhile, discomfort is wedged in my stomach that is either indigestion or my fledgling secret sense. Great Aunt Sadie looks at me, as though picking up on the message I'm receiving. She sends a message to Mama with her eyes, like we're all hooked up to the same telephone party-line. Until now, it never occurred to me that we could have an entire conversation using only our eyes.

Nothing ever happens in Katy's Ridge. Especially nothing big. Yet something is up. Something that has the smell of secrets all around it. Something that could change everything.

CHAPTER FOUR

Wildflower

After supper, our family congregates on the front porch. With the sun behind the ridge, it is chillier, but still warm enough to wear only a sweater. Lily sits on the porch swing between me and Aunt Sadie. She acted strange all through supper. It was Aunt Sadie who tapped my shoe under the table and drew my attention to it. Sometimes I'm so close to Lily, I don't realize the subtle things. But Aunt Sadie does. She knows whenever something big is going on with Lily and when Lily's thoughts are playing out like a thunderstorm behind her eyes.

A long time ago I learned not to ignore my secret sense. I check the sky to see if a storm is moving in, but there are no clouds in sight. I want to believe this premonition is nothing. Yet something has been pestering me all afternoon.

Behind us, Bolt, Danny and Lizzy toss a ball against the side of the house and take turns catching it while Janie looks on. Poor Janie. I want to pull her up onto my lap and make up for the first ten years of her life when she didn't have a mama.

On the other end of the porch, my nephew Nat sits reading a book. Does he suffer from similar losses? I think of his father, Nathan, all the time. About how he won over Mama early on, about how he helped us track down Johnny that day and how he made Amy much happier than she is now and more agreeable. Grief does surprising things to people. It breaks us down and makes us stronger, sometimes all at once. I've seen it in Mama, too.

"Will you sing us something?" I ask Lily.

If anything can be a healing salve it is Lily's singing. Even Mama calls her a natural. I imagine her musical talent comes from Daddy, the only other musician in the McAllister family. Daniel claps to encourage her, and the others tell her how nice it would be to hear a tune. No family gathering takes place these days without Lily singing a song.

"Sing Amazing Grace," Jo says. "It was Daddy's favorite. He'd love that."

Lily agrees and her mood appears to lighten. She stands and leans against the porch rail facing the house. It is a small stage. Too small. I can't help thinking she is destined for bigger things. Not that I've ever said this out loud.

Lily closes her eyes like she's gathering the song in her memory. She hums the tune first to warm her voice, like Daddy used to do before he sang. I've always wondered how she knew to do that. I like to think it's a part of him coming through her.

Amazing Grace, how sweet the sound, she begins. The words are soft at first, but then build.

Every time Lily sings, a lump of thankfulness catches in my throat. How can the ugliest moment of my life result in something so beautiful and pure? People say Lily's voice is as good as Kate Smith's, who sings *God Bless America* on the radio. Preacher used to say that pride comes before a fall. But there's nothing wrong with this kind of pride. The pride that comes from hearing something beautiful and being proud of humanity.

My sisters, brothers-in-law, nieces and nephews, are spellbound, as are Mama and Aunt Sadie. Whenever Lily sings everyone goes quiet, like they're walking around inside a church. She goes on to another verse and then another. The melody soars and my chest expands. For nine months she lived inside of me, and even though she's her own person now, her songs will be stored forever in my heart.

Earlier that day, Lily asked the one question I never know how to answer. Someday soon I will have to tell her the truth. It's amazing she hasn't found out already, given the *loose lips* in these parts. But at the same time, mountain people will keep a secret forever if their own shame is attached to it somehow. Everybody knew Johnny was trouble. Everybody. Yet nobody did anything. Guilt has kept that secret sealed, as surely as if it were in a bank vault.

Oddly enough, as we were walking home, Lily asked if I'd ever felt like moving away. Earlier today, at the cemetery, I was thinking about that very thing. I wondered if a place existed where I could go and totally be myself without anyone judging me. If so, I'd be tempted to pack all our bags this evening. However, I doubt such a place exists.

After Lily finishes her song, everyone stays quiet for several seconds like the song is somehow healing all the lonely places inside each of us. Finally, Daniel and the boys begin to whistle and all of us clap.

"Daddy would have loved that," I say, giving Lily a hug.

"You should sing on the radio," Jo says, and everyone agrees.

Lily's face colors and she lowers her head. Whenever she sings at church, all of us come to hear her—even me—even though it's a guarantee that Preacher will sermonize about heathens turning their back on the Lord. But, as far as I'm concerned, it was the Lord and the Church who turned their backs on me.

Moments after finishing her song, Lily sits on the porch steps while Aunt Sadie and I claim the porch swing again. The others talk. Yet I am not hearing most of it and rub the center of my chest.

"What is it?" Aunt Sadie asks.

"Do you remember those dreams I had after Lily was born?"

"They were more like nightmares," she says. "You were terrified for days afterward."

In the dreams, Lily fell down a ravine and died crashing against the rocks like Johnny did. Sometimes, I'd wake up screaming. But I haven't had them for years. Not since she was an infant.

We are all protective of Lily. Me. Aunt Sadie. Mama. Daniel. My sisters, too, but not as much, now that they have their own broods to watch out for.

"Are you having a premonition?" Aunt Sadie asks.

According to her, premonitions are just a fancy name for the secret sense. Along the same lines, June says I can foretell the future as good as she can if I take the time to pay attention.

"It may be nothing," I say.

Mama comes out of the house, her apron finally off for the day. She looks impatient with me, even though I haven't said a word to her.

"What are you brooding about now?" she asks me.

My irritation flares. The look we exchange has our history in it. A history neither of us has forgotten. Fourteen years ago, Mama and I made our amends in Daniel and Jo's barn. It was the closest I ever felt to her. Even though I know she would walk into a burning house to rescue me, as I would her, that doesn't mean we're close. If she had to choose, I still think she would rather have Daddy sitting here on the porch than me. It probably doesn't help that I've always looked like him, especially as I've aged. I sit before her, a constant reminder of what she's lost.

"Have a seat, Nell," Aunt Sadie says. "You're just ornery because you're tired."

Mama sits in the rocker reserved for her. I wish I didn't take her moods so personally. In the next second my secret sense twists my gut. I turn to Aunt Sadie, finally clear on what it's telling me.

"A stranger is coming," I whisper.

"A stranger?" Aunt Sadie turns to look down the path that leads to the house, as if someone might appear at any moment.

I think of all the hours I've sat on this front porch, looking down this hill waiting on Daddy to come home, and he never did.

"Whatever it is, we'll get through it," Aunt Sadie says to me.

Daniel turns away from Cecil and looks at me as if he might be needed. I smile so he'll think everything is fine. He sits in the rocker on the other side of the door, a toothpick stuck between his lips. His leg must be bothering him because he winces as he helps it bend. Bolt runs to the porch steps to ask if Daniel wants to shoot basketballs into the wooden hoop nailed into one of the oak trees by the house. Daniel declines. The valley on his forehead deepens, like he's thinking a father should play ball with his sons.

Lizzy yells for Bolt to return, but it sounds more like a whine. Amy has confided in me that she can't wait until Lizzy outgrows her childishness, but I'm not so sure she will. Meanwhile, Jo looks through a McCall's magazine, while Lily and Nat talk about books and Meg goes inside and brings out the transistor radio from the kitchen and sets it on the porch rail. She turns the knob to tune in the one station we can get here in the mountains that comes in from Nashville. Jim Reeves is singing his latest hit. From the look of things, it is a normal afternoon in the life of the McAllister family, but something doesn't feel normal about it at all.

A hint of winter blows in from the west, and I pull my sweater closer. Before long, we'll gather around the wood stove in the living room instead of the front porch. If a stranger is coming, they'd best arrive soon. Winter is a difficult time here. It's hard to imagine someone new coming to Katy's Ridge at any time of year. It's not the type of place that collects newcomers.

My secret sense vibrates at the center of my chest and causes me to stand. I look down the hill with anticipation. A woman wearing a white dress approaches. A white purse hangs over one arm and she has a red ribbon in her hair. Something about her seems familiar. As she gets closer I can see that her hair needs a good washing and her dress is faded and worn. The pattern on it is almost completely washed off.

When I finally recognize who she is, I gasp. I don't want the woman to come any closer. She is pale like a ghost, an apparition from the graveyard of my past. My bottom lip quivers like it knows something the rest of me doesn't. Lily looks at me, her expression alive with another of her unending questions.

The woman stops a few feet away from the porch.

"Can we help you?" I say. I search the past for the name of someone I haven't thought about for over a decade.

"Oh my heavens," Aunt Sadie says softly, before covering her mouth.

Mud is caked around the woman's white shoes like she's traipsed through every mud hole in Katy's Ridge to get here. She presses the stub of her cigarette into the soil with her dirty shoe. I step to the end of the porch, telling Lily to stay where she is. The woman looks at me like she's daring me to recognize her. The look in her eyes makes me shiver. A deep sadness has made a home there.

"Wildflower, do you remember me?" the woman asks.

It is odd to hear a stranger call me Wildflower. A name only used by close family when I was a girl. Most people call me Louisa May now, except for Daniel, and occasionally Mama, and my best friend, Bee Blackstone, who calls me Lou.

The surprise has turned me into one of the icicles that clings to the rocks behind our house in winter. I am frozen. Lily stands next to me. Is she being protective or just curious? Nobody else moves, except for Amy who nibbles on her fingernails. Even Daniel appears at a loss as to what to do next.

"Who is this, Mama?" Lily whispers. She takes my sweaty palm.

I'm not sure how to answer.

"I'm Melody Monroe," the stranger says. "I used to live here in Katy's Ridge. You may remember my brother, Johnny."

Melody Monroe trains her eyes on Lily, taking a long look. It reminds me of how her brother used to look at me when I walked down the road toward school or to the cemetery or to see Mary Jane. My heartbeat accelerates and a memory chases after me. I am running from the cemetery down the mountain path to get away from Johnny, my arms pumping wild. For years I've run away from these memories. Now a ghost of that long ago terror stands in our front yard.

CHAPTER FIVE

Lily

Great Aunt Sadie steps to the other side of Mama like we're all about to sing the hymn *A Mighty Fortress is Our God.* We are all steeped in hymns, even though none of us attend church anymore unless I'm singing. The last time we attended, Mama swore if she heard Preacher Evans say *Repent* one more time, while looking straight at her, she'd throw up her morning oatmeal on his suit. Even Granny misses most Sundays and has taken to saying her prayers on the back porch while she peels potatoes into a bucket.

"Can we help you with something?" Great Aunt Sadie asks the stranger.

"What's going on?" I ask. The look on Mama's face is one I've never seen before.

Uncle Daniel stands now, his bad leg collapsing until he rights himself again. My family has been turned into pillars of salt like Lot's wife when she looked back on Sodom, a story I heard in a rare trip to Sunday School.

I ask the question again, this time louder. Bolt, Danny and Lizzy have stopped playing ball and have turned into statues, too.

"Are you going to tell her, or am I?" the stranger says to Mama.

Mama snaps awake, as if a mountain lion has come down from the higher mountains and is threatening us.

"You're not welcome here. Go back where you came from." She points down the hill toward the road.

The woman doesn't move. "I'm only here for a visit," she says.

Whoever this woman is, she isn't welcome. My family is usually friendly to strangers. But not this one. Mama squeezes sweat into my palm again, and Great Aunt Sadie places a heavy hand on my shoulder as though I might get kidnapped.

In the westerns I've seen at the Rocky Bluff Theater, there's always a standoff between the good guys and the bad guys. If this were one of those movies, Mama would be in the role of Gene Autry, and the villain in this scene would be a woman who needs to clean her shoes.

Granny is the first family statue to come alive. She gets up from her rocker and walks into the house letting the screen door slam behind her. A few seconds later she returns with the shotgun she keeps next to the back door to scare away the foxes and bobcats from her hen house. Evidently this stranger is someone she sees as a threat.

"You've been asked to leave," Granny says. She raises the shotgun and points it straight at the woman.

I gasp. Mama taught me to never point a shotgun at a person or an animal unless I intend to kill them.

The woman lowers her head and takes two steps back, holding up an arm to prevent Granny from coming any closer.

All the McAllisters know how to load and shoot a shotgun, even me. Mama taught me around the same time I learned to drive the truck.

"No need to get upset, Mrs. McAllister."

"Why are you here?" Great Aunt Sadie asks.

"I'm only back for a visit," the stranger says. "We've still got land here."

"What's your real reason for being here?" Mama asks.

The woman hesitates and glances at me.

"I've been hearing things, and I wanted to check it out for myself," the woman says. She doesn't take her eyes from me.

"Hearing things?" Mama asks. "Like what?"

"Maybe now's not the proper time," the stranger says, glancing over at Granny who hasn't moved.

Uncle Daniel steps to the porch rail. "Whatever you're peddling, we're not interested," he says.

She offers Daniel a slight smile, as though recognizing him.

"I don't want any trouble, Mister Daniel," she says. "The only thing I'm peddling is the truth."

I doubt Aunt Amy has a fingernail left, and I've never seen Aunt Meg's eyes so big. Not even when she's telling a big piece of juicy gossip. Aunt Jo is now in the yard with the kids making sure none of them get any closer.

"Like I said," Uncle Daniel begins again. "We're not interested."

"Somebody, please tell me what's going on?" I say. This time I practically shout. If there's anything I hate, it's being the last to know something.

For the first time since the stranger arrived, Mama looks over at me. "It's something that happened before you were born," she says, as if this should be enough for me to drop it.

"What is it? What happened?" I ask.

My questions are met with silence.

"Y'all are acting like a bunch of cowards," I say, my frustration growing.

Mama shoots me a look that isn't the least bit cowardly.

From behind me the shotgun cocks. I can't believe the stranger is still within a mile of here. If Granny had a gun aimed at me, I'd be halfway to Rocky Bluff by now.

"If you want to talk, I'm staying at my family's place until Friday," she says directly to me.

"Why would I want to talk?" I ask, confused that she has spoken to me.

"'Cause it looks like you're not getting any answers from your family." Her lips form a straight line and nearly disappear.

Granny cocks the other barrel, and the stranger announces she's leaving. With a swift turn she walks down the hill, kicking up dirt and pebbles on the path. After she passes the Red Bud sisters, the stranger disappears out of sight. Everyone on the porch exhales at once and the statues come alive. Chatter begins.

"Are you all right?" I ask Mama. Her face is pale and her hands are trembling.

"I've been better." She offers a faint smile.

Mama is the bravest person I know and to see her scared makes me feel jittery inside. Great Aunt Sadie is taking care of her, though, and takes both Mama's hands, like she's giving her something solid to hold onto. Mama's eyes have that look she gets when she disappears into the past. Aunt Sadie makes Mama sit on the porch swing.

"You're safe, sweetheart," she says. "You're safe."

Safe from what? I want to ask. What does Mama need to be safe from?

My hands find their way to my hips. "Somebody needs to tell me what this is about," I say. My entire family turns toward me, even my cousins.

Mama looks straight at me, but doesn't speak.

My face grows hot. In that instant, I hate my entire family with their statue ways and how nobody talks. I fortify my hatred by telling myself this is one of the reasons I am perfectly fine leaving Katy's Ridge forever.

"Tell me," I say, my voice raising, giving them one more chance.

It's hard to believe that minutes ago I was singing a song about grace and everything felt right. But now, everything feels wrong. What hurts the most is that I'm being lied to by the one person in the world I thought I could count on—Mama.

A secret needs to be told. A secret that involves me. A secret, it appears, that Mama has no intention of telling.

CHAPTER SIX

Wildflower

A tremor runs through my body like a bird coming back to life that a cat has left for dead. My teeth chatter. It feels like it is twenty degrees outside and I am without a coat. It's been years since I've had a spell like this, probably since the night Lily was born.

"Have Daniel take Lily," I tell Aunt Sadie through chattering teeth.

Aunt Sadie pulls Daniel aside to speak to him and everyone leaves shortly afterward. Daniel and Jo take Lily to their house.

"Sit over here," Aunt Sadie says to me.

The memories come close together like labor pains, forcing me to remember what I've spent years trying to forget. The sound of Johnny running close behind me, and then finally catching up. The helplessness of being thrown to the ground, the breath forced out of me. The smell of the liquor on his breath.

"Wildflower, you're going to be all right," Aunt Sadie says. "Breathe deeply for me."

Aunt Sadie sounds like she's midwifing one of her expectant mothers. I remember the night she helped Lily come into the world. Giving birth teaches a woman how to surrender and just let life do to you what it insists on doing. However, I don't get the reward of a newborn at the end of this. What I'm giving birth to feels like something old that shouldn't still be alive.

Lily out of sight, I curl into a ball on the porch. Mama brings a quilt and Aunt Sadie wraps it over me. The wood feels cool on the side of my face, and I can smell the aging pine. Mama asks Aunt Sadie what she should do. The last time I heard that worry in her voice was when she and Daniel carried me home after Johnny left me for dead.

"Don't worry, Nell," Aunt Sadie says. "She needs to do this to get free of the ghosts. It won't last long. Maybe you could make her a glass of tea."

With that, Mama goes into the house, and I'm glad she's gone. Now it's just Aunt Sadie and me.

"What's happening?" My voice shakes to match the chattering of my teeth.

"You stored up all that hurt from years ago. It's good that it's coming out," she says. "Best thing you can do is not be afraid of it."

Aunt Sadie reminds me to take deep breaths of mountain air to soothe myself. The trembling scares me. I want to believe it won't last long. Mama arrives with tea and puts it on the porch next to me. Aunt Sadie asks her if we can be alone, and Mama goes into the house again, this time taking the shotgun sitting next to the screen door. I remember Johnny breaking into the house and Amy wounding him with the same gun. The next morning, Daniel, Nathan and I followed the blood trail and found Johnny dead at the bottom of the ravine. Dead from the fall, not the gunshot wound.

A breeze comes up that rushes below the floorboards. It carries the dank smell of the dirt that lives under the porch. I shiver like I'm shaking off a fever. At the same time, sounds and pictures of the past come without my bidding. Aunt Sadie sits next to me on the porch, running a gentle hand through my hair like she did when I was a girl. Waves of panic rise and then fall. I count them. Ten. Eleven. Twelve. I wait for more, but the shaking stops.

"Good girl," Aunt Sadie says.

Though I'm not a girl anymore, I feel like I'm thirteen again, the age of the memories. Aunt Sadie rubs my back, offering me every bit of comfort she can. I remember how solid she was after it happened. I'm not sure what I would do without Aunt Sadie. Then and now.

Time slows. My breath deepens. Minutes later, I make my way to sitting, the quilt falling from my shoulders.

"I feel better," I say.

"Good." Her face relaxes into a smile.

"What happened?" I ask her, taking a sip of tea.

"It must have been Melody Monroe showing up," she says. "It woke up all those memories that had been sleeping."

"I haven't felt that way since—" I can't say the words.

"I know," she says.

"It felt awful. Like it was happening again."

"You needed to release it," Aunt Sadie says. "You needed to rid yourself of that pain that got buried."

Mama comes back outside asking if I need anything. Though I am calm, she looks worried. I reach for her hand and squeeze it. I wonder if she ever gets jealous of the closeness between Aunt Sadie and me—her dead husband's sister.

Aunt Sadie and Mama help me to stand, and I feel almost normal again.

Mama goes back inside, and Aunt Sadie and I sit on the porch swing.

"Lily is upset with me," I say. "I don't blame her. She deserves to know the truth."

"You can't protect her forever," Aunt Sadie says.

"I just want to know why Melody Monroe is back in Katy's Ridge," I say.

"Maybe she's trying to rid herself of painful memories, too," Aunt Sadie says.

"You don't think she's come back just to stir up trouble?" I ask.

"If she has, it's worked. But it could also be for the best," she says. "Gifts come in surprising packages sometimes."

"I wish you wouldn't speak in riddles," I say.

"But you've always been good at riddles," she says to me with a wink.

I pause, unable to fully take in all that the day has brought. We slowly rock the porch swing and look down the hill.

"Did you know that Lily is almost the same age I was when it happened?" I say to Aunt Sadie.

She lets out a moan, followed by a sigh. "Oh my, I never thought of that."

"I was so young," I say.

Aunt Sadie takes a deep breath. "Nobody should have to go through what happened to you," she says, her words soft.

"Should I tell Lily the truth?" My question is in earnest now.

Aunt Sadie pauses for what feels like several minutes, but what might have been seconds instead.

"I honestly don't know," she says. "I wish I did. I imagine there will be tradeoffs with either choice you make."

"But what if Lily gets angry with me? What if she doesn't understand?"

"There isn't a child alive who doesn't hate their parents at one time or another."

I wonder how Aunt Sadie got so wise about children when she never had any.

"I don't remember hating Daddy," I say.

"If he had lived longer, you might have," she says. "Joseph wasn't perfect. He could be as stubborn as an ox sometimes."

To my surprise, I remember the mule that carried Daddy home on the stretcher that last time. Memories have come unbidden all day.

"Isn't it odd that Melody would show up fourteen years later? To the day?" I ask.

Aunt Sadie nods. "There's an invisible world out there that we barely take into account," she says. "A world full of mystery and coincidences."

However, it's the visible world I'm worried about. "What if Melody tells Lily what happened?" I ask.

"How would she even know?" Aunt Sadie says. "She was living in Kentucky with her aunt by then."

"Someone from Katy's Ridge must have told her about Lily," I say.

"I'm not sure who she's in touch with," Aunt Sadie says. "There wasn't a soul at Johnny's funeral."

Surprised, I turn to look at her. "You went to Johnny's funeral?"

She folds her arms, as if feeling a sudden chill. "It was just me and Preacher and a bunch of crows in the trees."

The hairs prickle on the back of my neck.

"Help me understand why you would go to the funeral of someone who nearly beat me to death," I say, trying not to feel betrayed.

After a lifetime of knowing her, I can't remember a single time I've been upset with Aunt Sadie. Until now.

"I felt sorry for him," she says, offering no apology.

"And you didn't feel sorry for me?"

"Of course I did," she says. Her eyes don't release me. "And if you recall, I was there for you the entire time." She pauses and looks at me. "Maybe all that hurt you stored up had anger in it, too."

At that moment, I am not willing to tell her she could be right.

"I believe that everybody should have at least one additional person present at their birth and at their funeral," she says. "I don't care what unforgiveable sin they've committed."

It is the midwife in her that sees it this way, and perhaps it is the little girl in me that is hurt that she could go to Johnny's funeral while I was in bed, unable to move, covered with cuts and bruises.

"I know you've been very loyal to me, Aunt Sadie." My voice is softer now. "It's just a surprise, I guess. A surprise on top of the shock of Melody showing up. I had forgotten she even existed. It never occurred to me that she might know about Lily and show up some day to see her and talk to her. It never occurred to me once."

"We'd like to think life is predictable, but it isn't," Aunt Sadie says, staring off into the distance.

All of a sudden I am tired of Aunt Sadie's wisdom and tired of a past that won't seem to rest.

"I need to go to work," I say to her, which is the only thing I can think of to say.

The day has contained too much history, and I need to get away. But I also need to talk to Bee and the mill is somewhere we can have privacy. I pretend I'm not angry at her, and give Aunt Sadie a hug. Then I follow the path that Melody Monroe took down the hill.

Twenty minutes later, Bee enters the small office at the back of the sawmill where I sit at Daddy's old desk. Sometimes I can still smell him here, as though he never left. One of his old flannel shirts hangs on a nail on the back of the door. I refuse to move it, even this many years later. On a rustic bookcase in the corner are several books and a collection of things my sisters and I made him when we were girls: clay ashtrays shaped like hand prints with his initials in the palms, acorn paperweights heavy with school glue, boxes made of sticks meant to hold letters, and brittle dried wildflowers filling ball jars.

Bee sits on the edge of the desk. Her father used to own the sawmill, but over the years he let me buy him out with a portion of the money that came in. Now, it is mostly mine. The mill is the first thing I've ever attempted to own, besides my truck. Bee's parents live in Rocky Bluff now, but Bee still lives in their house in Katy's Ridge near the elementary school where she teaches.

"What's happened?" she asks. "You look awful."

Bee is an expert worrier, and I try not to give her anything to concern herself over. But I need a friend to listen to me. Someone I'm not related to, and who didn't go to Johnny's funeral. My hurt feelings return. For some reason it feels like everything has changed in the last few hours.

"Two things happened today," I begin. "One is that I had a horrible fight with Aunt Sadie."

Bee smiles like she thinks I'm joking. When she figures out I'm not, she repositions herself on a chair near the desk, her posture arrow straight.

"She told me she went to Johnny's funeral," I say.

Bee grimaces. "Why did she do that?"

"It doesn't matter why," I say. "It's the fact that she did it at all."

Bee touches my arm. "Calm down," she says. "I'm sure she had her reasons. Aunt Sadie wouldn't do anything to hurt you on purpose. You know that."

"I do know that," I say. "That's why I was so shocked."

Bee nods her understanding.

"But that's not the biggest shock, Bee. There's more."

She looks at me with renewed worry.

"A stranger showed up at the house a little while ago. At least I thought it was a stranger at first."

"Out of the blue?" asks Bee.

I nod.

"Well, don't keep me in suspense. Who was it?" She adjusts her sweater, and I notice the latest bumblebee she's stitched onto one of her blouses.

"It was Melody Monroe," I say.

Bee lets out a soft gasp, "Melody Monroe?" She pauses. "What is she doing back in Katy's Ridge?" she asks.

"I'm not sure, but she showed up on our doorstep right after supper. She mentioned Johnny."

The look on Bee's face confirms that I'm not overreacting.

"Are you okay?" Bee asks again, reaching her hand toward mine.

"Not really," I say. "It was like seeing a ghost, and I had this strange reaction afterward. I couldn't stop trembling."

Bee scoots to the edge of her chair. "What did Melody want?"

"She spent a lot of time looking at Lily, and then mentioned Johnny's name like she was threatening to tell." A brief quiver returns.

"You look flushed," Bee says. "Are you sure you're okay?"

I tell her about my reaction after Melody left and how Aunt Sadie said it was a way to release old hurts. I tell her Aunt Sadie said it was a good thing, but she looks doubtful.

"How did Lily react?" she asks. "Did she say anything after Melody left?"

"She was full of questions about who Melody was, of course, and didn't want to let it go."

"Sounds like her." Bee taught Lily in school, back when she still called herself Becky Blackstone instead of Bee.

"Can you blame her for wanting to know who her father is?" Bee twists a strand of thin long hair and then pushes it behind her ear.

I walk to the window and back again, something I do when I'm at a loss.

"Pacing won't help," Bee says, like she is an expert on going back and forth.

She wears one of her navy blue skirts with a white blouse and a yellow sweater that perfectly matches the yellow of the quarter-sized bumblebee stitched onto her collar. Bee has offered to stitch a wildflower onto the bib of my overalls to honor my nickname, but I've declined.

"You were sweet to come over," I say, but Bee is distracted, as if visiting a part of her past, as well.

"I taught Melody before she moved away," she says. "It was the year her sister Ruby died. They were such a sad pair, those girls. Melody didn't talk to anybody but Ruby at school, and then after Ruby died she quit talking altogether."

"I was in Ruby's grade, remember?" I say.

At first, she looks at me as if this can't possibly be true, but then nods as she remembers.

Bee is six years older than me and she was just out of teacher's college when she came to teach at the small elementary school in Katy's Ridge. I was in eighth grade and she taught me for one year before I went off to Rocky Bluff High School. She was *Miss Blackstone* then.

"Ruby's funeral was so sad," Bee says.

I flash on the oak tree where Ruby hung herself and shudder. I was always afraid of dying young back then. Not because of Ruby. But because two years earlier I overheard Mama tell Preacher during a home visit that she had given birth to a baby named Beth who died right before I was born. After that, death felt too close. It could have been me that died instead of Beth.

"I went to the Monroe house once," I say to Bee. "It was easy to feel sorry for them. Good luck just couldn't find them."

"The father showed up at school one time when I was alone," Bee says, her voice low. "He didn't do anything, but I had a feeling that he wanted to. It was probably good Melody moved away," she continues. "I just hope wherever she went was better."

"Given the way she was dressed today, I'm not so sure."

Bee frowns.

"Maybe I should tell Lily about Johnny before Melody does," I say.

"Do you really think Melody would have that much nerve?" Bee asks.

"It looked like it today."

We pause, and I lean against Daddy's desk.

"Maybe you should just play it by ear," Bee says. "Maybe that *secret sense* you're always talking about will tell you if it's the right time or not."

We say our goodbyes. I'm not convinced I need to rush out and tell Lily about her father. I'm also not convinced I need to keep the secret.

When I go home, I find Lily at the kitchen table playing rummy with Mama. Rummy is Mama's favorite game and she can play for hours, causing her opponents to drop out from sheer fatigue.

"Who's winning?" I ask.

Lily's lips are tight and she doesn't look at me. Over the years, we've had a few spats that provoked a pout or a snarl at most, but she's never refused to look at me. She's not the type to punish with silence. That would mean she couldn't ask questions.

Mama gives me a look that says: *She's just like you. See what I've had to put up with?*

I pour myself a glass of tea and think of the willow tree up at the cemetery. I want Daddy to help me make sense of what I should do. Losing him was horrible. But losing Lily, even for an evening, feels like more than I can bear.

CHAPTER SEVEN

Lily

Refusing to look at Mama, I fume in silence. Between my huffing and sighs of exasperation, I play cards with Granny, who isn't in the mood for niceness, either. We don't talk, and each take turns slapping down our cards on the kitchen table like we're pissed as rattlesnakes over the hand life has dealt us. Mama finally leaves, tossing a sigh into the discard pile.

"You finished punishing her yet?" Granny asks me.

It's unlike Granny to take Mama's side. "Who's punishing who?" I say. "I have a right to know, and you know it."

If I had any nerve at all I would go over to that Melody woman's house and ask her what in the hell she has to tell me. *I'm a big girl,* I tell myself. *I can handle it.* At the same time, I wonder if I can.

"I wish we had a telephone so I could call Pearl," I say to Granny, who lifts an eyebrow as if she's studying me. "We're practically the only family in Katy's Ridge that doesn't have one." *It's 1956, for God's sake,* I want to add, but Granny will not tolerate cussing in her kitchen.

"Once you can pay for it, we'll get one," Granny says.

"We live in the Dark Ages," I say, after discarding a jack of hearts.

I fume in silence for Granny's benefit, too.

"Most families have telephones and television sets by now," I continue. "I've watched Ed Sullivan at Pearl's house and can't believe all the good things we're missing."

"If you don't like it here, feel free to leave," Granny says, studying her cards.

Picking a fight with Granny is never a good idea, so I let it drop.

When the crickets tune up for the evening to sing their songs, I want to tell them to shut up. For the rest of the evening, I avoid the living room where Mama is reading and take an extra-long bath hoping she's waiting to get into the bathroom.

When I dry off, I put on my pajamas and then go into our bedroom. Mama follows me in.

"Can I brush your hair?" she asks.

I stand in our bedroom with my hands on my hips, wondering how long I can stay mad at her if she insists on being nice. She pats the bed.

I sit with a huff and bounce on the worn out springs just to irritate her, but she isn't the least bit irritated. My hair is long enough that I can sit on it if I'm not careful. Mama said she used to have hair as long as mine, too, but now she wears it short to avoid accidents at the sawmill.

Hair brushing is something we rarely miss. I take my place at the foot of the bed and Mama sits behind me. With slow, gentle strokes, she brushes my hair as if it is made of birds' nests that will fly apart if touched too roughly. Over and over, she sweeps my hair back and gathers it and then lets it drop. I close my eyes. This rhythm is like a lullaby. My breathing deepens, and I expel the last of my anger with a sigh.

How is it that even without a daddy, I feel completely loved?

"I'm sorry, Mama."

"I'm sorry, too," she says.

Mama puts the brush on the bed, and I turn to see her head bowed like she's praying.

"Does this mean that you and God are on speaking terms again?" I ask.

She lifts her head and looks at me, her eyes shiny with unshed tears.

"Maybe someday we will be again," she says, like it's a secret wish she's not sure will get fulfilled. "I don't want you to hate me," she adds, her voice soft.

"I don't hate you, Mama," I say, although twenty minutes before I would have sworn on a Bible I did.

She leans over and rests her head on my shoulder.

"We need to not have secrets from one another," I say.

She raises her head and her eyes find mine.

"I'm not so sure I agree," she says.

I start to ask why, and she answers as if she's already heard my question.

"It's my job to protect you, Lily, in the best way I know how. When you're a parent, that's what you do."

"Remember when you used to read me fairy tales at night from Granddaddy's book?" I ask.

She nods. "It was a book he used to read to me and my sisters at night," she says.

"Well, if there's a kingdom where secrets are kept, you're the queen," I say to her. "And the castle where you keep those secrets has a deep moat with alligators in it."

She laughs. "That's probably true," she says. "But you've kept secrets from me, too, haven't you?"

I pause, remembering my plans to leave Katy's Ridge as soon as I am out of high school.

"I take that as a 'yes,'" she says, her smile brief.

She looks at me in that way she always does, like she's recognizing somebody she used to know.

"My secrets are nothing bad," I say, thinking, *at least nothing bad to me.*

"Listen, sweetheart, you're as entitled to your confidences as I am to mine."

She says this like she's closing a loop on a sweater she's knitting to keep it from ever unraveling. "A mother never knows everything about her daughter, and a daughter never knows everything about her mother. It's just the way it is."

In my imagination, I hear a snap, the jaws of the alligator in the moat.

"But what if your secrets involve someone else who has a right to know?" I ask.

"Oh, Lily," she says, as though I'm intent on making her life harder than it already is. But I detect a little give in the fabric of her protection of me.

I pick up the hairbrush and motion for Mama to turn so I can brush her hair, too. Her hair is short, but thick, and she's tender-headed, so I am as gentle with her as she was with me.

"Telling secrets has consequences," she says, as though the matter isn't entirely closed.

"But not telling them has consequences, too, doesn't it?" I ask.

She turns and looks at me.

"You have to decide whether telling the secret is going to hurt anybody or not," she says. "If telling it gives you relief, then you just pass that hurt onto other people. In that case, it was probably selfish to tell."

"So you don't want to tell me about my daddy because it might hurt me?" I ask.

Mama sighs.

"Lily, it's been a really long day. I just can't do this right now."

Mama stands and takes the brush from my hand and places it on top of the old bureau that she and her sisters used to share. Before I have time to crawl under the covers, she turns out the light.

Through the thin walls, I can hear Granny getting ready for bed. The rocking chair in her room begins its faint crackling against the wooden floors. Sometimes Granny rocks deep into the night. Tonight, I wonder if she's thinking of Granddaddy, who died fifteen years ago today. Or maybe she's wishing she'd pulled the trigger of that shotgun.

As I ready for sleep, I think of the stranger with the muddy shoes and the look on Mama's face at the time, like a ghost had appeared right in front of her.

My cousin, Bolt, told me years ago that the Monroe land was haunted. It lies beyond the crossroads over near Sutter's Lake. A girl hung herself in an oak tree on that property.

Tomorrow after school, I want to find the stranger's cabin. She may know something about my daddy.

Mama reaches over and touches my arm in the darkness. "Are you still awake?" she whispers.

"Yeah," I whisper back. I'm glad I'm not angry at her anymore. I've never been able to stay mad at her for long.

"I love you, Lily," she says.

"Your secret sense knew the stranger was coming, didn't it?" I ask.

"It did," she answers.

"Do you think I'll get the secret sense someday?"

"Even if you don't, you have other very special gifts, Lily McAllister."

"Like what?" I say, but I know she's talking about my singing.

"Go to sleep," she says, turning to face the wall.

I close my eyes, but I can't quit thinking about the stranger. I'm convinced she holds pieces of the puzzle I've been trying to solve my entire life.

"If you don't tell me, I'll ask her," I whisper. It sounds like a threat, though I don't mean it to. Or maybe I do.

The mattress squeaks as Mama turns to face me again. I imagine her raised brow along with that don't-even-think-about-it look.

"I'm serious, Lily, don't go looking for trouble," Mama's voice breaks out of a whisper.

In the next room, Granny's rocker stops. Has she heard us? The wooden floors announce her movement across the room, followed by the metallic moan of the iron bed that receives her.

"I just want the truth," I whisper back. "When you're ready," I add, knowing it's best not to force things. If Mama feels pushed into a corner she fights back like a bobcat.

"I'll think about it," she says, as though too tired to fight.

I smile. A tiny victory.

According to Mama, everything in nature has a timing to it, and she taught me to respect the timing of things. You can't open a cocoon before its ready, or the butterfly will die. You can't force a flower to bloom by pulling it apart. You can't force the river to flow faster than it does. You can't force people to move faster than they want to, either. If Mama says she'll think about it, she will. But that doesn't mean I'll get what I want. At least I know now who to go to for answers if Mama denies my request—the stranger named Melody Monroe.

CHAPTER EIGHT

Wildflower

After a fitful night's sleep, I go into the kitchen the next morning to find Mama already at the table. Four quilt squares sit next to her as well as a needle with thread marking where she stopped the night before.

"I made it strong," she says, holding up her coffee cup. Did she have trouble sleeping, too?

My dreams were full of chase scenes. Lily running through the forest, fleeing from an unseen assailant. Sometimes I wonder if dreams are my secret sense just coming out in a different way.

"You're up early," Mama says. "You got a meeting I don't know about?"

I pause long enough to wonder if I should tell her the truth. The truth wins out. "Actually, I'm going to go by the Monroe place and talk to Melody."

Her voice starts off loud and then goes to a disapproving whisper: "You're going to do what? Why would you do that?"

Mama is protective of all her children and until I had Lily, I took her way of caring as an insult.

"It may be the stupidest thing I ever do, Mama, but I can't just sit around and wait for the shoe to drop."

Mama looks at the kitchen door as if to make sure she won't be overheard. Her words come out in a whisper again: "Do you think Melody Monroe knows that Johnny is Lily's daddy?"

"That's what I need to find out," I say. "I don't know what she knows. But when she was here yesterday, she couldn't take her eyes off Lily and that concerns me."

"You want me to go with you?" Mama asks, glancing over at the shotgun by the door.

"I don't want to scare her," I say. "I want to have a calm conversation."

"I don't know if that's possible with that woman," Mama says with a scoff. "My guess is she's here to make a mess of things."

"Maybe she is," I say. "That's what I want to find out."

"You be careful," Mama says.

I grab a biscuit left over from yesterday and fold two pieces of bacon into the center of it and wrap it into a napkin.

At the front door, I yell a quick goodbye to Lily, who is getting ready for school. She yells back the same. At least she's still speaking to me. I remember how Mama and I barely spoke for weeks after Johnny attacked me. Back then, I thought Mama's silence might kill me. Even the simplest people are complicated, and I don't know that I'll ever understand most folks. I'm not sure I even understand myself.

At the bottom of the hill I slide into my pickup and let it warm up while I eat my biscuit. I toss the crumbs outside for the birds. I drive in the opposite direction of the sawmill toward the Monroe place. The paved road changes to dirt and gravel and then to just dirt. No matter how slow I go, the shocks on my old truck squeak and moan. With the ruts and potholes, it's like riding a wild horse who refuses to be tamed. I pull over and park where the road becomes impassable. A few yards away, I find the remnants of an even narrower dirt road that leads into the forest.

The last time I was here I was Lily's age, or maybe a little younger. On a post to the left of the road is a rusty white sign that once had *No Trespassing* painted on it. Now it reads *o es-passin*. The road is grown over and looks like a mud farm at best. Standing water sits in deep craters, and it takes some doing to avoid the puddles. It reminds me of jumping hopscotch squares in elementary school. I think of Bee. I could never spend an entire day with a bunch of kids like she does.

I walk deeper into the woods. Even with the leaves halfway off the trees, it is still dark. I shudder and think of the dream I had the night before of Lily being chased. My stomach rumbles with the strong coffee and biscuit. I shouldn't be here. I have work to do at the mill. But I need to ask Melody about her intentions.

Nothing much has changed about the Monroe place except that, with no one cutting trees for firewood, the forest is denser. Wisteria vines have captured the front porch and threaten to overtake the rest of the house. Even from a distance the old wood smells rotten. The floor boards of the porch visibly buckle in places with green vines reaching for sunlight between the boards. A three-legged stool sits next to an old washing machine with rollers. A stack of firewood is covered with a white fungus that stretches its fingers in every direction and looks almost as rotten as the porch. At the bottom step I stomp the mud off my boots to announce my arrival, and call out Melody's name. On the step next to me is a graveyard of cigarettes twisted into the dark, damp wood. The cabin reeks of sour cigarettes and rot.

Several long seconds later, the door opens just enough for Melody to peek outside. Even though it's after 9 o'clock, she looks like she's just woken up. I remember the first time I came to this cabin, when Melody and I were both girls. Daniel was with me and my best friend, Mary Jane. Daniel had asked Melody where Johnny was, so he could tell him to leave us alone.

"You wanted to talk with me?" She wipes her eyes.

"I do," I say. I pause long enough to wish I'd pondered a strategy on the way over. "I'd like to know your plans."

"My plans?" she says with a short laugh, like she's never had a plan in her life. Even though there's a chill in the air she opens the door wide. "You drink tea?" she asks. She disappears into the cabin.

"Sure," I say, even though I just had coffee.

I test the porch steps before I climb them, grateful my feet don't break through the boards long overdue for being replaced.

A shiver splits my ribcage when I step inside the house. I've never been in the Monroe cabin and the smallness of it feels like what I imagine a prison cell is like. I wonder how an entire family could have lived in it. In the next second it occurs to me that four of this family of five are dead, leaving only Melody behind.

Melody stands at a small wood stove with a pan of water on top heating to a boil. A small table with two chairs is in front of a cracked window that offers the only light in the room. Mama's kitchen looks fit for royalty compared to this.

"I guess I gave you quite a jolt yesterday," Melody says, inviting me to sit at the table.

I thank her and take a seat in an uncomfortable chair whose woven seat has almost busted through. With the door open, the dampness of the forest permeates the room. I half expect mold to climb up my ankles if I sit still long enough.

"You gave us all a shock," I say.

"I bet I did," she says with a grin that quickly fades.

If history had been gentler with both of us, perhaps we would have been friends. Yet right now she feels more like an enemy than anything, and I need to determine what weapons she has.

A bed takes up a corner of the small room, the old mattress torn and spitting out its stuffing in different places. A threadbare blanket lays across the bed to serve as a sheet and a faded quilt covers the top. A smaller bed, without a mattress, is on the opposite side of the room. I wonder where Johnny and the girls used to sleep. This cabin is barely big enough for Melody and me.

In the last decade, I've reached the beginnings of forgiveness for what Johnny did to me. I've even begun to forgive myself, the hardest task of all. But seeing Melody again makes me feel like the ground I've fought for all these years is crumbling underneath me.

"Why are you back here?" I ask, sounding harsher than I intend. "I mean, if you don't mind my asking."

She takes a sideways glance at me, as if to determine whether she should answer. Then she lights a cigarette with a match from a box of kitchen matches kept in a small metal box. The fingers on her right hand are yellow and tough from holding cigarettes.

"After my aunt died, I found an old letter addressed to her from Doc Lester," she begins. "My aunt lived in Katy's Ridge when she was younger and they used to be friends."

It is hard to imagine that Doc Lester has friends, even old ones, given I typically think of vermin whenever his name is mentioned. I'm not the only person in Katy's Ridge who feels this way.

"Doc wrote my aunt after Johnny died." She takes a seat at the table and unfolds a letter from her dress pocket as if to offer proof.

A wave of nausea hits, and I hold my stomach to calm the wave.

"You okay?" Melody asks.

"I've been better," I say. I remember the tremors that shook through me yesterday like an earthquake, an unexpected reaction to Melody showing up at our door.

"The tea should be ready," she says, getting up from the table. "I'm afraid I don't have cream and sugar."

"That's all right," I say. I never drink hot tea anyway. But it gives me a reason to sit a while.

After putting a pinch of leaves into a small cloth bag, she steeps it in the water that has just boiled. Melody gathers cups and saucers to put on the table. One cup is chipped. The other is missing a handle. Their flower design is just as faded as her dress. Yet both hint at beauty and better times. Then she returns to the stove and waits for the leaves to finish steeping. Melody doesn't speak, but stares out the window like I do sometimes when I'm remembering something from a long time ago.

A ragged potholder hangs from a nail near the stove. She grasps the pot with it and pours the tea into each of our cups. Then she sits at the table to join me. The chair beneath me has a hole in the weaving, and I hope I don't bust right through it and end up on the floor.

The tea tastes bitter and stale like it's been sitting in a tin for a long time.

"Lots of ghosts in these parts," she says, looking around the room.

I nod. We sit in silence for several seconds, as if paying our respects to the spirits of the dead who are everywhere. If I didn't feel the need to protect Lily, I would have already left.

"My aunt didn't tell me that Johnny died," she begins again. "I had to find out from the letters. All this time, I imagined he was still living in this cabin, up to no good."

I wonder if she's come to Katy's Ridge for answers.

"Do you remember when it happened?" she asks me.

"It was a long time ago," I say, thinking it was more like a lifetime.

"You know what's odd?" she asks, without waiting for an answer. "It's odd to me that Johnny died by falling down a mountain. Johnny knew these hills up, down and sideways. He would never have been that reckless."

Her eyes don't leave mine, as though she's challenging me to a game of truth or dare.

"From what I heard, it was winter," I say. "The footbridge was icy." These are the facts. But what I don't tell her, is that I would have killed Johnny myself if he hadn't fallen.

Her eyes narrow. "How do you know this?" she asks.

"I know because Daniel and Nathan found him," I say, which sounds innocent enough.

She sits straighter in her chair, as though curious. "They must have been looking for him to find him at the bottom of the ravine. It's not like there's a clear view."

Melody is clever, and I search the past for the truth. I was the one who spotted Johnny at first. I saw something shiny at the bottom of the gorge. Johnny was wearing the gold medallion he had stolen from me. Later, I thought that Johnny taking the necklace was his way of getting his mama back. Lily wears it now, unaware of its history. I wanted to give her a piece of the gold Mary. But I wonder now if I was also giving her a bit of her father.

I force myself out of the past. "Why did you come back, Melody?"

She squints from the cigarette smoke. Then drops the butt in an empty jelly jar with an inch of water in the bottom. It gives a short hiss.

"Like I said yesterday, I came back to sell the place. Not that anyone would have it."

Melody glances around as if calculating the cabin's worth.

"In his last letter to my aunt, Doc Lester said she might want to come and meet Lily. He said she was a very special girl. Imagine my surprise to learn I had a niece."

I exhale, hearing the imaginary other shoe drop. Melody looks at me like a cat waiting for an apology from a mouse.

You'll get an apology when hell freezes over, I want to tell her.

The only sunlight in the room is hidden by a cloud and her face falls in shadow.

"Listen, I can't imagine that you actually wanted to have Johnny's child," she says. "He forced himself on my sister, Ruby, too." She glances out the window toward the oak tree.

At the time of Ruby's death, news of her unborn child flew through Katy's Ridge like a flock of sparrows going from tree to tree. I remember seeing Ruby in that small coffin, knowing she had a tiny unborn baby still in her belly. Over a decade later, I still shiver with the thought.

Secrets get buried all the time. I'll keep mine buried, too, especially if they might cause Lily to suffer. I clinch my jaw. I've spent the last fourteen years making sure that my shame didn't touch my daughter, and Melody could erase all that in a day.

My thoughts capture me, and I'm startled when Melody begins speaking again.

"Did it ever occur to you that we might like to know that Johnny had a child?" she asks.

"I didn't think you'd care," I say, though in truth, it never occurred to me that Johnny's family had any rights to my child.

"My aunt is near death and would like to see her," Melody says.

"I thought you said your aunt was dead."

Melody's eyes dart toward the door, as if looking for a way out of her lie.

"I meant to say she's dying," Melody says.

"She even sent money for the bus, so I can bring Lily home." She pulls a few bills from her tattered dress pocket. I'm not sure which story to believe.

The sun returns but offers little comfort. "Lily's home is here," I say.

It never occurred to me that a member of Johnny's family might get curious and come looking for Lily. Or that the news would ever go beyond Katy's Ridge.

However, if there is anyone who might want to bring trouble to the McAllister family, it is Doc Lester. He hates Aunt Sadie, and was less than useless after Daddy's accident. Not to mention his suggestion to get rid of Lily before she was born. I'm not sure what he had in mind, but if she were a kitten he probably would have drowned her in a bucket. His treatment of us since then hasn't been much better.

I always thought it would be Preacher who would condemn me to eternal damnation and treat me accordingly. But even he has managed to swallow whatever judgments he has about me and Lily, which I imagine are considerable. Perhaps it helps that Lily sings so beautifully in his struggling choir and often sings solos that bring the old widows of Katy's Ridge to tears. Tears that guarantee to up the totals in his collection plate.

"So you haven't told her who her father is?"

Melody's eyebrows arch toward the sagging ceiling that has a greenish tint. If Mama were here she'd take a scrub brush and a bucket of bleach to it.

"I don't blame you," she quickly adds. "I'd make up a story myself before I'd say Johnny was the father. Hell, that's like admitting you had a thing for Hitler."

Her giggle sounds childlike, as though all these years she's never left this cabin. Even today, she's barefoot, like the last time I saw her when she was a girl. At least we have one thing in common. It appears she hates Johnny as much as I do. I can't imagine hating one of my sisters as much as she hates her only brother.

Melody puts the wad of dollar bills on the table as though offering to buy her. My scalp tingles and my secret sense gives me a nudge to get out of there. But I can't go just yet. I need to get what I came for.

"Are you going to tell her?" I ask.

She smiles and I remember Johnny's crooked teeth.

"I might," she says. "Don't you think she deserves to know?"

Lily has said similar things.

All of a sudden the dark cabin feels like it might swallow me.

"I guess I'll leave it up to Lily," I say. "But if you really care about her—" The words tighten my throat. Melody doesn't even know Lily. There's been no time for caring to grow.

Silence fills the room. It is Melody who studies me now, as if disappointed my fear doesn't give her more pleasure.

"I'll leave it up to Lily, too," she says finally, and folds the money into her pocket. "If she asks, I'll tell her what I know. If she doesn't, I'll leave it alone."

A lone cicada sings, trapped in this cabin for so long it has no idea whether it's day or night, summer or fall.

"But what about your dying aunt?" I ask. "I thought she wanted to see Lily."

She hesitates. A smile comes and goes so quickly I question whether I've imagined it.

"I can always keep the money and tell her Lily changed her mind after I'd already bought the bus ticket," she says.

The deep breath I take makes her smile again, as if she realizes how she's held me hostage.

"Lily is a great kid," Melody says, and I wonder how she would know that after only laying eyes on her for the first time yesterday. "No doubt that's your influence. Though Johnny wasn't all bad, either."

Her generosity surprises me.

"From what Ruby told me, he was actually a sweet boy before Mama died. He was my older brother, by about six years, so we weren't really close. By the time I knew him he wasn't that nice."

She looks around like her family's history is recorded on the walls like ancient cave paintings. A history she would rather not revisit, either.

"Do you mind if I ask you something?" she begins again.

"No," I say, though the opposite is true.

"Does it bother you that she looks so much like Johnny?" she asks.

Though everyone must think it, no one has ever spoken these words. Lily is Johnny's child, if only in looks. She is tall, thin and has his intense eyes. Eyes that won't let you get away with anything. Eyes that penetrate and see the things you wish they didn't see.

I stand. "To me, Lily looks like Lily," I say.

What I will never tell Melody, is that it did bother me at first. Immensely. Even when she was small, I could see Johnny in her bone structure, her way of standing. If Johnny was still alive, all Lily would have to do to confirm paternity would be to look at him. But Johnny isn't living, and nobody—until now—has even brought it up.

"I've got to get to work," I say. I stop at the door and turn before leaving. "So you promise you won't tell Lily anything unless she asks you?"

"That's right," Melody says.

Something causes me to linger. I want to give her something more so she might keep her promise. "I hope life has been okay for you, Melody. You know, in recent years."

She stares into the teacup resting between her hands like June Sector does when she reads tea leaves. I imagine her tea is cold now, yet she holds it as though it warms her hands.

"It could have been better, I guess," she says.

We end our conversation with the pleasantries that often begin one. But something tells me that the trouble is far from over.

CHAPTER NINE

Lily

The morning is crisp and the dew makes the path down the hill slippery in places. When I reach the bottom, Mama's truck is gone, and I wonder why she felt the need to leave the house so early. At the road I hesitate, wondering what I'll miss at school today, and then turn toward the old Monroe place. I have never skipped school before. Not once. But today I have a higher quest. I need to find out the truth.

With every step my guilt rises with the oatmeal in my stomach. I stop at the crossroads where one road leads to the elementary school and the other leads to the mill, and rethink my decision. Even though I've missed the bus, I could still go to the mill and make up a story. I could tell Mama I wasn't feeling well at first, but that now I would like to go to school. Then either she or Uncle Daniel could drive me into Rocky Bluff.

Going to the high school is the only break I get from the smallness of Katy's Ridge. While the population here hovers around fifty, Rocky Bluff has almost 1500 residents, and is a metropolis in comparison. Still, it's not like me to break the rules.

A truck drives around the bend, and I'm relieved it's not Mama. The driver slows when he sees me. It's my Uncle Cecil. Not my favorite person. The truck idles as he rolls down his window. From the passenger side, Janie looks at me with her flat expression. Uncle Cecil's birthmark reminds me of my geography teacher saying the Soviet leader, Khrushchev, was a scary man.

"You miss the bus?" Uncle Cecil says.

I pause long enough for a fresh wave of guilt to crest. "I'm helping out at the elementary school today," I say.

Janie turns her beige face toward me like my 'helping out' is news to her.

"Hop in. That's where we're going." He leans over Janie and opens the door so I can get inside.

"Actually, I'm enjoying the walk this morning. Mama says walking is good for me." I give him a smile, surprised by how easy it is to lie.

Uncle Cecil shrugs and closes the door before giving me a short wave and driving away. He is new to the family, but is nice enough, and I can't believe I've just lied to him. It's not like I can get away with it, either. If Janie doesn't tell, it will come out when he tells Aunt Meg that he saw me on the road this morning. There is no way I won't get in trouble for this, but I can't seem to stop myself.

For the longest time I stand at the crossroads kicking rocks from one side to the other. A feeling comes over me that I've had more than once. A feeling that someone is watching me, even though nobody is around. A gust of wind brings down a flurry of leaves that scoot along the road and gather in a dusty whirlwind before dancing away. I pull my sweater close and remember the stranger from the day before with her mud-caked shoes. The thought of her gathers me up in her whirlwind, and I turn in the direction of the Monroe property. Since I'm probably already in trouble, I might as well do what I set out to do.

Around the bend in the road, I hide my lunch pail behind a boulder, planning to pick it up again on my way home. A few steps later I take off my heavy sweater and tie it around my waist. The sun, having risen above the ridge, is now warming up the day. When I get to the dirt road off the main road, Mama's truck is pulled off on the side.

What's Mama doing here? Her empty coffee cup sits on the seat of her truck. Is this why she tossed and turned all night? Was she dreaming up a plan to visit the stranger? I take off down a narrow dirt road that is pocked with mud puddles.

One summer, Bolt and Nat and I went in search of the empty Monroe cabin. We'd heard for years that it was haunted and wanted to check it out. Back then we were in the midst of a dry spell so it wasn't this muddy.

In no time, mud cakes around my good shoes Mama bought me for my birthday last July. My feet get heavy, and I wonder how the stranger managed to keep her shoes as clean as they were. At this rate, I'll be scrubbing mine for hours, removing the evidence of where I've been. To avoid the deepest mud holes, I perch on mounds of grass when possible, leaping to the next clump of grass. Several leaps later, I come upon the small cabin. When I see Mama standing in the doorway talking to the stranger, I duck behind a large sycamore tree. I am too far away to make out any of their words.

A circle of oak trees guards the house, and I remember the story of the girl who hung herself. The place would feel creepy even without knowing the story. The dark forest makes this place look like a Hansel and Gretel fairy tale. I half expect to see breadcrumbs in the mud, leading the way out of the forest. If I were smart, I would probably follow them.

The wind pushes the cabin's bitter smell in my direction. This old house has been in the process of falling down for years. Patches of light green moss grow on the roof and vines as thick as three fingers hold the house hostage. I wonder if I can get close enough to hear what Mama and the lady are talking about. I hide behind trees and underbrush, inching my way closer to the cabin. I crouch at the right side of the porch behind an old rusty washing machine. I listen to Mama's lower voice and the stranger's higher one. A duet in a minor key. Although I can't make out any words, I can tell from the way Mama's holding her body that she's not happy.

When Mama walks out the front door, I drop to my knees to stay hidden. She takes the path back to her truck, and the look on her face is one I've never seen before. Regret? Sadness? Cold mud soaks into my bottom of my dress. Now I've ruined my dress, as well as my shoes. Trouble piles on top of trouble.

Seconds later the stranger steps out on the porch without shoes, wearing the same dress from yesterday. She mumbles something under her breath about teaching Mama a lesson, and then goes back into the house. I can't tell if she's disappointed or angry or just acting normal.

I keep an eye on Mama, just in case she comes back, prepared to dive into the dark recesses under the porch. I don't move until her truck starts up and the gravel spews as she drives away. Then I stand and look down at the red Tennessee clay pressed into my knees, as well as the mud damage to my shoes.

I sit on an old log next to the house and lean against the rotting wood to decide what to do next. Not only have I skipped school, but I've ruined my things. The woman inside the cabin begins to sweep. I contemplate whether I should just walk away or knock on the door.

Warmth comes to my face. I decide to make the best of all the stuff I've ruined, and stand and brush myself off. Then I make a wide circle back through the woods so I can approach the house as though I'm just now showing up.

When I get to the porch steps I call out 'hello.'

The stranger comes to the door, broom in hand.

"Does she know you're here?" She looks out into the forest, the way Mama left.

"No," I say.

"So you were hiding out here the whole time?"

"Not the whole time," I say.

She gives a slight grin like I remind her of somebody.

"I wondered if you'd have the guts to show up," she says.

When her grin grows into a smile she looks younger and not nearly as scary. She is pale, like her life has seen very little sunlight. "Come inside," she says. "Leave your shoes at the door."

"You have something to tell me?" I ask, not moving. I don't even want to think about what Mama would do if she knew I was here.

"You willing to listen?" she says back.

"Depends on what you have to say," I answer.

"Come inside," she says. She goes into the house leaving the door open.

I can't move. It's like my feet are anchored to the earth with mud, and I've been made a prisoner.

"Come on," the stranger says, from inside the house.

I think of Hansel and Gretel again. Is there a big stove in there that she'll throw me into?

You read too many fairy tales, I tell myself.

I wish I had Mama's secret sense. It would tell me what to do. But the secret sense is a language I've never learned to speak. At least not yet.

The rickety steps lead to an unstable porch. It helps that I just saw Mama leave here alive and well. I approach the door not knowing what I might find inside. The stranger sits at a small table in the corner. A chair is pulled out where I imagine Mama sat. I take a seat and glance around the small, dark room.

"Could you tell me your name again?" I ask, feeling bold. "I don't remember from yesterday."

"Melody," she says, in a sing-song voice, like she recognizes the irony of someone so sad having such a beautiful name.

Her feet are dirty but the floor is clean from the sweeping.

"Where are you from?" I ask. This is not a question I ever get to ask in Katy's Ridge since few people visit here.

"I was born here in this cabin," she says. "But when I was a girl, I was sent to live with my aunt in Louisville, Kentucky."

In my mind, I put Louisville on my list of places to visit someday. I would travel there now if the opportunity presented itself.

"Why'd you come back?" I ask.

"You ask a lot of questions," she says. "Anybody ever tell you that?"

"Just about everybody tells me that," I say, looking away from her grin.

"It's okay. I'm not mad at you or anything," she says. "You skipping school?" she asks, like it's her turn to find out things.

I nod, and lower my head. Skipping school is nothing to be proud of.

"We can keep it a secret if you want," she says. "I'm good at keeping secrets."

I wonder if this is true.

Two teacups sit on the table. I hope she doesn't offer me anything to drink.

"When you came to the house yesterday, you said to come see you if I wanted to talk."

She nods.

"Why would I talk to you? What do you want to tell me?" I ask, looking up at her again.

"There's two more," she says, as if catching me at something.

"Two more?"

"Questions," she says.

"Listen, I can go if you want," I say, standing.

"No, no," she says. "I want to get to know you." She motions for me to sit again.

"Why?" I say, before I can catch myself. But we both smile this time.

"You can call me Melody if you want," she says.

I nod, but I'm not ready to call her anything.

"You may be related to someone I used to know," she says.

"I take it you don't mean Mama," I say.

"No," she answers. "I think I knew your daddy."

My breathing goes shallow. All these years I've wanted this question answered and now that it's as close as the cracked teacup sitting in front of me, I'm not so sure I want to know. If I listen to what she has to say, it feels like it might change everything. And maybe not in a good way.

Dozens of questions rush forward wanting answers, but I don't speak.

"Would you like to know more?" she asks, like she sees my predicament.

I say I do, but I'm not so sure. All of a sudden, my heart beats like it has a race to run.

She walks over to the door like she's making sure Mama isn't coming back. Then she turns to face me again. She isn't wearing a slip, and her dress—backlit by the sun—reveals her scrawny legs.

"I think your daddy was my brother, Johnny Monroe." She grins like she takes pleasure from saying it. "He was a couple of years older than your mama and they went to the same school. At least before Johnny dropped out in sixth grade."

Over the years, I'd imagined that my daddy was smart like Granddaddy. Maybe he even had a college education, which would be a first in my family. It never occurred to me that he might be a sixth grade dropout.

"That was the year our mama died," she says, as if feeling the need to give a reason. "She died of TB when I was six."

Melody glances at the bed like that's the last place she saw her mother alive.

Tuberculosis is feared here in the mountains. Several people have died from it. I wonder if the tuberculosis germs are still living in that bed. Or maybe they are circulating in the air. I hold my breath for a few seconds until I realize I've probably already breathed them in anyway.

A part of me wants to run out of the cabin and keep on running until I make it back to Granny's kitchen. Another part of me feels bolted to the floor. The two parts battle it out in silence.

What if she's just making this up? Great Aunt Sadie says you can tell from someone's eyes whether they're telling the truth or not. If they're lying, their eyes dart like hummingbirds drinking from flower to flower.

"What are you thinking about?" she asks me. Her voice sounds caring, but her expression reveals something else. If I had to guess, I'd say she's getting pleasure from somebody else suffering for a change.

"What was he like?" My voice sounds shaky at first, but I smooth it out.

"The truth?" she asks.

I nod to avoid the words shaking again.

"Your daddy was mean as a snake," she says, her eyes holding steady.

After a short gasp, I have the beginnings of a coughing fit. Melody brings me a glass of water that is slightly brown. The father I imagined was kind, never mean. She reaches over and pats my hand as though life disappoints all of us, so I might as well get used to it. I challenge myself not to pull my hand away, even though her touch is as cold and clammy as a fish out of the Tennessee River.

"How do you know for sure he's my daddy?"

"I don't know for sure," she says. "On account of he's not here to ask. He died right before you were born."

"What killed him?" I ask, as another of my fantasies dies. This one being that my daddy isn't dead at all, but is living somewhere around here and will show up any day to apologize for not being better in touch.

"He fell down a mountain," she says. "At least that's what your mama told me."

"Mama told you that?"

"She sure did. Right before you got here."

I want to know why Mama kept this from me for all these years and then tells Melody the first day she sees her.

"But how do you know he's even my daddy?" I ask again, my voice getting stronger.

She pauses. "You know Doc Lester?"

I nod. My family hates Doc Lester, especially Mama. She won't let him get near me with his doctoring. If Aunt Sadie can't find a remedy for whatever ails me, Mama says she'll take me to see the doctor in Rocky Bluff, even though he charges two dollars for an office visit.

"Doc wrote a letter to my aunt in Louisville saying that Johnny had a daughter. He said her name was Lily. That's your name, right?"

I start to stand, and the chair I'm sitting in crashes to the floor with me in it. I'm lucky the old floor is half rotten or I might have knocked myself out.

"You all right?" Melody leans over me on one knee.

Flat on my back, I take in this person, with bad breath to accompany her bad teeth, who is quite possibly my aunt. The thought occurs to me that I've got plenty of aunts already, what do I need with one more?

"You're wrong," I say. "Doc Lester lied to you." I scramble from the floor, my head throbbing. Once upright, the dizziness sets in followed by the tears that threaten to come.

Within seconds, I bolt out of the cabin, hearing Melody call out my name. The mud slows me down as I run through the woods and toward the road. Even though I heard her drive away ages ago, I want Mama's truck to still be there. By the time I reach the crossroads, it feels like my lungs might burst from my chest. I stop running and lean over to slow my breathing. Once I can stand up straight again, I try to decide what to do next. I take off walking in the direction of the mill where Mama works. She has some major explaining to do.

CHAPTER TEN

Wildflower

My hands are still trembling when I park my truck outside the sawmill. I will do anything to keep Lily safe, yet I'm not sure how to protect her from the truth. I leave my muddy boots at the side door and walk into the office in my socks. Daniel sits at the desk we share, working on the ledger where we keep track of all our orders. Orders that promise to grow leaner as we head into the winter months. Silas—who made Daddy's coffin and is an old family friend—only works two or three days a week. He cuts the lumber, and with the help of his son, delivers it to wherever it's needed.

The day before, Daniel assured me that Melody wasn't up to anything and would be gone soon. But he wasn't in that cabin with her. Nor did he catch her in the lie about her dead or not-so-dead aunt.

When Daniel starts to get up, I motion for him to stay seated and pull another chair next to the desk.

"I need to talk to you," I say. "It's serious."

He puts down the pencil and turns to look at me, his face showing immediate concern. Ever since Daddy died, I've relied on Daniel to help me figure things out.

"I've just come from the Monroe place," I say. "I talked to Melody, and if Lily asks, she plans to tell her who her daddy is."

"Good lord," Daniel says, his voice soft. He closes the ledger and takes off his glasses that he uses to see the small numbers.

"I don't trust her, Daniel. Melody Monroe is up to something. I am certain of it."

"Sounds like you may be right," he says.

We pause, as if taking this in.

"The timing is uncanny, isn't it?" I begin again. "She shows up on the anniversary of Daddy's death, which is also the anniversary of—" I don't want to say the words. But Daniel knows as well as I do what happened on that first anniversary because he and Mama found me in the woods and carried me all the way home.

I flash on the feeling of being carried in his arms and Mama's voice calm and steady saying not to give up, that we'd be home soon. Then I wonder how something that happened so long ago can still be so fresh in my memory.

"Uncanny is a good word for it," Daniel says, his forehead creased.

We exchange looks, unprepared to fight old battles. Daniel studies the eagle tattoo on his arm, as if remembering the war from which Amy's husband, Nathan, didn't return. The shrapnel in his leg causes him pain, although most of the time he tries to pretend it doesn't. On the days it's hurting him, he chews aspirin like they were peppermints.

"There are ghosts out at that place, Daniel. It's creepy. Bad things have happened in that cabin. You can just feel it. Like it's seeping out of the walls or something."

Daniel looks thoughtful, like he's trying to make sense of things. "From what I can tell, broken families are everywhere," he says. "The Monroes are one of those broken families. Whatever good was there at one time died away. In some ways, they never had a chance."

"I think you're right," I say.

"Tell me what you two talked about," Daniel says.

"She wanted to know how Johnny died," I tell him. "I didn't mention that he may not have died in the first place if we hadn't been chasing him."

"Johnny brought this on himself," Daniel says. "He threatened you. Then he broke into the house. There was a reason he was being chased. We were trying to keep you safe."

"I'm not sure Melody would see it that way," I tell him.

"It was his choosing," Daniel says. "If he hadn't come after you, he would still be alive."

I remember the Monroe cabin and wonder if choosing has anything to do with all that happened there. Sometimes life has nothing to do with choice.

"Daniel, why did I lie to Lily all these years? I should have told her the truth the first time she asked me." An unexpected sob catches in my throat.

"You didn't lie to her," he says, leaning closer to pat my hand.

"Not saying is the same as lying," I say. "She's asked me for years who her daddy is, and I've refused to tell her. Nothing kindles a fire like the flames of silence."

"You're being too hard on yourself," Daniel says. "You were just trying to protect her. Anybody in your position would have done the same thing."

"Anybody?"

"Anybody," he says. He acts certain, but Daniel is loyal to a fault. I'm not sure I can trust him to tell me when I'm truly in the wrong.

"I should have made up a story. Anything to throw her off track. It was the secretiveness that was wrong. It just made things too enticing."

"Tell me exactly what Melody said when you talked to her," Daniel says, repositioning his hurt leg.

"She said Lily has a right to know, and that if Lily asks her, she will tell her."

"Maybe Lily won't ask."

We exchange a look.

"Right. When has Lily ever not asked?" he says.

"Lily not asking is like laying odds that the sun won't come up tomorrow morning," I say.

"Not very good odds," Daniel says, looking thoughtful again. "Well, she's at school now, so at least it won't happen anytime soon. You'll have a little time to prepare."

I glance at the ledger that documents all the revenue and expenses of the sawmill.

"Do you think I should offer Melody money not to tell Lily?"

"Trust me," Daniel says, "you don't have any money to offer her."

"Maybe I should have reasoned with her more," I say, biting my bottom lip.

"It's easy for parents to think they didn't do enough," Daniel says. "But when is anything ever enough? More love could always be given. That goes for compassion and kindness, too."

"It's clear I messed up, Daniel."

He pauses, "If you really feel that way, then maybe telling Lily makes sense."

"It's going to hurt her," I say.

"Life hurts us all," he says.

"For years, Lily's built up these fantasies about who her daddy was," I begin again. "You know what a big dreamer she is. Always has been. She expects life to turn out okay no matter what. I was that way, too, remember? Until that day—"

"Bad things happen to everybody," he says, patting his leg. "When are you going to get it into that thick skull of yours that you didn't do anything wrong?"

"I may never get it," I say, lowering my eyes.

Daniel stands, grabs his cane that is hooked on the handle of the desk drawer and puts a hand on my shoulder.

Tears come.

"If Daddy had been alive, he would have protected me from Johnny," I begin. "But then Lily wouldn't exist, and I'm not sure who I'd be without Lily. How can the worst thing to happen in my life, give me the best thing to ever happen? I just don't get it."

"I don't get it, either," he says. "Life is a mystery to all of us."

Daniel goes back to the ledger. I need to tell Lily the truth before Melody does, but this thought scares me almost as much as the other secret of my life coming to light. I just don't want Lily to have to grow up as fast as I did. But I have to prepare Lily for the world. Otherwise, what kind of parent am I?

The telephone rings and gives us both a start. The voice on the line is the secretary from the high school. I listen and then thank her, telling her that I'll handle it. I hang up the phone.

"I may be too late in wanting to do the right thing," I say to Daniel. "Looks like Lily skipped school today. For all I know, Lily is already at Melody's learning the truth about who her father was."

Daniel stands and cusses. I wonder if he's cussing because of what I just told him or if his leg is hurting him.

"I don't want to lose her, Daniel. There for a while, Mama almost lost me. If I lost Lily, it would break my heart."

"It would break both your hearts," he says, handing me my coat.

I put on my muddy boots and run outside to my truck, retracing the way I came thirty minutes before. After the truck jolts to life, I shift the gears from first to third, pushing the old truck as fast as it can go toward the Monroe cabin, wondering if my relationship with Lily is strong enough to bear the truth.

CHAPTER ELEVEN

Lily

When I arrive at the sawmill, Mama's truck isn't in front but Uncle Daniel's is. I can't quit thinking about what Melody told me. I find Uncle Daniel sitting in the office doing the books.

"Where's Mama?" I ask.

He stands, a grimace crossing his face from the pain in his leg. "She just left. She's out looking for you. I'm surprised you didn't see her."

"Why is she looking for me?" I ask.

"The school called," he says. "She knows you didn't go today."

I moan. Who gets caught the one time they skip? *You do,* I say to myself. You with the mean daddy who dropped out of school in sixth grade.

"Can you take me over to Great Aunt Sadie's?" I ask him. I'm not sure why I want to go there, except I need to talk to someone. Great Aunt Sadie is who Mama goes to when something is bothering her, either her or Uncle Daniel.

"Wouldn't you rather stay here and wait on your mama?" he asks.

I cross my arms, trying to keep my anger from spilling out all over Uncle Daniel. "Can you take me to Great Aunt Sadie's or not?" I ask. "I need to talk to her. It's important."

"Why don't you tell me about it? Maybe I can help," he says.

"No thank you," I say.

I love my Uncle Daniel, but he's not the one I need to talk to. I need to talk to Mama. But if she's not around then I need to ask Great Aunt Sadie why Mama lied to me all these years. Although, if what Melody said is true, maybe she was too embarrassed to tell.

Uncle Daniel limps out to his truck with me following close behind. His truck is newer than Mama's but is still old, and a Chevrolet instead of a Ford. On the dashboard are photographs of my Aunt Jo and my cousins, Bolt and Nat. Uncle Daniel starts the engine and puts it into gear. He drives slow, and I wonder if he's stalling for time, hoping we will meet Mama on the road.

"I'll tell your mother you're at your Great Aunt Sadie's," he says.

"Don't tell her anything," I say.

He glances at me while he drives. "You know I can't do that, Lily. I never keep secrets from your mother."

I huff, and Uncle Daniel rubs his bad leg like I'm making it worse. We ride along in silence until he tries to make conversation again, but I'm not in the mood. Great Aunt Sadie is the one person in my family I can count on to tell me the truth. If this Johnny Monroe character is my father, I want to hear it from her lips.

"Did you know that woman who showed up yesterday?" I ask, thinking Uncle Daniel probably knows everything, but he's under Mama's spell and sworn to secrecy.

He stops on the side of the road, letting the truck idle. Then he turns and looks at me like he's weighing the checks and balances on one of his ledgers.

"Melody grew up here," he says. "I knew her family for years."

"Tell me about them," I say.

Uncle Daniel taps the steering wheel, like he's drumming up the past.

"Arthur Monroe, Melody's father, served in World War I and got gassed and supposedly was never the same," he begins. "Arthur couldn't get work, and they were really struggling. I used to take them vegetables from our garden every now and again, and your grandfather used to take them eggs and whatever he thought would help."

I wonder if this Arthur Monroe is my other grandfather.

"The mother died pretty young, and there were three children," he continues. "An older boy, Johnny, and then two girls, Ruby and Melody. Melody was the youngest. I hadn't seen her since she was a little girl. Skinny little thing. Really quiet. The other sister, Ruby, died young, and then Melody was sent off to live with relatives. She's had a rough life, that's for sure," Uncle Daniel concludes.

"What was the brother like?" I ask, not telling him why I want to know.

Uncle Daniel pauses again, and winces as though his leg is bothering him, but he hasn't even used the clutch. "Johnny was a sad case," he begins again, "especially since his daddy used to slap him around."

"How did he die?" I ask. It is a simple question, except I may be talking about my daddy.

"Accident," Uncle Daniel says. "He fell."

I wait for more. "If that's the long answer, I'd hate to hear the short version," I say. I try to be funny, like Mama is sometimes, but Uncle Daniel isn't amused. He rubs his other leg like that one is suddenly hurting, too. I wonder how far to go with my questions, but then he starts the truck again like he's finished. We are quiet for the rest of the ride.

When we turn to go down the road to Great Aunt Sadie's house, Uncle Daniel tells me he's not going to lie to Mama about where I am.

"Tell her I'll talk to her when she gets home after work," I say.

He says he will.

"Give me a call if you need a ride home," he says.

I say I will and get out of the truck.

As I approach the house, Great Aunt Sadie comes out of the barn carrying a baby goat. For an old lady, she is still strong. She smiles when she sees me like I am a friend she hasn't seen for a while. A hawk feather sticks out her brown fedora, her long, white hair captured under the hat.

At the end of the driveway, Uncle Daniel gives the truck horn a quick toot and waves to Great Aunt Sadie. I hadn't realized he was watching.

"To what do I owe this pleasure?" she says.

She delivers the baby goat to my arms. "Isn't she a beauty?" she asks, before I have time to answer. "I'm taking her to the side yard so she can hang out with the other kids for a while and give her mama a rest."

The faint smell of mama's milk is on the kid's breath, and I can feel its beating heart against my chest.

"Baby animals make the world softer somehow," Great Aunt Sadie says. "Birth of any kind is a miracle when you think about it."

For the first time that day I think of Crow and wonder if I'll have a family someday.

When Great Aunt Sadie opens the wooden gate to the side field, I put the goat down and she wobbles off to meet her siblings and cousins. My great aunt hasn't asked why I'm not in school or why I might want to visit a day after I just saw her.

"You need to talk?" She has a way of knowing things even if you don't speak them. "Let's go inside," she adds, with a nod.

Unlike Uncle Daniel, whose allegiances are clearly drawn, Great Aunt Sadie is as loyal to me as she is to Mama. She brought us both into the world. We make our way into the kitchen and wash the goat smell off our hands.

In contrast to the Monroe cabin, the room is full of light and living things. Different herbs line the window sills and English ivy crawls from pots toward the light. She likes to bring outside things inside, and on warmer days she practically lives outside.

An abandoned wasp's nest is on the top of the tall kitchen cabinet and a small robin's nest with two broken blue shells sits at the center of the table. I take note to see if there's anything new and spy a fragile snakeskin resting on the ledge near the door. Several smooth white stones are stacked nearby.

"Thirsty?" she asks.

I nod.

She gives me a glass of pure well water from a white pitcher. I drink it all at once.

"You had lunch?"

"Not yet," I say, knowing it won't be long before I have a feast before me.

As expected, she cuts up potatoes and onions and fries them in butter on the stove and tosses in herbs from the windowsill. Then she takes four eggs sitting in a basket and breaks them in the middle of the potatoes and onions. She slices two big pieces of bread from the loaf sitting on the counter and places them in the oven to brown. Then she sets the strawberry preserves that Granny made on the table. Her food always tastes different than Granny's, with different flavors that taste like surprises.

Plates in front of us, she tosses her hat on a nearby chair, and her hair falls to her shoulders.

"Bless this food we are about to receive," she says, with a wink toward the ceiling like she and God share the kitchen.

I hadn't realized how hungry I was until the food was before me. Somehow finding out secrets steals an appetite away, at least until enticed by a lunch like this one.

"Okay, out with it," she says, after a few bites. "I know you've got questions or you wouldn't be here."

I pause long enough to form the words. "Does it count as a lie if someone knows something you should know but they don't tell you?"

"Is this a riddle?" she asks, dead serious.

I pause again to figure out how to make it clear.

"Like if someone has a secret that involves you, but they don't tell you about it, is that still a lie?"

"I guess it's a lie of omission," Great Aunt Sadie says. "Why?"

"I went to see Melody Monroe," I say, my confession unplanned.

Sadie stops mid-chew.

"What did she say?" she asks, her voice veering towards what could be mistaken as a low growl.

"She said that her brother, Johnny, is my father."

Her fork falls on the plate with a sharp clang, making us both jump. Then her eyes grow serious. "Does your mother know you talked to her?"

"Not yet."

Great Aunt Sadie wrings her hands long enough for her food to grow cold, and the wrinkles on her forehead have multiplied. I don't like seeing her worried. It makes me wonder if I am wrong for seeking out the truth.

"Keep in mind, Lily, that nothing is as it seems," she says, finally. "You may think you know the story and it can turn out to be something else entirely."

"Did all of you know?" I ask.

"Did all of us know what?" she says.

"Did all of you know who my father was? Did all of you keep it from me?"

She pushes aside her plate, the eggs and potatoes of little interest to her now. "You need to talk to your mother," she says.

"But she's the one who lied to me." I tell myself to stay calm.

Her look has kindness in it. "First of all, you need to hear the whole story before you make up your mind about things," she says. "You know your mama wouldn't knowingly do anything to hurt you. You know that, Lily, don't you?"

I don't answer and push my plate away, too. It's true that Melody may be lying, but that doesn't change the fact that my entire family has been lying to me by omission for the last fourteen years. Mama being the one who omitted the most.

"Melody said her brother, Johnny, dropped out of sixth grade and was meaner than a snake. Is that who my father was? A lowlife who didn't even finish elementary school? Why was Mama with him? Was she that hard up?"

Great Aunt Sadie rises, placing her fists on the wooden table. "Don't you ever talk about your mama like that." Her eyes don't waver from mine.

I swallow. It's the first time she's raised her voice to me.

"Your mama is one of the bravest souls I've ever met on this earth," she says. "And she does not deserve one moment of your criticism."

I lower my head and agree.

"I've said too much already," she continues. "You need to talk to her, and not make harsh conclusions until you hear the whole story."

Her lips form a stern line and her eyes appear darker than their usual gray.

"I guarantee you that Melody Monroe wants something out of this," she begins again. "I could see that look in her eyes when she showed up at your house yesterday. That girl has had a hard life. Her daddy wasn't right in the head, and her sister was one of the saddest souls I've ever seen. You be careful, Lily," she continues. "You be careful who you trust and who you don't trust. Your mama has stood by you every day of your life. You need to hear her side of the story before you go jumping to conclusions."

Two robin's eggs shells sit on the windowsill. More than ever, I want to fly away from Katy's Ridge and never return. For the first time, I don't care how much my leaving will hurt Mama. Even after Great Aunt Sadie told me not trust Melody's words, I somehow know it is true that Johnny Monroe is my daddy. And no matter how much people defend Mama, she should have told me these things a long time ago.

CHAPTER TWELVE

Wildflower

After arriving back at the mill, I find Daniel still sitting at Daddy's desk. "Lily knows about Johnny," he says.

I close my eyes and shake my head, not knowing whether to cry or cuss. "Where is she?"

"Sadie's," he says.

"What should I do, Daniel? Should I go to her?"

"I don't think so," he says. "I think she needs time to get used to it. Sadie will help with that."

It's hard for me not to rush over to Aunt Sadie's house, but I need to think about what to do next. I don't know how much she knows, or what Melody told her. That will have a lot to do with how I respond.

Unable to get anything done at the mill, I drive to June Sector's house. I need a friend to talk to and Bee is still in school. All morning I've been thinking about how to tell Lily the truth, but Melody has beat me to it. I hate to think of Lily in that broken-down cabin, and I am relieved to know she's now over at Aunt Sadie's.

I park in the grass near the house, next to the Sector's old Buick, and walk toward the door. When I reach the porch, Horatio, June's husband, greets me—his tall, thin frame towering over me. Horatio is full Cherokee and his wife, June, is white. Until I gave birth to Lily, they were the primary outcasts in Katy's Ridge.

"Still got that good luck charm I gave you?" Horatio asks the same question every time he sees me.

From my pocket, I pull out the small leather pouch with the star ruby inside to show him that I still carry it everywhere I go. The ruby was a gift from Horatio after Daddy died. For years now I've felt that Lily was my good luck charm, a gemstone in the midst of a sea of ordinary rocks.

"June around?" I ask.

"Out back," he says.

A moment later, Crow comes out of the house to greet me.

"I didn't know you were home," I say.

"I'm on military leave," he says.

I remember when Crow was a toddler running around the yard. Now he's taller than his daddy and handsome—dark hair, blue eyes—blessed by the best parts of his parents.

"Does Lily know you're home?" I ask. It's no secret she's had a crush on him since she was in third grade and he was in seventh.

"Pearl asked her over for supper." He smiles, like it's something he's looking forward to.

Since Daniel said Lily wants to talk tonight, I'm wondering how she plans to do both.

"I'm here to see your mom," I say to Crow.

"She's out back," he says, sounding like his daddy.

When I walk around the side of the house, I find June hanging laundry on the line. A breeze blows the clothes like sails on giant sailboats I've seen pictures of in Daddy's books.

"You got time to talk?" I ask.

"Sure," she says, as if she's been expecting me.

June continues hanging the line, and I grab a wet blouse from the top of the clothes basket. I shake the water and wrinkles out and hang the blouse on the line.

"What's up?" she says.

"All hell is breaking loose," I say.

She glances over at me. "What do you mean?"

June has always been easy to talk to, easier than anyone in my family, and maybe even easier than Bee.

"Melody Monroe came back to Katy's Ridge yesterday," I say.

June's eyes widen, confirmation that I'm not imagining how bad this is.

"Why in the world would she come back?" June asks.

"Doc Lester wrote a letter telling her she had a niece."

"He sticks his nose into everything," June says, hanging several pairs of white socks on the clothesline.

I agree.

Doc Lester has called June a witch on more than one occasion because she reads palms and tea leaves. He's said similar things about Aunt Sadie.

"How do you know she's back?"

"She showed up at the house yesterday."

"On the anniversary?" June's eyes widen again.

I nod. "There's more," I say. "I went to see her this morning and told her that if she cared about Lily she wouldn't tell her anything about Johnny. But I just heard from Daniel that she already did."

June snaps the wrinkles out of one of Crow's uniform shirts and finishes the last of the laundry. She offers me one of the chairs Horatio made for the backyard. Then she joins me. The spot overlooks a valley with the soft mountains circling like ancestors. I take a deep breath.

"I've always loved it here." I tell her.

June looks out over the mountains, as if she hasn't seen them thousands of times before. "Does Melody know what happened?"

"I'm not sure," I say. "She knows Johnny is Lily's father because she asked me what it was like that Lily looked so much like him."

"She said that? Oh, honey, I'm so sorry." She pats my hand. "Should have known Doc Lester would be at the center of this mess."

"To be honest, I'm surprised it has stayed a secret for as long as it did," I say.

"Mountain people can be loyal even when they shun you." June grins, but then gets serious again.

"Isn't it strange that Lily hasn't found out before now?" I say. "Looks like somebody would have told her."

"That child's been protected her whole life," June begins, "and not just by you. Sometimes I think your daddy is watching out for her, too."

Tears threaten to come and June takes my hand.

"Don't worry, you'll get through this," she says. "You've been through much harder things."

"But, June, what if this leads to that other secret coming out?"

She looks at me. She knows exactly what secret I'm referring to. "Then we'll deal with that, too," she says, her tone resolute.

"Have you thought about confronting Doc Lester?" she asks.

"And say what?" I ask. "He's basically told a secret that everybody in Katy's Ridge already knows."

"Except Lily," June reminds me.

"Except Lily," I repeat. "I'm beginning to see the unfairness in not telling her." I can tell June things I've never told anyone. Not even Bee. For some reason, I feel totally safe with her.

"What else did Melody tell you?" June asks.

"She wants to take Lily to Kentucky to visit an old dying aunt who wants to meet her. But something doesn't feel right."

"Then don't let her go," June says.

"Don't worry," I say. "I have no intention of letting her go."

"Does Nell know Melody is back?

"Mama pulled a shotgun on her yesterday and had it cocked before Melody finally got the message to leave."

June laughs. "She protects her own, your mother."

I nod. "I wonder what Daddy would do about Melody," I say to June.

"He'd probably try to reason with her," she says.

I pause. "Actually, I think Daddy probably would have told Lily the truth a long time ago, when she first asked," I say. "But I didn't have the courage for that, evidently."

We look at the mountains, as if they might hold answers to my current situation.

"By the way, Lily didn't go to school today," I begin again. "She went over to the Monroe cabin and now she's at Aunt Sadie's."

"Well, if anybody can talk sense into her, it will be Sadie," June says.

I agree.

"You need to talk to Lily, too," June says. "It's time."

"I know," I say, "but that doesn't mean I want to do it."

"I know," she echoes.

"Why did I think I could keep this secret indefinitely?" I ask her.

She glances back at the house. "A time comes when we can't protect our children from the world anymore."

"That's exactly what Daniel said," I say.

"Well, Daniel's right," she begins again. "We can't prevent them being hurt. The best we can do is be around to help pick up the pieces if they fall."

I thank June for being here for me.

"When does Crow leave?" I ask.

"Tomorrow, late," she says, with a quick inhale. "Pearl invited Lily over for supper. That okay with you?"

"Sure," I say. "Though she hasn't said a word to me about it yet, and she told Daniel she wanted to talk to me tonight."

"She's got other things on her mind, I guess," she says. "We'll have plenty, regardless. You're welcome to come, too," she adds.

I thank her again, not knowing what my evening may bring. "June, what if Lily hates me after this? If Mama kept a secret from me for fourteen years, I'd be furious."

She stands, looking over at the laundry on the line. "She won't stay angry for long," June says. "She knows how much you love her. Hell, everybody in Katy's Ridge knows how much you love her."

"Do they?"

"That's another reason they've probably kept quiet all these years," she says. "They've been struck speechless by how much you love that girl. Don't underestimate the power of love when it comes to healing things."

We walk together to the front of the house where Horatio and Crow sit on the porch. In the distance, Pearl walks down the road with two of her siblings. School is out.

"You stay safe," I say, and give Crow a hug.

He promises he will.

Pearl walks up to the porch and smiles at her brother, happy he's still here.

"You see Lily today?" I ask her.

She looks away.

"I know she skipped school," I say. "They called."

"I haven't talked to her since yesterday afternoon when I came over to your house," Pearl says.

I realize that was before Melody made her appearance. "She may need to talk to you later," I say. "Something big has happened."

Pearl grins like she's itching to know what happened. Sometimes I wonder why Pearl and Lily are friends. Pearl seems younger, somehow. Lily is quieter. She might even be called shy, if not for her singing. When she sings, she changes. She fills with life. She's happy when she sings, and her constant questioning stops. It's as if the answers flow from her then, and she is totally herself. The feeling visits me again that whatever is going on is far from over, and that no secret is safe.

CHAPTER THIRTEEN

Lily

After talking to Great Aunt Sadie, I decide to go to the mill to talk to Mama. When I walk I usually sing something, or at the very least I hum a tune, but today I don't feel like singing. I can't remember another time when this was true.

As I come to the crossroads, I stop long enough to grab my school books and the lunch Granny packed for me that morning from behind the boulder. I take a bite out of the apple from my lunch and glance down the road that leads back to the Monroe place. I wonder if the woman, who could be my aunt, is still sitting in that dark cabin.

In the span of one day, I am in more trouble than I've ever been. I skipped school. I went to a stranger's cabin without telling anybody where I was going, and I lied to Uncle Cecil. According to Daniel, the school called so Mama already knows about the skipping. Right now, I don't even care if I have to do extra chores for an entire year. I deserve punishment.

Whenever I act like Mama, Granny likes to say that the apple doesn't fall far from the tree. Maybe getting in all this trouble is me being like my daddy. I toss what's left of the apple as far as I can into the woods, wishing I'd never gone to Melody Monroe's.

I need to ask Mama flat out: *Is Johnny Monroe my daddy?* And if he is, she needs to tell me her side of the story, like Great Aunt Sadie said.

When I get to the mill, it is late afternoon and Miss Blackstone's car is parked out front. Uncle Daniel and Silas—who help out—are gone. Miss Blackstone was my elementary school teacher for years, since all of the grades are in one room. For as long as I can remember, she's been Mama's best friend. Like Pearl and me, they spend a lot of time together talking. It suddenly occurs to me that I haven't given Pearl an answer about coming to supper. Crow is only home for two more days, and I almost forgot because of everything else that's going on. But first, I need to deal with Mama.

Miss Blackstone's Ford sedan is a newer model, black with white trim. Her family has enough money for newer cars. She wears store bought dresses and always buttons the top button of her blouses. She is tall and lean and doesn't have much of a figure. Whenever I was bored at school, I would study her,

like you study someone you admire. If becoming a world renowned singer doesn't work out, I might teach school when I
grow up. Miss Blackstone said I was smart enough.

Besides the older widows at church, Mama and Miss
Blackstone are the only unmarried women in Katy's Ridge. As
far as I know, Miss Blackstone has never dated, and appears
about as interested in the possibility as Mama.

I think of Melody Monroe. I didn't see a ring on her hand,
either, making her a maiden aunt if she's anything at all.

Please, God, don't let me be related to her, I say to myself.

With no saws running, the double doors in front are
closed and the mill is quiet. I walk around to the side door, a
short cut to Mama's office. A small window is on the outside
wall, about six feet from the ground. I want to see what kind
of mood Mama is in before I talk to her, so I stand on a large
log to see inside. A twinge of guilt causes me to pause, as I
add spying to the list of bad things I've done today. If Johnny
Monroe was kin, I'm collecting my inheritance awfully fast.

Through the window, I see Mama in her office talking to
Miss Blackstone. They are both smiling, a good sign that this
may be the time to talk. Mama is never this happy at home. I
lean closer to hear, but their voices are muffled. Seeing them
together invites a prickle of goosebumps onto my arms. It reminds me of the time I accidentally saw Granny stepping out
of the bath tub. Seeing all that flesh that was usually hidden
under a dress and apron was shocking to me. Her breasts

sagged like flour sacks, and I remember the light brown V of hair between her legs.

Mama and Miss Blackstone are different together. Miss Blackstone, who was serious at school, is smiling, too, like there's no place she'd rather be than talking to Mama. I think of my friendship with Pearl, and how we're never this happy. Pearl irritates me when she goes on and on about boys, and she has the patience of a flea on a dog when it comes to listening to me. Pearl is probably looking for me right now. I remind myself I need to see Crow before he leaves, but I can't pull myself away from watching Mama be so happy.

I feel like Pumpkin waiting at the door for scraps. But every time I start to step away from the window, I get pulled back to the scene. Their movements tell a story. They touch each other occasionally. A hand on an arm. A finger pointing that the other one grabs. It is Mama's playfulness that surprises me most. Though I've known her playful, it's mainly been with me, not other grownups.

If anything, Mama can be way too serious. Yet when she puts the worry down—like now—she looks like a totally different person. A beautiful person. I like that Miss Blackstone brings this out in her, and surprise myself with the wish that I could someday make her this happy, too. The closest I get is when I sing.

Captured by the scene, I forget why I'm here. As much as I know it isn't respectful to spy on people, I can't seem to walk away. Something is about to happen, and if I turn away I'll miss it. The whole day has felt like this. I wonder again if this is the secret sense Mama's talked about. My life feels like one of those radio series Granny loves to listen to. A mystery is about to be solved, and somehow Mama and Miss Blackstone are part of the mystery, too.

The desk is the biggest thing in the small room. A couple of wooden chairs sit along one wall. Chairs I used to build a fort when I was a little girl and spent time in Mama's office. Now Mama and Miss Blackstone laugh, and I try to remember the last time I saw Miss Blackstone even chuckle. Maybe it was the time Crow stuck a piece of chalk up his nose and pretended it was an elephant tusk. Crow was four grades ahead of me and sat at the other end of the room, and was always trying to make us laugh.

Every now and again I realize how pretty Mama is. Not the way Aunt Jo is pretty, in that movie star way, but Mama has her own beauty that's hard to describe. It's like she fits perfectly in her skin, and possesses an ease I hope I have someday, instead of always feeling so awkward. It's hard to see how I'm like her when I look in the mirror. For the first time I wonder if she's been looking at me my entire life and remembering someone *as mean as a snake*.

Mama would be upset if she knew I was spying on her. She's cautioned me more than once that I might regret overhearing things. I imagine those regrets go for seeing things, too.

Mama moves closer to Miss Blackstone, her hand touching her arm. For a long time, they just look at each other, and then Mama touches her face. Gripping the window ledge, I lean closer to the glass to make sure it's not a distortion. Through the dirty panes, I see Mama lean forward and kiss Miss Blackstone on the lips. Not a quick peck between friends, but a kiss I imagined I'd have with Crow someday after we got married. I remember the romance novels I found hidden in the closet that belonged to Aunt Meg. Books I sneaked and read on the flat boulder back behind the house. Books whose stories seem mild compared to what I'm seeing now.

My breath fogs up the window, and I lean back to erase my presence. In my awkwardness, I jerk back and lose my footing, unable to right myself. When I fall, I knock over a wheelbarrow nearby that clunks to the ground. I land on sawdust so I'm not hurt, but I'm certain I've been heard.

Within seconds, the door opens and Mama looks down at me, her face as red as mine feels.

Mama's expression spells out bad news like a headline on the Rocky Bluff newspaper. Miss Blackstone stands behind Mama, almost a head taller. Their kiss replays in my mind. I didn't know women kissed each other like that.

"Lily McAllister, how long have you been spying on us?" Mama says. Upon hearing my full name, I know I am in trouble with a capital T.

"Not long," I say, but the truth is, I've been standing there long enough for my whole life to change. From now on, I will always look at the two of them differently.

Brushing sawdust from my clothes, I get to my feet. For the second time that day I get the urge to run. This time I do.

CHAPTER FOURTEEN

Wildflower

Lily takes off running, and I know better than to take off after her. She can easily outrun her boy cousins, as well as me.

"Oh my God, what have we done?" I say to Bee.

Bee covers her mouth, as though to keep herself from screaming.

I pick up the wheelbarrow, giving it a kick as I do.

"Should I go after her? Should I try to explain?" I ask.

Bee sends a frantic look in my direction. "I don't know what we should do," she says.

We exchange desperate looks.

"I was afraid this would happen," I say to her. "I was afraid someone might see us. But I didn't think anyone would be around."

"Let's just stay calm," Bee says. She rests a hand on her neck like she does when she's thinking and stares at the floor. "Do you think Lily will tell anybody?" She looks at me.

"I don't think so, but how would I know? This has never happened before."

We go back to my office. I sit at Daddy's desk while Bee paces the room. I search for solutions written on the wooden floors.

"We've been so careful," she says. "Spacing out our visits. Not spending too much time at either of our houses. Early curfews."

"What if Lily never speaks to me again, Bee? What if she hates me now?" I bury my head in my hands.

"That doesn't sound like Lily," Bee says, her voice softer now.

"This is my fault," I say, looking up at her. "I told Daniel to tell Lily to come by and see me. Then I forgot about it. When you're around I forget about everything." I glance at Bee and my face colors again.

"You'll talk to her," Bee says. "You'll tell her how important it is that nobody know."

People finding out is Bee's biggest fear. Mine is having the people I love turn their back on me.

"We're not criminals," I say.

"It's the mountain laws of Katy's Ridge we've got to worry about," she says. "The people here are frightened of anything they don't understand. They surely won't understand this."

We pause in our panic. We are as far away from each other as we can get in the small room. Her at the window. Me now standing by the door. My face has not cooled down. I remember reading *The Scarlet Letter* and wonder what initial I will have to sew onto my clothes for this transgression. I walk over and sit at Daddy's desk. It is the desk version of trying to fill someone's shoes. It is too big for me. For the first time I'm glad he isn't alive to see my possible downfall.

"What is wrong with us?" I say, the tears starting now. "Why can't we be normal?"

"Hush, Wildflower," she says, her voice softer still. She rarely calls me Wildflower anymore, and I am surprised by how much comfort the name offers.

We've had this conversation many times before. I've spent hours wishing I was different. Wishing I didn't love Bee the way I do. I've fallen to my knees many times, not a soul to comfort me, except for the woman I can't help loving. Somehow, I don't think Daddy would condemn me. He would love me regardless. It would never occur to him not to. Though I doubt Mama would ever understand. This is the kind of thing that might finally break us apart forever. As for Aunt Sadie, I feel safe from judgment, but she may feel hurt that she didn't know. I haven't had the courage to speak to her about it. Not yet.

When it occurs to me how many people could be hurt, I lower my head and a tear drops into my lap. "Maybe we should end this, Bee. End it before anybody else finds out."

She stops her pacing and walks over to the desk. "Is that what you want to do?" she asks.

When I finally look up, tears glisten in her brown eyes. "No," I say, even though I'm not so sure. "All I know is I can't bring any more shame to my family, Bee. Remember Lily's birth? The whispers in church?"

"That was Johnny's shame, not yours," she says, her voice raised. "You fought back as hard as you could and you still nearly died."

Bee can get like this. Protective. Supportive. Refusing to let ignorance win. Even my own. "I haven't forgotten," she begins again. "I came to see you after it happened. Remember? He beat you up so badly you couldn't move. You have not brought shame on your family, Wildflower McAllister. You have not!"

She takes my chin and raises it so our eyes meet. Her bottom lip quivers and a tear slides down her cheek. I look away. It feels unbearable to see her in pain, a mirror of my own.

"As for us, we try to be honorable people," she continues, her knuckles rapping on the desk. "We go out of our way to be helpful. We love our families—"

Bee's tears flow now. I hand her one of Daddy's handkerchiefs from my pocket. To see someone experiencing so much sorrow feels almost unbearable to me. She blows her nose and wipes the tears away, but they keep coming. I can't help but think that I'm the cause of her unhappiness. I apologize and she tells me to stop. Then I hold her, feeling her body quake, until her tears finally stop. It doesn't seem fair that so much pain could come from loving another person. But it does.

Minutes later, I remember the look in Lily's eyes. She is hurting now, too. The hurt of not understanding what she saw. Shame threatens to overpower me again. I push it away. Life can be such a mess sometimes. Daddy always said that people will do the right thing if challenged, that goodness will win out. But I'm not so sure I believe that anymore. From my experience, people choose meanness at about the same rate as they choose goodness. It's the conflicts in life that test us to see which side we'll choose.

"What do we do now?" Bee asks, pulling me from my thoughts. She looks beaten and afraid.

"First, I need to find Lily and talk to her," I say.

"What will you tell her?" Bee asks.

"I'm not sure." I grab the keys to my truck off the desk and kiss Bee lightly on the lips, glancing up at the window where Lily watched us. I'm surprised I didn't see her.

"Let me know what happens," she says.

"I will if I can," I say. "But I may not come back here today." The only place I can use the telephone to call Bee is from the sawmill. It's too big a risk to call her from one of my sisters' houses. I wonder if Mama will ever give in to having a telephone installed at the house. She was slow to see the benefits of indoor plumbing. It was Daddy who could talk her into the 20th century. But I have much bigger problems at this moment than telephones.

"Were you serious about breaking up with me?" Bee's eyes are rimmed with red.

"I didn't mean it," I say. "It was just a reaction to the day. It's just sometimes I think it would be easier."

She turns away, and I apologize again. However, if it came to having to choose whether to have Lily in my life or Bee, chances are Bee wouldn't like my answer.

CHAPTER FIFTEEN

Lily

I can't remember the last time I ran like this. Away from the one person I thought I could count on. A part of me wants to run all the way to Rocky Bluff and then to the first city I can find. Chattanooga or Nashville or maybe even Knoxville. Then I will finally be rid of Katy's Ridge forever. What I didn't anticipate is that I want to rid myself of Mama, too.

Is Mama in love with Miss Blackstone? I ask myself.

The thought tastes bitter in my mouth, like the goldenseal or dandelion that Great Aunt Sadie uses in her strong tonics when one of us is sick.

My hair flies wherever it wants to go. I wish I had on my old shoes instead of the new ones that aren't fully broken in. They would be easier to run in. But these will do. I slow down long enough to take the dirt road to Pearl's house. I have so much to tell her. Too much. But I can't tell her about Mama. I can't run the risk of everybody in Katy's Ridge finding out.

But I can tell her what I found out from Melody Monroe. Although that feels like old news now. News I found out a hundred years ago instead of this morning.

Shame pumps through me as I run. Followed by hatred. I have never hated Mama before, not for one second. But I do now. I hate her for not telling me about Johnny Monroe. I hate her for kissing Miss Blackstone. I hate her for not being like everybody else.

At school, most people my age have mothers who stay at home. Or they work as school teachers or nurses. They certainly don't work at sawmills or run their own businesses. And they certainly don't kiss another woman.

"I hate you!" I yell as loud as I can on the way to Pearl's house.

Spit mixes with my fly-away hair. The road is not muddy like on the way to the Monroe place, but I slow my pace. I feel tired from the day. Tired from running like a colt out of a barn into an unfenced pasture. My heartbeat echoes in my ears. My day was already spoiled with the visit to Melody's. And now this. I flash on Mama looking into Miss Blackstone's eyes and touching her face and then shake my head to wipe away the pictures. In the next instant, I decide I hate Miss Blackstone, too. Up until twenty minutes ago, she was probably one of the five people I most admired in the world, along with Mama. But now, I never want to see either of them again.

My lungs burning, I slow to a walk. When I reach Pearl's house, I knock on the door, winded and close to tears.

June Sector opens the screen door, an old diaper slung over her shoulder like she's been cleaning.

"Lily, are you okay?" she says when she gets a look at me.

"I'm fine, ma'am," I say, thinking that I'm getting good at being a liar, which is probably a Monroe family trait.

"You don't look fine," she says.

"Is Crow still here?" I ask.

Seeing Crow again may be the only thing that can redeem one of the worst days of my life. The only thing that comes close to competing is when I got my period in eighth grade on a day I wore a white dress to school. Miss Blackstone went with me to the bathroom and helped me wash out my dress, and then loaned me a Kotex pad and a sanitary belt and one of her big sweaters to wear over the dress. Thankfully, Miss Blackstone is tall so the sweater was almost as long as my dress. I tremble with the thought. Then I remember Mama kissing Miss Blackstone and shudder.

"Crow is out hunting with his daddy," June Sector says. "Does your mama know you're here?"

I tell her no.

The Sectors are friends of Mama's. I've played with Pearl and her brothers and sisters since I was in diapers. No wonder Mama is friends with every outcast in Katy's Ridge. She's one, too. I guess I didn't want to see it, because that makes me the daughter of an outcast, and one of them. I'm not sure why this never occurred to me. I guess I didn't want to see it. After all, the reason Mama is an outsider is because she had me.

June Sector hasn't moved from the door and looks at me like she's trying to get a reading.

"I'm actually here for Pearl," I say, standing straighter, doing my level best to act normal.

She calls for Pearl.

Rumors have spread for years that June Sector is a witch. But I've known her for as long as I can remember, and I've never seen her do anything witch-like. No brooms or caldrons or black clothes are in sight. Although to some people even having the secret sense is suspect, so telling fortunes is even worse. Backward ways, Mama calls them. Everybody has backward ways, she says, even people in big cities. But I don't trust what Mama says anymore. My list of reasons to leave Katy's Ridge is growing.

When I look up from my thoughts, June Sector is still at the door. "Are you staying for supper, Lily?"

It's only then I remember I'm supposed to come to supper tonight. I can't believe I forgot about this in the midst of all the other trouble. Any other time I would have been dreamy all day with anticipation.

"I haven't asked permission yet, but I guess so," I say. At that moment, I don't care if Mama gets mad at me. I wish I could leave with Crow tomorrow and go to Korea, or anywhere far away.

If Granny finds out Mama has been kissing Miss Blackstone, I doubt Mama will be welcome to live at the house anymore. Will I have to go, too? What will we do then? Mama always tells me there are consequences to our behavior.

Well, Mama, what are the consequences of this? I want to ask her. My confusion deepens.

Even though I've seen Mama and Miss Blackstone together hundreds of times, I've never seen them smile at each other the way they did at the mill. I've never seen them hold hands or even touch. For them to be so different behind closed doors means it's a secret what they're doing, and maybe it's a dangerous secret at that.

When Pearl arrives, her hair is wet from a bath. She pulls me to the side porch where we can't be overheard.

"Lily, what's wrong? You look horrible. Have you been crying?"

I'm not sure what to say, or where to start.

"Talk to me," she says in a half-whisper. "Where were you today? You didn't come to school."

"Long story," I say, finding my voice again.

It really is a long story. I haven't even told her about the stranger who visited yesterday. A stranger named Melody, who could very well be my aunt, the sister of my daddy. My daddy being a stupid snake, as it turns out. It also turns out that Mama may be something even worse.

All of a sudden, I don't want to call him 'daddy' any more. It's like he hasn't earned it. A daddy is what Bolt and Nat have in Uncle Daniel. A daddy is what Pearl has with Mr. Sector.

It's someone who has been around and helped you with things.

My thoughts are still running even though I'm standing still. If it's okay for two women to kiss, then why have I never seen anyone doing it before? And why would Mama hang around with someone snake-like? Questions overwhelm me. Questions I may never find out the answers to since Mama—who I plan to never speak to again—is my main source for answers. I'm not even sure what Great Aunt Sadie would have to say about this.

"Talk to me," Pearl says. "You're acting like you've seen a ghost or something."

"Not a ghost," I say, thinking the apparition that's shown itself is actually a side of mama I never knew existed.

"Tell me what's happened." She grabs both of my shoulders and gives me a shake. I have to resist knocking her to the ground.

"Are you mad at me?" she asks. Her lips form a pout.

"No," I say. "I've just had a really bad day."

"I wish you'd tell me what happened," she says. "We're best friends."

I pause. I can't tell Pearl. Pearl's loose lips could sink a fleet of battleships, and no matter how angry I am at Mama and Miss Blackstone, I don't want them to get in trouble.

Seconds later, Crow and Mr. Sector come out of the forest each carrying a rifle and two rabbits. Rabbit stew is probably on the menu for supper. Crow smiles when he sees me and it

reminds me of how Mama smiled at Miss Blackstone. I wonder if I'll ever be able to get that picture out of my mind.

Crow seems older than when he left to join the Army a
year ago. His eyes linger on mine, as though he's noticing how
much I've grown up, too. I even have a bit of a figure now.
Though, honestly, not that much of one. I couldn't be Lana
Turner if I tried.

Pearl gives me a poke in the ribs that nearly knocks me off
the porch, and Crow grins at me again.

"See, I told you he likes you," she whispers.

I imagine Cupid's arrow aimed at my heart, but I don't
have time to fall in love right now. My whole life is collapsing
in a heap on the floor like a steamer trunk emptying itself of
secrets. Not to mention that I'm about to disown Mama.

CHAPTER SIXTEEN

Wildflower

Running up a hill reminds you real quick how old you are, but I need to find Lily. It will be dark in an hour. When I arrive, instead of Lily, I find Mama sweeping the front porch. A ritual she does every evening for three seasons of the year. Out of breath, I stop at the bottom of the steps and lean over.

"What is it?" she asks. Her frantic voice and the alarm in her eyes give me a snapshot of history—the day they brought Daddy up this hill for the last time. The day that changed all of our lives in an instant. My biggest fear is that *this* day will change all our lives, too. Especially mine and Lily's, and maybe Bee's.

My breath still labored, Mama snaps her broom to attention. "Louisa May, if you don't tell me this instant what's going on I'm going to swat you with this broom."

"Is Lily here?" I ask.

"No she isn't," Mama says. "What's wrong?"

"I just need to talk to her." A stitch grabs my side. I lean over again to give myself relief.

"You don't run all the way up that steep hill just because you need to talk to somebody. What's happened?" she asks again.

I make sure I'm not within swatting distance. Mama is almost as dangerous with a broom as she is with a shotgun.

"You two have a falling out?" she asks, a hand on one hip.

"Yes, Mama, you could say that we've had a falling out."

I wait for her to look pleased, but she doesn't.

"Sometimes I think you spoil that girl," she says instead.

Now that my breath has returned, I feel riled. "The only thing I've spoiled Lily with is love," I say.

We exchange a stare like old times.

Mama begins to sweep again, with a fierceness that was absent before. But then she stops, like she's thought better of it. After Daddy died, she gritted her teeth and kept going, determined to plow through to the end of the row. Yet, as she ages, I've noticed her jaw loosen, as if she's given up some of her fight.

"She'll be home directly. It's almost supper time," Mama says. "That girl doesn't miss a meal."

My shoulders relax. I'm glad we're not going to fight. I don't think I could take two members of my immediate family angry at me. Not today, anyway.

I remember what June said earlier about inviting Lily over to supper. "She may be eating at Pearl's tonight," I say, to the sound of the broom hitting the wooden floor.

The swish stops. "Well, I wish somebody had told me that," Mama says. "I've cooked enough for three people."

Truth is, Mama always cooks for six, as if Daddy and all my sisters still lived at home.

"Of course, you two never think of me," she adds.

"You know that's not true," I say to her.

My anger kicks up dust again that no broom can touch. But it's not Mama that I'm angry with. It's the world. A world that says Bee and me loving each other is wrong and needs hiding. A world where women aren't always given a choice. A world where mothers and daughters don't talk about things and misunderstand each other.

"I don't want to fight, Mama, I'm just worried about Lily."

"What did you two get in a tiff about?" Mama leans her broom against the house and sits in her porch rocker like she's all of a sudden tired. I forget sometimes that she'll soon be fifty years old.

Before answering her question, I play with the idea of being honest. What would life be like if every single one of us just told the truth? My bravery rises and falls with the swiftness of a chimney sweep.

"It's nothing really," I say. "Just a misunderstanding. If she shows up here at the house, just tell her I'm looking for her."

Mama rocks, and I catch a glimpse of her in her old age. Frail. Tired. Ready to meet up with Daddy again. Sometimes it feels like I will always be the girl I was at thirteen, and Mama will always be the same age she was back then. But time keeps rocking on. All of us in the rhythm of growing older.

My thoughts swing from Mama to Lily. For the first time I realize that—unlike me—Lily probably won't stay in Katy's Ridge her whole life. She doesn't talk about it, but I know from the books she reads that she wants to travel. She can name every state capital in the U.S., learned from a map tacked inside the bedroom closet we share. The same closet I shared with my sisters when I was growing up. Pretty soon it will be me sitting on this porch, rocking into my old age, finally getting a bedroom to myself and waiting for Lily to find time in her busy life to visit me. I don't want anything to push her away before she's ready, and this thing with Bee might give her a reason to leave too soon.

Meanwhile, Mama looks at me like I'm a place she'll never get to visit, the distance between us too great. I wish I could send her an imaginary postcard that says *I love you* and *wish you were here.*

"Don't wait supper on me, Mama. I need to find Lily, and then she and I need to talk."

"Well, don't talk her ear off," Mama says. "Not everybody thinks that talking is the cure for whatever ails a person."

"Yes, Mama," I say. I walk up on the porch and give her a kiss on the cheek.

She shoos me away like I'm a gnat circling her head, but then her mood changes, as if I'm not the only one thinking of a time when she won't be here anymore. She takes my hand and looks at me. I can't remember the last time she did such a tender, simple thing. Her touch is cool, her skin rough. She has the hands of someone who has scrubbed floors her entire life, as well as labored at a thousand other things.

"I know you haven't spoiled that child," she says.

Her words are soft, forgiving and unexpected.

"Lily is the luckiest girl in the world to have you as her mother," she begins again. She strokes my hand like she's rubbing a cool lotion into all the dry, cracked places of my soul.

My eyes water. "Thank you, Mama. That means a lot to me. It truly does."

The look she gives me is full of tenderness. I soak it in, remembering the night in the barn so many years ago, the first time I saw the love at the center of her fierceness.

"Now, go find your daughter and bring her home," she says. She pats my hand and the door to her softness closes. Yet, in a day that has shown no mercy, her tenderness feels like a moment of grace.

As the sun drops behind the mountain, I say goodbye to Mama and head back down the hill. Sometimes, we feel about as different as two people can be. Yet, over the years, we've worked at finding a path to each other, if only for moments at a time. Sometimes you don't even have to leave home to travel great distances.

CHAPTER SEVENTEEN

Lily

Mama's truck travels up the dirt road to the Sector's house and pulls up into the worn spot in the yard where people park. The driver's side door opens with a loud squeak. Worry dances across Mama's face. As only Mama can do, she strides up the walk. Proud and determined.

In the late afternoon sun, I stand on the porch and fortify myself for what's to come, making an effort to not look scared.

"I've been looking all over for you," she says to me.

Compared to Crow and Mister Sector who have just returned from hunting, Mama is tiny, though she comes across as someone who is six feet tall. She greets all the Sectors and then shoots her worried look toward June before it settles on me again. I shoot her back a look that bypasses worry and goes straight to sheer meanness.

I am not speaking to you, my look says. *I may never speak to you again.*

My expression stops her at the steps.

"We need to talk," she says to me.

"No we don't," I say, realizing I just broke my vow to never speak to her again.

Looking at her now, I see more than my mama, I see a stranger. Someone who hides things from people like the names of fathers and the people she's in love with.

"What's going on?" June asks her.

"You wouldn't believe me if I told you," Mama says.

However, the look they exchange tells me that maybe June knows. If that's true, she doesn't seem the least bit shocked or surprised.

I have never been so confused in my life, and if I weren't so worn out from running here I'd take off again.

"We need to talk, Lily," Mama says again. "Get in the truck. I'll take you home."

"I'm having supper here," I say.

"You are?" Pearl says, like it's news to her.

Meanwhile, it bothers me that Crow is a witness to all this. For someone who doesn't know what happened, I could come across as hateful. Then it dawns on me that given who my daddy is, hatefulness may be another family trait, just like lying. I ball up a fist ready to scream, or better yet, punch someone. Preferably Mama.

"We can do supper another time," June Sector says to me.

"We can't do it another time. Crow will be leaving tomorrow," Pearl says, her tone approaching a whine.

My face turns hot all over again, as though my private undergarments are hanging on the Sector's clothesline for Crow to see. Mama tells me with a look that this isn't the time or place to air our laundry, dirty or clean, and that I'd best be getting in the truck.

I cross my arms, refusing to go anywhere, and increasing the amount of trouble I'm in.

Pearl is wide-eyed, like she's wondering what's got into me. Meanwhile, Crow and Mr. Sector stand holding the dead rabbits, and Crow is staring down at his Army boots like they could use a polish.

"Lily McAllister, I want you in that truck this instant." Mama's finger points like an arrow toward the beat up Ford she bought third-hand. Her eyes tell me that I don't want to know what will happen if I defy her. As much as I am ready to leave Katy's Ridge forever, I'd like to leave with Mama's blessing, not a curse.

Silent, heart racing, I saunter over and get in Mama's truck. I slam the door, putting so much anger into the slam that the truck rocks, the shock absorbers singing in the choir with the squeaking door.

Mama and I have never had a fight this big, much less in front of people. She gets in the driver's side of the truck and starts it. The truck sputters and clunks to life like it always does. Uncle Cecil is the only mechanic this old truck has ever seen, and he isn't even a real mechanic.

As she puts the gears in reverse and backs out, I wish I could put the day in reverse and start it all over again. This time I'd go to school like I'm supposed to, and not go anywhere near Melody Monroe. If I'd done that to begin with, I'd be about to spend the entire evening with Crow.

Sometimes one decision can set your life on a totally different path. Mama's told me this before, but it's the first time I've ever understood it. If I had inherited Mama's secret sense, I probably would have known today would turn out this way. Instead, I've been ignorant and embarrassed myself in front of Crow and his family.

Even though the day is cooling, I feel hot and roll down the window. I shake my head in disbelief that this much trouble could happen in the 24 hours since that woman showed up in Katy's Ridge. She's like a bad luck charm, if there is such a thing. Yet at this moment, Melody Monroe seems the least of my worries. Mama wants to talk. And I'm guessing it's about what I saw at the mill, not what Melody Monroe told me.

Instead of going home, Mama pulls off on the side of the road near the river. It's a place she's never taken me before, and I thought I knew every inch of Katy's Ridge. I wonder if Granny is waiting supper for us, and figure both of us will be in plenty of trouble if she is. Then I think about all the complaining I've done over nothing ever happening in Katy's Ridge. Turns out I didn't know how lucky I was.

CHAPTER EIGHTEEN

Wildflower

Talking to Lily at home isn't an option since Mama is an expert at overhearing things. And the sawmill is definitely out, given what just happened there. I pull off at a place by the river where Daddy taught me to fish. The first fish I caught was a catfish. It was ugly as sin, as Mama would say, but was a delicacy once it was fried in cornmeal. My stomach growls just thinking about it, but my hunger will have to wait.

"Why are we stopping here?" Lily asks.

"We need to talk and we need privacy to do it," I say.

"But it's almost dark and it's getting cold," she says, as if these are things I haven't noticed.

I'm hungry and tired and have no idea what I'm going to say to my daughter. From behind the seat, I pull out one of my old jackets and hand it to her. She puts it on.

"It smells like you," she says, like she's forgotten for a moment how much she hates me.

Lily pulls the smell close. She used to crawl into my lap when she was a little girl to smell the back of my hands and my hair, as if memorizing my scent. She is a creature of smells and songs.

What I forget sometimes is that it hasn't been that long ago that Lily was a little girl and a person in need of a mother. At fourteen, she's already practicing to be a woman. The same age I was when I had just given birth to her. If anything, seeing Lily now helps me see how young I was to have a baby. Too young. Mama had Jo when she was eighteen, but there are plenty of girls in the mountains having kids at fifteen and sixteen and dropping out of high school to raise them. Mama made sure I finished. She refused to let me be one of those girls. She kept Lily during the day so I could. She said it was what Daddy would have wanted. But she must have wanted it, too.

The day has wrung me out like a dishrag. I feel too tired to clean up the mess I made at the sawmill by not being discreet. No matter how hard it is, it's important that Lily and I talk. That last morning I saw Daddy alive, my secret sense told me to run after him and tell him how much I loved him. Unfortunately, I talked myself right out of it. I told myself I'd have plenty of time to tell him later. Well, life doesn't always give us a *later.* You have to make time to say things that need to be said.

I ran away the day Daddy died, just like Lily ran away from the sawmill. Sometimes running is the only thing we know to do. It was here that I ran, to this place by the river. A place I haven't returned to in years. Somehow, Daddy's death seems to have set everything in motion that has happened since. Not only what transpired with Johnny, but also all that's happened today. It reminds me of all those begets in the Bible that Daddy used to read to me and my sisters when we were trying to get to sleep at night. So-and-so begat so-and-so. Everything and everybody connected to what came before.

"It's getting dark, so we'll need a few things," I say to Lily. "Hand me those matches in the glove box."

Lily opens the compartment and digs out the matches. When she tries to shut it the latch doesn't grab and she slams it four times until I put my hand on hers. I latch it easily, knowing how to finesse it closed. Lily's angry look returns.

We get out of the truck and I grab the flashlight I keep in the back.

"Stay close," I say.

Lily huffs.

Who can blame her for being upset? To protect her, I've deliberately kept things from her for years. Or maybe it was more to protect me.

As we take the skinny path to the river, the flashlight offers circles of light for us to follow. Crickets voice their surprise at seeing us. The sun has dropped further behind the hillside and the river holds the last of the light. A sliver of a new moon has risen and it promises to be as dark a night as it gets in these parts.

"Gather sticks and branches for a fire," I tell her.

Thankfully, she doesn't sass me.

We rummage around the trees along the riverbank for dropped branches that we break against our knees and throw in a pile. After arranging them, I light a match and place the flame at the bottom.

"Would you like to sit?" I ask Lily. My nerves feel as jumbled as the mound of sticks I've just laid.

She shrugs and then sits near the fire, positioning the coat to sit on instead of the cold ground.

In the dim light, Lily pulls something out of her pocket. It is a sandwich wrapped in waxed paper, a toothpick piercing the thin covering like a safety pin to hold it all together. It looks like it's been in her pocket for a long time. She tears the sandwich down the middle and hands me half. It is one of Mama's leftover chicken sandwiches, with a generous helping of mayonnaise. The bread is soggy, but at that moment I've never tasted anything better. I thank Lily for sharing. When we finish, we lick our fingers and dry them on our coats, then we sit in silence as the river gently laps the shore.

"I wish you hadn't run away," I say.

Lily doesn't answer. The only other time she was this quiet was last spring when I told her about the birds and bees, as it is commonly called. She finally confessed to reading Meg's romance novels hidden in the bedroom closet, and figuring it out on her own. Compared to the awkwardness we are experiencing now, that talk feels like nothing.

A fish jumps near the riverbank, a flash of silver in the dark water that echoes the silver of the moon. Water continues to lap gently at the shore. I am ready for this day to end, but I have things to say if Lily will listen. At least I don't have to worry about her running away this time. It is too dark to go anywhere.

The ground is cold underneath me and the fire warms my face. I throw another stick on the flame and an owl hoots in the distance, as if to ask what we're doing in his territory. I imagine him swooping down with silent wings to capture my words before I have time to speak them.

The last time I sat at this spot was the day Daddy died. My heart was breaking. At least nobody is dead this time. I take a deep breath, knowing I can't put off talking to Lily any longer. It is too cold to take the time to grow the courage I need or choose perfect words.

Still I hesitate.

Lily looks at me, her face a mixture of shadow and firelight. She wants this to be over, too. At least that's what I tell myself.

"Bee and I—Miss Blackstone and I—love each other," I begin, surprising myself with my honesty. "We've loved each other for a long time. Almost ten years now." My voice falters. "Nobody knows. We're afraid people won't understand. Not that it's any of their business, anyway. But we love each other, Lily. We truly do. And I don't see how that's anything different from what your Aunt Jo and Uncle Daniel have."

"Except they aren't ashamed," Lily says. "That's the biggest difference, isn't it?"

I turn to look at her, wondering how she became so wise. She's right, of course. It isn't the same. Like dew on a foggy morning, shame covers every aspect of my life with Bee.

"The world is a complicated place," I say. "At your age, you're not meant to understand everything."

"Do you understand it?" she asks.

I pause. "Actually, I don't. I wish I did."

"You need to stop this," Lily says. "You need to never see her again."

Her words surprise me. They sound hard, like Mama's get sometimes. But I don't blame her for saying them. I've said the same thing to myself.

"I wish I could," I say. "Bee and I have tried to break it off many times."

"Try harder," Lily says. She pokes the fire.

"It's not as easy as it sounds," I say.

"That makes no sense at all," Lily says with another huff. I can't believe how much she sounds like Mama.

"All I know is that I'm a better person when Bee's around. A happier person," I say, determined to hold my ground.

The fire in Lily's eyes grows wilder. It is obvious she is confused and doesn't understand. I'm not sure I understand, either. In fact, I feel exhausted from all the years I've spent trying to be normal.

My shoulders drop. Emotion chokes out my words. I tell myself not to weep, but I am too tired to resist. The tears come. Not of someone grieving, but of someone defeated.

The crossness leaves Lily's face. She apologizes. I seldom let Lily see the side of me that isn't strong. The side that is just as lost as everybody else about how to love and be loved.

"It's not your fault," I tell her, my tears slowing. I use the handkerchief Bee used earlier to dry my face, and then sit straighter. "The funny thing is, it all feels so natural. Like I've loved Bee my whole life."

My confession brings her into my arms. Our reunion brings more tears. I think of times I've held Lily while she cried. The result of scraped knees, hurtful friends and the rejections life brings, either real or imagined. I got fighting mad at whoever hurt her, and at this moment I feel fighting mad at myself. I wish I could be different.

"You shouldn't have to deal with anything like this," I say to her. "I've spent fourteen years trying to protect you from hard things."

Lily releases our embrace and sits back to stare at the fire.

"I'm not sure if I can get used to seeing you and Miss Blackstone together," she says thoughtfully. "But I think it would be the same if you fell in love with a man."

I exhale, not even realizing that I'd been holding my breath.

"I don't want to share you," she continues. "But I don't want you to be alone, either. Nobody should be alone."

She looks off into the darkness, her thoughts taking her far away.

Meanwhile, a ripple of gratitude washes over me, and the crickets turn up their volume to remind us they are here. It has been unusually warm this fall and the cricket season has been extended. I imagine this concert offers one of their last songs before winter.

For the first time this evening, I think about Melody Monroe. Daniel said Lily went over there this morning, which means we have more to talk about. It is perhaps the most important conversation we will ever have. But it seems neither of us have the strength for that one. At least not now.

"Nobody else knows about you and Miss Blackstone?" Lily asks.

"The Sectors know," I say. "Sometimes Bee and I go over for lunch on a Saturday so we can have time together where we don't have to worry about people seeing us."

"You mean Pearl knows?" Lily asks.

I nod.

"But Pearl never said a word to me, and she's never, *ever* been able to keep a secret."

"Well, she's kept this one," I say.

"Crow knows, too?" she asks.

I nod again.

"Then why didn't you tell *me*?" She looks hurt again.

"Because of what happened today," I say. "I was afraid it would scare you or make you hate me."

A possum sticks her long nose out of the brush to investigate the fire, a welcome distraction. Her beady eyes take us in, and she sniffs in our direction. She hisses at us before turning away and disappearing into the underbrush.

Bee was one of the few people in Katy's Ridge who didn't turn away from me when I was carrying Lily. My best friend Mary Jane wouldn't have anything to do with me after that. Or maybe her parents wouldn't allow it. But it was hard losing a best friend. It helps to have a big family. But we are meant to have friends, too. So it was a lonely time. People just stopped talking to me. Or did their best to avoid me.

For months after Lily was born, Bee came over every Saturday morning to help me with her. She'd bring a loaf of banana bread that her mother made. Then we'd talk about books and about different things that were happening in the world. We could talk about anything. We became really good friends. It was years later before we admitted our feelings had grown into something more than a friendship. I remember how hard those days were. Both of us feeling crazy and bad. Feeling drawn together one minute and denying it the next.

Lily wraps her coat closer, and we stare into the crackling fire. Her confusion hasn't left her face, but it would be impossible—at least before we have our other talk—to explain how it was when I was pregnant with her.

"For a while, I didn't think I'd ever see Bee again," I say, reaching toward the fire to warm my hands. "She moved to

Nashville to teach," I say. "I was heartbroken, but I understood."

"How old was I?"

"It was the summer of your third birthday."

Sticks collapse into the fire and sparks fly. I toss on more branches realizing how cold we'd be without the flames.

"I remember when she came back," Lily says. "It was such a relief not to have Mr. Collins anymore."

Lily had Mr. Collins for first and second grade. He was unmerciful in how he disciplined the boys, and Lily feared him. I don't think there was a single student or parent who wasn't relieved when Bee returned.

"She told me she couldn't stand living without me," I begin again. "Truth is, I was having a hard time living without her, too. To find somebody you truly love is a rare thing, Lily, and isn't to be taken for granted."

She turns away, and I wonder if she's thinking about Crow, her crush of many years.

A nearby bullfrog begins a throaty, vibrating call.

"Can we go home now?" Lily stands. "Granny might be worried about us."

"Do you have any more questions?" I ask.

"No," she says.

"Well, whenever you do, I'd be happy to answer them," I say.

"Okay," she says back.

She has listened. That's all that I could ask for. If she is stunned or hurt by the news, she doesn't let on, and her anger seems to have died away like the fire. I trust her not to tell anyone what we've talked about. I imagine she wants to keep it a secret as much as I do.

With my boot, I sweep a layer of sandy soil over what's left of the embers. The world slowly becomes dark again. The moon winks at us. I turn on my flashlight and lead us back to the truck. Cold air nips at my cheeks, reminding me that winter will be arriving soon. The sounds of the river fade, and Lily is quiet. Too quiet, I decide, as we get into the truck. But I honor her need for silence.

Within a couple of minutes, we arrive back home and get out of the truck to climb the dark hill to our house, the flashlight growing dimmer with every few steps. Our footsteps join the sounds of our breathing, mine heavier than Lily's. As we walk the familiar path, I think of Bee. We will have plenty to talk about the next time we get together. I squeeze the buckeye I always carry with me. Bee and I found them on a walk together one day over at Sutter's Lake. We each carry one. Buckeyes are good luck when carried in a pocket and are even known for curing headaches.

We ascend the steepest part of the path and see our house, the single bulb on the porch calling to us like a beacon. Mama will be upset with us for coming home so late. But she will have also saved us supper in the oven, a plate covering it to hold in the heat and moisture. Some things I can count on with Mama.

Walking up the porch steps, I am reminded of the year the country fair came to Rocky Bluff. It was the first time I ever rode a roller coaster. Today has felt just as harrowing.

CHAPTER NINETEEN

Lily

Mama falls asleep fast, her breathing deepening into her usual light snore. After what happened at the mill today, we didn't even have a chance to talk about my visit to see Melody and what I found out there. In some ways it feels like an entire week has been crammed into this one day. All that's happened weighs heavy on me like Great Aunt Sadie's quilt that Mama put on the bed tonight. No matter how much I wish for it, sleep refuses to come.

I try to imagine loving someone and having to keep it a secret. I think of Crow. Not everyone in Katy's Ridge is accepting of the Sectors. If I married Crow, people might look at me the same way. Not to mention any children we have.

It dawns on me how difficult the world can be if you're the least bit different. Who is it, exactly, that decided that white people rule the world, and everybody else is out of luck?

Or maybe it's that men rule the world and women don't get to rule anything, except maybe the kitchen and the babies.

My frustration pushes me out of bed.

Mama startles awake. "You okay, sweetheart?" she asks sleepily.

"Can't sleep. Going into the living room to read," I whisper.

"Make yourself warm milk," she whispers back, and then mumbles like she's talking to someone in her dreams.

The bedroom dark, I've long since memorized every inch of it. I know the floorboards that creak and the way to turn the closet doorknob so that it doesn't stick. I slide on a pair of corduroy pants Aunt Amy made for me to go with a wool sweater that was a gift from Great Aunt Sadie. I grab my shoes and socks to put on in the kitchen. Once I make it to the hallway, I find my way through the house with the help of the light in the bathroom that Granny leaves on with the door cracked. I am good at being quiet. As the resident night owl, it's required.

In the kitchen, I open the refrigerator and drink milk right out of the bottle. I take the last slice of apple pie left over from the anniversary. The clock on the wall reaches its hands toward midnight. After putting on my socks and shoes, I slip on Granddaddy's old coat that Granny puts on to go feed the chickens. Then I step out onto the back porch.

The chilly night air prickles my face, but otherwise I feel warm in the coat that used to swamp me with its size. To the right of the back door is the small bench where Granny keeps a big flashlight. I test it to make sure the batteries are good. A warm glow lights the way ahead. For a moment, I shine the artificial light under the porch and see Pumpkin and his kin curled next to each other, unmoving, only mildly curious about why I'm not curled up in my own bed.

The moon is of no help tonight as I walk around the side of the house where the two bedroom windows are. I step as lightly as I can, not wanting to wake up Granny and her shot-gun. It is only when I get to the Red Bud Sisters that I let myself make my usual walking noises. Meanwhile, the crickets throb in the forest, their voices weak with autumn. Like my bedroom, I know every inch of the path down the hill. Yet it looks different at night and things scurry away out of sight.

The night shift, Mama calls them. Those animals that do their hunting and visiting at night.

When I get to Mama's truck, I touch the hood, as though it might still hold warmth from hours before. However, it is as cold as the night.

The sound of my footsteps on the pavement keeps me company as I walk. I note the distinctive sound of the soles of my shoes, mixed with my stride. Just like no two fingerprints are ever alike, that probably goes for footsteps, too. I skip a few steps just to break up the rhythm and think of a song I heard on the radio by a new singer named Elvis Presley. Music is what keeps me company best, yet no sound comes. Any songs I might sing seem to have been stolen by the events of the day.

As I pass Aunt Jo and Uncle Daniel's place, a single light outside the barn produces a whitish yellow glow. Dew moistens my face and the flashlight illuminates the fog that gathers along the river. The world is completely quiet, and it feels like a dream I might be having if I was sleeping right now.

I begin to hear other footsteps echoing in the night and pause mid-step, searching for sounds in the darkness. Nothing. I tell myself I imagined it. Besides, who in the world would be out here walking in the middle of the night except me? The whispers start again as I pass the old trail that leads to the cemetery. It seems odd that Mama didn't hear the whispers, too. Usually she's the one that notices things like that. She tried to convince me it was the wind in the trees at the bottom of the ravine, or the shape of the hillside that made the whispers, but I didn't believe that for a second. The flashlight falters, and I refuse to get scared. I shake it to renew its strength. It flickers twice, then a third time, but continues to light the way. In the distance, at about eye level, a tiny red glow is suspended in the woods. It looks like a lightning bug that's on fire, with a red glow instead of gold.

The whispers get louder and the red glow grows more intense. I stop walking, my heart looking for a way to escape my chest.

"You hear it, too?" a voice says. I jump like someone's goosed me.

I recognize the voice and shine my light toward the woods and see Melody Monroe. She is smoking a cigarette at the entrance to the path to the cemetery.

"Hear what?" I say.

She sits in the pitch black of night without a flashlight or anything.

"Turn off that light," she says. "It's hurting my eyes."

Reluctantly I do, and the darkness gets darker.

"You hear that?" she says, from inside the darkness.

"Hear what?" I repeat, my frustration growing.

"The whispers," she says, herself whispering.

A sudden chill passes through me.

She inhales and the red tip of her cigarette glows brighter like a monster with a single red eye.

"Yeah, I hear it," I say.

"Who do you think that is?" she says.

"Who?" I say.

Our two voices reach toward the night. I wonder if this is what it's like to be a ghost and not have a body that's yours anymore.

Whenever Melody inhales her cigarette, the faint glow outlines her face. Underneath the smell of cigarettes, I smell something sour, like moonshine.

"Who do you think is whispering to us?" she asks again, her words slurring.

I don't answer and wonder if I should continue on to the Sectors or turn around and go back home.

"I think the whispers are your daddy," she says. "I think it's Johnny."

I gasp, before I can stop myself.

"Your mama told me today that he slipped on icy rocks and fell down the mountain," she begins again. "It would be around here where they found him. Near that old footbridge. You know the one?"

"I know it," I say.

"Maybe we should get closer so we can hear him better," she says.

A shiver of cold caresses my neck, and I reach for the gold medallion Mama gave me and find it missing. I search my pockets and then shine the light on the ground. Melody whines for me to turn it off. Mama is going to kill me for losing it, but I'll have to search for it another time. I'm not going anywhere near that footbridge, not in the middle of the night, and not without my necklace to protect me and certainly not with Melody Monroe who smells like a giant jar of moonshine mixed with stale cigarettes.

"What do you think Johnny's trying to tell us?" Her words continue to slur. "Do you think he's trying to tell us who his murderer was?"

"Murderer?" I ask.

Melody laughs.

"Oh, that's right, your mama said he fell."

She is silent now, as though letting her words have time to sink in.

"So, what are you doing out here in the middle of the night?" she asks.

I could ask her the same. "I couldn't sleep," I say. "I was just taking a walk."

She lights another cigarette off the one that's almost finished. Then she flips one of the tiny red glows to the ground.

She stands and then stumbles toward me. I take a step back and feel her reaching toward my arm.

"What are you doing?" I say into the blackness.

"I'm going to introduce you to your daddy."

She lunges forward and this time grabs my arm instead of air. "Hey, stop it!" I say. Her grip is strong for someone who has been drinking all night.

"Johnny would like you," she says. "Probably like he liked my sister."

The laugh that follows doesn't have any humor in it. Melody seemed much nicer in the light of day.

"Come on, girl," she says, trying to drag me.

"Let me go!" I jerk away and she loses her grip. I turn on the flashlight and shine it right into her eyes. She winces and puts her hands up as protection from the light. It's then that I realize how weak she is, and the fear I felt moments ago drifts away on the cold breeze.

"Well, if you're not going with me to hear what Johnny has to say, I guess I'll go by myself," she says. "Knowing Johnny, he'll probably give me an earful about how your mama was the one that killed him. But knowing Johnny, he probably deserved to get killed."

"Mama would never kill somebody," I say.

"You'd be surprised what people will do," she says, as though she's had experience in being surprised. "You be careful," she adds. "All sorts of ghosts out here."

But she is the one stumbling around. She is the one that needs to be careful. I think of the footbridge she will have to cross to make it to the cemetery and wonder if she can stay upright long enough to cross it. She goes in that direction, and I call out for her to be careful. She trips and cusses and then pulls herself up again.

When her footsteps finally fade, I turn on the flashlight again, grateful to have the way illuminated. At the boulder where Melody sat are the butts of several cigarettes, as though she'd been sitting there a long time.

How dare she say that Mama killed someone. Mama would never resort to violence to solve anything. Granny might, but not Mama. I tell myself to forget about running into Melody Monroe and try to shake the creepiness away, but it sticks to me like the falling dew.

Halfway between both places, I wonder whether to go back home or to the Sectors. In the next second the wind picks up, and the whispers return, this time louder. I listen for a message on the wind that will solve this mystery once and for all.

CHAPTER TWENTY

Wildflower

In the dream, Lily is about to fall into the ravine. Over the years, I've had this dream a dozen times and was reminded of it yesterday before Melody Monroe arrived. It always gets my heart racing. Awake, I tell myself it isn't real. That everything is all right. But something feels terribly wrong. To reassure myself, I reach a hand over to Lily's side of the bed. I roll over and touch the other side of the mattress. I sit up in bed.

"Lily?" I call, not caring if I wake up Mama. "Lily?" I call louder.

I get up and turn on the light, stepping into my slippers and then putting on my robe. I open the door and find Mama in the hallway.

"What's wrong?" she says, shotgun in hand. Her long gray hair drapes down her back. I hadn't realized Mama's hair had grown so long.

"Are you sleeping with that thing now?" I ask, pointing to the shotgun.

She doesn't answer.

"Do you know where Lily is?" I ask.

"No idea," she says. "Maybe she's reading in the kitchen."

I follow Mama into the empty kitchen. A plate sits by the sink, evidence that Lily has had a snack. Mama never leaves even one plate or cup unwashed before bed.

I turn on the back porch light and step outside. Winter is close. I can feel it in the breeze. "Lily?" I call again.

Mama steps outside, too. "My flashlight's gone," she says. "And Joseph's coat."

"Where would she go on a night like this?" I ask, more to myself than Mama.

"You two have a fight?" Mama says.

She sits the shotgun next to the door, perhaps ruling out foul play unless I've caused it.

I pause to think, rubbing warmth into my arms. "I brushed her hair before bedtime. I thought we were back on good terms."

"It's hard to know with Lily," Mama says. "She's much quieter than you are about things."

We go back into the house. "I wish we had a telephone," I say to her. "Now I've got to wake up Daniel and Jo."

"Who would you call?" she asks.

"Pearl, I guess."

"June would have sent word already if Lily was over there. She wouldn't want you to worry."

Mama's right. June would have sent Horatio over here in the middle of the night just to set my mind at ease.

"Where is she, Mama?" I ask.

With no answers, she looks as worried as I feel.

To make sure we haven't missed her, Mama and I search in every room. Our house is small enough that it doesn't take long. There are no real hiding places in this house. The closets are small and have too many things inside to hide a person. Quilts are stored under the bed. I go to the front door and turn on the porch light and go outside. I call Lily again. Then I remember Melody Monroe standing in the yard. Could she be at Melody's?

I run into the house and throw on my clothes from the day before. Mama studies my every move, telling me not to panic, but she doesn't look that calm, either.

"I'm going to drive over to the Monroe place and see if she went over there," I say.

"Surely she wouldn't have," Mama says.

Lily's whole life has turned upside down in these last two days. I'm not sure what she will do anymore. I take the flashlight I used the night before and go into the kitchen to find new batteries. Luckily Mama has one package left.

"Do you want me to come?" Mama says, looking around for her shotgun.

"It's on the back porch," I tell her, "but no, I don't want you to come."

She looks relieved.

"Maybe you should go get Daniel," she says.

"No need to wake everybody up, at least not yet," I say. "Let me go over to Melody's and just make sure she's not there."

It's the fastest I've gone down the hill in a long time. The truck complains when I start it, like an old man not wanting to turn over and get out of bed. I don't give it time to warm up before I pull out and drive down the road toward the cross-roads. I park where I did the day before and head into the woods with the flashlight. I can't imagine what Melody might have told Lily. We never got to talk about that yesterday. Melody has no way of knowing the whole story, anyway. Though from what she said to me, she has guessed some of it.

After a day of sunshine, the mud is less sloppy in places but it is still slow going. The cabin door is open and the light is on. It looks like somebody might have just stepped out to get a piece of firewood for the wood stove. I call Melody's name. Then Lily's.

"You in there?" I ask, stepping onto the front porch. My heartbeat quickens. I wonder if Melody has a shotgun she keeps close like Mama does.

An empty jar of moonshine sits on the table, as well as the same faded china cup with the chip on the handle. There's a letter beside the cup, and I step close enough to read it. It's addressed to someone I don't recognize, probably Melody's aunt, and it is signed Lester, short for Doc Lester. I pick it up and hurriedly try to make out his messy scrawl.

Doc Lester writes Melody's aunt that she might want to meet Lily. That she is a special young lady. He tells her that she sings at the church, and then he says something about me. I shine the light closer. *Her mama doesn't deserve her. She's a bad influence*, he writes. *As her next of kin, you should come and take her back with you.*

His words frighten me. There's never been any love lost between us, but I never thought he hated me enough to think me unfit.

I search the room to see if Melody's things are gone. Could she have taken Lily back to Kentucky on the bus tonight? My body tenses. But her open purse is still on the bed, revealing the wadded dollar bills she offered me earlier. She hasn't gone far without any money. But where has she gone on this dark night? I go outside again and up the slight rise to the outhouse. I pass the huge oak tree where Melody's sister Ruby hung herself when I was twelve. A branch, as big as I am, has broken off and fallen to the ground. I shine a flashlight into the top of the tree and remember Ruby's funeral—easily the saddest I've ever attended, aside from Daddy's. A shiver climbs the back of my neck.

At the outhouse, I call Melody's name again. Something scurries away, and I catch the tail of a raccoon in the beam of my flashlight.

If Melody and Lily are together, where would they go? My secret sense answers me and I stop cold. Half running, half trying not to trip, I make my way back to the truck. I drive past our house and driveway and stop on the road at the beginning of the path to the cemetery. Cigarette butts are tossed next to the boulder in front of the gnarled dogwood tree that marks the beginning of the path. I remember the dream that woke me earlier. Lily falling. Lily falling into the ravine. Forcing myself awake before she landed.

Aiming the flashlight up the path, I begin to run. Every few yards I call out Lily's name. When I get to the footbridge, I stop to catch a jagged breath. I shine the light down into the ravine, but its beam doesn't reach the bottom. I call for both Melody and Lily, my shout edging toward a scream. But the forest is quiet. Dead quiet. I remember how Lily said she heard whispers here, and I wonder what the ravine would have to say if it could speak. Would it tell the story of Johnny's death? Johnny lying dead at the bottom. My gold medallion around his neck? Sadness reaches for me in the darkness, as if tapping me on the shoulder to get my attention. It is an old sadness. One I haven't felt in a long time.

The wind shifts in the trees, and the sound of the rushing water drifts from below. I remind myself that a forest at night isn't a scary thing for me. Daddy would take me fishing in the middle of the night or he'd take me and my sisters to a dark meadow to count lightning bugs. Daddy made nighttime seem magical instead of scary. Yet the darkness tonight feels different. The night is hiding something from me.

Searching for relief from my panic, I shine the flashlight into the forest. It feels like someone is watching me, but I see no one. I call out Lily's name. I wait, listening for an answer. When none comes, I turn around and retrace my steps, pleading with the angels and demons of the past to not let history repeat itself.

CHAPTER TWENTY-ONE

Lily

After walking down the middle of the dirt road that leads to the Sector's house, I question what I'm doing here. Not being able to sleep was part of it, and then running into Melody Monroe. But also, I want to see Crow before he leaves.

One light is on in the kitchen window of the small farmhouse. It occurs to me how easy it would be to spy on people if a person wanted to. I turn off my flashlight and let the kitchen light guide me in. It could be anybody in that kitchen. Horatio or June, or any of their four kids, Crow being the oldest.

Please, God, let it be Crow, I say out loud.

Mama says she and God aren't on speaking terms anymore. But how can you see a gold Mary and be mad at God at the same time? Aren't they related? I step closer, grateful that the curtains were left open. A lone figure sits at the kitchen table reading a book, his back to the window.

Thank you, I say, looking up into the starless night.

I tap on the window and shine the flashlight to light up my face. Crow smiles. He opens the kitchen door.

"What are you doing here?" he whispers.

"I couldn't sleep," I whisper back.

"I couldn't either," he says. His smile feels as bright as the flashlight I've just turned off.

He invites me to sit at the kitchen table. I've never seen Crow in his pajamas. He asks if I want a cup of coffee, and I say yes even though I never drink it. He asks if I want cream and sugar, and I say yes to that, too. Truth is I'd probably say *yes* to anything Crow suggested. I pretend I know what I'm doing and add cream and sugar until the liquid turns the color of Crow's skin. I take a sip and then turn away to make a face, unsure how anyone could drink something so bitter.

Before Crow joined the Army, his black hair dropped down into his eyes and he had this habit of tossing his hair to the side so he could see. Now his head is completely shaved, and I miss the long hair that made him so much of who he is.

"I'm glad you came," he says, as we continue our conversation in whispers.

His grin reveals the dimple he was famous for at Rocky Bluff High School. Despite his mixed race, he played on the football team and was quite popular. The number of touchdowns he got on Friday nights mattered more to the townspeople than who his daddy was. Although, that didn't mean girls were allowed to date him. At least that's what Pearl told me. I find myself hoping she doesn't wake up and find me here or this time will become all about her.

"Don't tell Pearl I was here," I say.

"I won't," he says, showing off his dimple again. "Best not to tell anybody."

I nod, thinking about what Granny would do if she found out I was sitting with Crow while he was wearing his flannel pajamas. Not that Mama would like it one bit, either.

"Hey, you want to go out by the creek?" he asks. "There's a couple of chairs out there and we won't have to whisper."

I think of the voices near the footbridge, and wonder if there's any truth to my daddy trying to get messages to me.

"It's cold outside," I say. "You probably wouldn't want to wear just your pajamas."

He goes to change. While he's gone I get familiar with the kitchen clock shaped like a rooster whose tail clicks back and forth with every second that goes by. I try another sip of coffee and rush over to spit it out in the sink. I pour the whole cup down the drain and wash out the cup and dry it and put it back in the cabinet so no one will know I was here. Listening to all those detective radio shows with Granny has taught me a few things about hiding evidence.

After Crow returns in regular clothes and a coat, we go out the kitchen door. Once we're outside, I turn on my flashlight again. Crow takes my hand and leads me to the creek. He's never held my hand before and despite the growing coldness of the night my body feels warm. The sound of the creek gets louder with each step and we stop at two wooden chairs sitting on a little rise. When I've visited Pearl, I've seen her parents sit out here in the evenings. We sit and the dew on the arms of the chairs soaks into my palms. I pull Granddaddy's coat closer and turn off the flashlight to save the batteries so I can get home.

In the daylight, this is a beautiful spot and even now the sound is beautiful, a trickling melody flowing between river rock. We don't have to whisper any longer, but the words have escaped us.

Finally, it is Crow who speaks first. "I don't want to go back," he says, as though the darkness has invited honesty.

"What?" I say, unable to hide my surprise. "I thought you liked the Army."

"I like getting paid," he says. His words have a smile in them, even though I can't see it.

"Don't you like going to new places?" I ask, thinking I would sign up this minute if I could.

"Not really," he says. "I'd rather be right here in Katy's Ridge. That's why I couldn't sleep. I don't look forward to leaving tomorrow."

The dream Pearl and I have had forever is that Crow comes with us to live in a big city where we would all live together. A dream from which I now feel rudely awakened. How are Crow and I going to end up together if he never wants to leave Katy's Ridge? All of a sudden I wish I was home and in my bed. This day has gone on too long. But at the same time, I like sitting with him here in the dark.

"How long do you have left?" I ask.

"Another year," he says, like a year is a long time away from home. "Why couldn't *you* sleep?" he asks.

I pause, feeling protective of Mama, but then remember that all the Sectors know.

"I just found out about Mama and Miss Blackstone," I say. "Actually, I found out accidentally. I was spying on them and saw them kiss."

Something about the near total darkness of the new moon invites confessions, and I wonder what he would confess to me if he had a chance. But perhaps he already has, about wanting to stay in Katy's Ridge forever.

"Are you okay?" he asks.

"Well, not okay enough to sleep," I say, with a short laugh.

The darkness is like wearing a blindfold, and I wish I could see his face to see his reaction to my words. Instead, I can only feel the nearness of him—the warmth of our arms sitting close to each other on the chairs.

"Your mama and Bee are good people," he says. "I don't see any harm in them loving each other."

"But what will people say?" I ask.

He pauses, and I wonder if he's upset with me. "Do you know how many people like me there are in the Army?" he asks. "Half-Cherokee and half-white? If I cared what people said, I'd be miserable."

He moves his arm, and I feel his warmth go away. "But how do you not care?" I ask, my question genuine. "I care if people like my singing. I care if people might judge Mama and treat her badly. Aren't those normal things to care about?"

His warmth returns and, even wearing a coat, the hairs on my arms reach toward his.

"I don't pretend to have any answers, Lily." His voice softens. "I just don't want you to get hurt, is all. People can be mean, so you got to at least pretend that you don't care. Otherwise, it lets the mean people win."

I wonder if it's true that my father was famous for his meanness. At least his sister thinks so. I won't confess any of this new information to Crow tonight. What he might think is another thing I care about. Not that he would judge me for it. At least I don't think so. I also won't tell him about the whispers near the footbridge. This seems too crazy to confess to anyone, much less someone I want to like me.

In the cool darkness, his fingers reach toward mine. We clasp hands with intertwining fingers, and I can hear the blood rushing in my ears. Not that I'm scared. It's more like I'm too excited to sit still, and at the same time don't want to move. We listen to the sound of a mountain stream singing its song in the middle of the night. Crow is eighteen and feels a world older than me. While I have only been as far as Rocky Bluff, he's left Katy's Ridge. He's been on a plane. He's flown to other countries. Even Melody Monroe went to Louisville, Kentucky to live with her aunt. It's hard to imagine that all

Crow wants to do after seeing the world is come home to boring Katy's Ridge.

The new moon peeks through the trees. My face is cold compared to the warmth of Crow's hand. I've waited for years for him to realize he loves me. But none of that matters if it means I have to live in Katy's Ridge forever. A thought that causes my throat to tighten.

I hope Mama doesn't wake up to find me gone. I should have left a note just in case. I wouldn't want to worry her. But she was exhausted when she went to bed, so I doubt she'll wake up before morning.

"I'd better get back," I say.

He releases my hand so quickly I have to resist reaching for it.

"Try not to give your mama a hard time," he says, as though finishing all he meant to say. "Bee's a good person."

He stands, his shape towering over me like a mountain.

"I do want Mama to have someone in her life who loves her," I say. "I just don't want her to get hurt."

"We all get hurt," he says. "No way to avoid it."

Crow acts more mature since he went away, and I wonder if that's what happens when you enlist in the Army.

"Let me walk you to the road," he says.

The flashlight stays in my coat pocket. We've made peace with the darkness, and I can make out the shapes of things now. In the span of an hour, I've become a nocturnal animal.

After hearing my footsteps alone on the way here, it is intriguing to get in step with another person. At the paved road, we stop. Given he's going to leave for Korea tomorrow, we have goodbyes to say. However, we both appear too awkward to say them. Crow pats me on the shoulder and says he'll see me later, and I repeat the same thing back to him. It's the best we can do and it will have to be enough.

As I walk toward the house, the night feels colder. I pull Granddaddy's jacket close, and wish for about the hundredth time that I had known him. I turn on the flashlight again, letting it lead me home. In the quietness, I remember the feeling of Crow's hand in mine. I've never held hands with a boy. A boy who is almost a man.

When I pass the boulder, the whispers call for me again. If my father has something to say to me, he will have to wait. All I can think about is sleep.

As I climb the hill to our house, I notice every light is on. Mama is standing on the porch looking frantic, a flashlight in her hand. It is only then that I realize how much trouble I am in.

CHAPTER TWENTY-TWO

Wildflower

The light from the other flashlight bounces up the hill. It is Lily. My relief comes out as anger.

"You scared the life out of me," I say, when Lily reaches the porch. "Where have you been?" I clutch the top of my robe, suddenly feeling the cold air again. "Were you at Melody's?"

"I was at Pearl's," Lily says, avoiding looking at me, which means there's more to the story than she's saying. "Why would you think I was at Melody's?" she asks.

I pause. I don't have an answer, except that my worst fear was that Lily was already in Kentucky.

She steps inside the house and leaves her shoes at the door. Inside, she tosses Daddy's coat onto the back of the sofa. I resist yelling at her to put away her things.

"By my watch, it's three in the morning," I say, following her into the kitchen. "What were you doing at Pearl's? I woke up at 1 o'clock and couldn't find you."

Mama stands at the kitchen table, where she's been holding a prayer meeting all by herself.

"I made coffee," she says to me. Then she stands and gives Lily a look like she's glad she's not her. It is unlike Mama to stay out of things, but I'm glad she is. "I'm going back to bed," she adds, and closes the door so Lily and I can talk.

"Was Pearl up in the middle of the night?" I ask.

Without answering, Lily gets a glass of milk from the refrigerator, drinks it down and then places the glass in the sink. She seems tired, but also distracted. Not to mention, silent.

"I don't care how angry you are," I begin again. "That gives you no excuse for taking off in the middle of the night without leaving a note."

"I'm not angry at you," she says.

"Then why would you go to Pearl's?" I ask.

Lily hesitates. Her shoulders drop. "Don't get mad," she says.

I wait. Anytime a conversation is prefaced with *don't get mad*, I know it's something guaranteed to anger me.

"I was actually talking to Crow," she says.

"In the middle of the night?" My voice reaches toward a shriek, and I sound like Mama.

Lily turns to face me. "I couldn't sleep after all that happened yesterday, so I went to see Pearl but she was sleeping."

Lily's words race to explain. "But then I saw Crow was in the kitchen so I knocked on the window, and he invited me in. He was having trouble sleeping, too."

"What did you two do?" I forget how much I like Crow, and that I've known him since he was a baby. He is a man now. Eighteen years old while Lily is fourteen.

"We just talked." Lily's cheeks flush.

I tell myself not to overreact, and my worry returns about history repeating itself. Until now, it never occurred to me how much I fear Lily finding herself with a baby at fourteen. I stand and go to the sink, washing her glass, not knowing what else to do.

"What did you talk about?" I ask, trying to stay calm.

"We talked about how lucky you are to have Bee," Lily says. "And about how it doesn't matter what people say. And how everybody gets hurt, whether we want to or not."

"You talked about all that?" I ask.

"That, and about how he can't wait to get back to Katy's Ridge." Lily sits at the table. She seems to have matured overnight. For a few seconds, I get a secret sense that somehow life will be kind to her.

"I was selfish for wanting things different," Lily says, looking at me.

"Selfish?" I ask.

"You should get to love whoever you want to," she says, as though convinced.

Lily stands, and I wonder if I imagined what she just said. She tells me she has to go to bed, and kisses me on the cheek before leaving the kitchen. I pour myself a cup of coffee and sit back at the kitchen table. I feel grateful to Crow, and really all of the Sectors. I allow myself to fantasize about it being a different world, where Bee and I don't have to pretend we're only friends.

For years, I've feared what might happen if Lily found out. By the time I went to bed last night I had decided that she would warm to Bee eventually, if we were patient and lucky. It never occurred to me that her acceptance might come so fast, though it sounds like Crow's response helped. Of course, her understanding could also be short-lived.

While searching for Lily, I questioned whether I should break it off with Bee. That seemed the safest thing to do. I have a business here, and if anybody else finds out, I could lose it. I know these people. It took them nearly a decade to grant me eye contact after Lily was born. Then I remember my next set of worries: Melody Monroe. I want her to leave. Sooner rather than later. And if she comes near Lily again, Mama won't be the only one looking for the shotgun.

After the sun comes up, Mama comes into the kitchen where I remain sitting.

"Louisa May, did you not go back to bed?"

"Couldn't sleep," I say.

Mama puts on her apron, as she does first thing every morning, and sits in her place at the table. I pour her a cup of warmed over coffee and place it in front of her. A cat scratches at the kitchen door, as if noting that the McAllister Diner is now open.

"Will you let Pumpkin in?" she asks.

"I thought you hated cats," I say, remembering a time when she threatened to drown them all.

"I do," she says. "But this old boy and I have become friends."

Secrets everywhere, I say to myself, including my own.

Mama drinks her coffee without speaking as Pumpkin sits in her lap. When you've spent your whole life with someone, surprises are rare.

"You're awfully quiet this morning," Mama says.

It isn't like her to notice my quietness.

The cat arches his boney backside and lifts his rump to enjoy the last benefits of Mama stroking him. Pumpkin and I exchange a look, and I can almost hear him bragging about how he won her over.

"How did your talk go last night? Before Lily pulled her disappearing act."

Directness is not like Mama.

"It went okay," I say.

She knows better than to ask me details. We McAllisters aren't big talkers.

"Where was she last night?" she asks.

"She was with Pearl," I say, deciding a half-lie is better than the truth in this instance.

"Growing pains?" To Mama, no matter what age you are, every problem in life has something to do with growing pains.

"In a way," I say, thinking that Lily has certainly grown in knowledge about me and Bee.

Mama lowers her voice. "Is it about that Melody woman?"

I pause. "I went to see her yesterday morning."

Mama stands, dumping Pumpkin off her lap. He lands on his feet, but looks up at her like he should have known not to trust her. She opens the kitchen door and shoos him outside. He turns and looks at her with what I take as disgust.

"You went to visit that woman?" Mama says, now standing over me.

Mama is not an overly large woman, but the force of her question causes me to scoot back in my chair.

"This isn't the day to test me, Mama."

Our eyes lock, like our horns have plenty of times. But neither of us wants to fight.

She backs off and sits in her chair.

"I went to ask Melody what she was going to tell Lily."

"What did she say?" Mama asks.

"She said she wouldn't tell Lily anything unless Lily asks."

"And you think Lily won't ask?"

I sigh.

Despite Mama's grumbling, I don't have the energy to tell her that Lily skipped school yesterday and that she's already talked to Melody. Nor will I tell her what Lily saw at the mill.

"I don't understand why Melody Monroe would show up in the first place," Mama says. "Is that place of hers even livable?"

"Barely," I say. "You should see it, Mama. It's so small and sad. I can't believe a whole family used to live there."

Mama nods. "Mabel Monroe used to take in people's laundry, and they sold practically everything they had just to get by. Your Daddy would drop things by to help out. He even gave them two good laying hens," she continues. "Arthur worked for a while at the mill, but he only came half the time, so Joseph had to let him go."

This is the most I've ever heard Mama say about the Monroe family.

"What else did Melody say?" she asks.

I hesitate, wondering how much to tell her. "She wants Lily to visit Kentucky. Evidently her aunt sent money so Melody and Lily could go back on the bus."

"Over my dead body," Mama says. "Don't you dare let that child go anywhere near those people."

I nod. For once in my life, Mama and I are in full agreement.

A knock on the front door breaks the growing tension. Mama stays in the kitchen, tidying up, and I go to see who it is. When I open the door, Bee is standing on the porch.

"What are you doing here?" I say, surprised to see her.

"I brought banana bread." She holds up the basket that looks like her mother packed it. Like me, Bee is not much of a cook, but her mother is. "I was worried," she adds in a whisper.

Bee is dressed in her Sunday best, even though it's only Saturday. I forgot how concerned she must have been, not hearing from me last night, but I was certain she would already be in bed by the time Lily and I got back to the house. I was also too tired to go back to the mill or to Daniel and Jo's to use the phone.

"I'm not sure this is a good idea," I say to her.

"Are we okay?" Her eyes don't leave mine.

Mama steps up behind me and Bee beams a smile at her.

"Anybody in the mood for banana bread?" Her eyebrows raise with the question.

Mama invites her inside and tells me to go get dressed. Greeting guests in a housecoat and slippers is never encouraged. Granny leads Bee into the warm kitchen, and I go into the bedroom to change. Lily is sleeping, her head covered to shield her from the morning sun making its way into the room.

I get dressed, run a brush through my hair and pull it back with a rubber band. When I glance into the small round mirror on the wall by the door, I practice a smile, even though I don't feel like smiling.

When I go back to the kitchen, Mama has put on a fresh pot of coffee and is just unwrapping the basket with the banana bread inside. She makes the noises she only makes for company, telling Bee how sweet she is to bring banana bread by. Mama can be practically friendly sometimes, and not just at church. Perhaps Bee has encouraged her by wearing church clothes to the house.

After filling coffee cups, Mama returns to the table where Bee and I sit. I feel jittery after all the coffee I've had, not to mention the secret sitting here in the kitchen between us.

"Banana bread is my favorite," I say to Bee, as if this is something she doesn't know.

"I remembered that," Bee answers.

At that moment, we act like acquaintances instead of what we really are. At least Lily knows now, and is reaching toward acceptance, thanks to Crow. When I try to imagine Mama's reaction if she knew our secret, all I can see is a shotgun pointing toward Bee. I shut down my imagination before she has time to pull the trigger. Whatever the scenario, I can't imagine it would be good.

"Did Louisa May tell you about the stranger who came to visit us two days ago?" Mama asks Bee. Whenever Mama calls me by my given name, I wonder if I'm in trouble. When I was younger, I wished sometimes that *Jane Eyre* had been her favorite book, instead of *Little Women,* since Charlotte is a much more glamorous name than Louisa May. At least to me.

"Lou—isa did tell me," Bee says, with an awkward glance in my direction. When we are alone together, Bee calls me Lou, and it isn't like her to slip and call me that in front of someone.

"That Melody woman stood there in the front yard as brazen as a hussy," Mama says. Calling someone *hussy* is as mean as Mama gets in front of company.

"I remember her brother Johnny. I went to school with him," Bee says. "We were in the same grade."

I turn to look at her. "I'd forgotten about that," I say, which is true. Somehow, I always think of Bee teaching school, not being taught.

Mama mumbles something under her breath about Johnny that I decide to let drop.

Bee glances at me periodically to determine if we are okay, and I try to reassure her with a glance that everything is fine. Though I'm convinced nothing will be fine until Melody Monroe leaves Katy's Ridge for good.

A railroad of secrets chugs along underneath all the polite conversation, while the three of us enjoy the banana bread. We are only one secret away from Mama throwing Bee out of her house, and probably me along with her. If I liked drama, this might be exciting. But as it is, I'm trying not to choke on the banana bread.

CHAPTER TWENTY-THREE

Lily

Voices wake me, and I try to decipher who is here. The smell of banana bread propels me to get dressed. When I enter the kitchen, I expect to see Great Aunt Sadie, who often brings over whatever she's made that day, but instead I find Miss Blackstone sitting at our kitchen table.

Seeing her reminds me of the kiss and a grumpiness descends like the fog that is just now rising along the river valley. Talking to Crow last night helped with the situation, but I didn't anticipate how I would feel seeing the two of them together again.

I greet Miss Blackstone, sounding less than thrilled, and Granny sends me a look that reminds me to respect my elders. I offer a 'sorry' as I sit at the table. This is more than I wanted to face this morning, especially after so little sleep.

While I take a piece of banana bread, I push away the scene that replays of Mama and Miss Blackstone in the mill office. I wonder if a person can wash out their eyes with soap to clean away something they've seen. Mama looks like she's seeing inside my thoughts and isn't pleased. I try to remember how happy she looked when she and Miss Blackstone were together, but this does little to soften my mood.

Mama and Miss Blackstone exchange cautious looks, like they're afraid I'll tell Granny their secret. But I have no desire to see World War III erupt right in the middle of the kitchen.

The conversation steers toward safe things. Mama and Miss Blackstone glance at me like they've known me my whole life, but I've all of a sudden become a stranger. While I've seen them together hundreds of times, I've never given it a thought. But now I'm remembering everything. Sometimes on Sunday afternoons they'd read together in the living room. Other times they'd go into Rocky Bluff together on a Saturday to see a movie or to run errands. Mama would often be invited over to Miss Blackstone's house for supper, and she wouldn't get home until after I'd fallen asleep. Later she'd say they'd played a long game of Scrabble that Mama won. She'd even throw in the words she won with like zenith or cosmos. Maybe if I'd had Mama's secret sense, I would have known about them a long time ago.

After finishing her coffee, Miss Blackstone announces that she'd best be getting home. Mama stands, almost too eager to walk her to the door.

I need to talk to Pearl and wish for the thousandth time we had a telephone. I want to tell her I know about Mama and

Miss Blackstone and ask her how she managed to keep it a secret.

After they leave, Granny wipes her hands on a dishtowel and then stands staring at me, her hands on her hips. She's caught me lingering again, and I wonder if it's too late to make a quick exit.

"You've been different since that Melody woman showed up," she says.

"Have I?" I say, surprised she noticed.

"You'd best stay away from her, Lily. That whole family is bad news. The Lord would be smart to smite the whole bunch of them."

"But I've already talked to her," I say.

"You what?" Granny's voice gets as big as her eyes. "Why in God's name did you do that?"

"Because I wanted answers," I say.

"Damn it, Lily McAllister, why do you and your mama always go looking for trouble?"

Until this moment, I had never heard my grandmother say a cuss word. Not once. And for some reason it gives me permission to say what I really want to say.

"Is it true?" I ask. "Is Johnny Monroe my father?" My question surprises even me. It's the one I'd intended to ask Mama yesterday, before I saw what I wasn't supposed to see.

Granny's lips form a thin line in the sand, daring me to cross.

"Is it true?" I ask again, knowing I'm crossing the line.

She takes a wooden spoon from beside the stove and uses it to point at me. I get a sense of what it must have been like for Melody to stare down Granny's shotgun. Then Granny's eyes get watery like she might cry and the answer suddenly scares me even though I haven't heard it yet.

"He hurt your mama," she begins. I expect her loud voice, but the words come out soft. Somehow this feels even more dangerous. "Johnny Monroe doesn't deserve to be your daddy."

I swallow hard. When I look up, Mama is standing in the kitchen doorway.

"What's going on in here?" she asks.

"Lily and I were just talking," Granny says.

Mama looks at me like she's wondering if I told Granny about Miss Blackstone.

I shake my head, no.

Granny puts her wooden spoon back on the stove and then goes over and starts to scrub the sink like she's trying to scrub her memories clean.

Granny's words soak into me: *He didn't deserve to be my daddy. He hurt Mama.* More clues to the mystery of who my father was. The blank chalkboard of my past is filling up with words. Words I never expected to see written there: *Mean as a snake. Dropped out of school. Hurt Mama bad.*

Meanwhile, in fourteen years of life, I've never felt so lost. I cross my arms in front of my chest and think about how Mama is all of a sudden a stranger to me. Is anybody as they seem? Maybe everybody in Katy's Ridge is just walking around pretending they are somebody they're not. All these years I've imagined my father was a good man. But it seems I was wrong. Dead wrong.

Another knock on the door causes everyone to jump.

"This place is becoming busy as a beehive," Granny announces, not hiding her irritation. "Lily, see who that is," she says. "Maybe somebody's brought sausages to go with the banana bread." She looks toward the ceiling as though God is getting special pleasure in irritating her, and then she starts to make more coffee. I go to the front door and open it.

At first I think it's a stranger, but then realize it is Crow wearing his uniform. It's the first time in my life I feel like swooning from the beauty of someone. But then I remember he has no ambition other than to live in Katy's Ridge after he does his time in the military.

"What are you doing here?" I say.

"I wanted to make sure you got home all right," Crow says.

Crow isn't like his nickname, except for the blackness of his hair. Real crows are mischief makers and hang out in groups. Their squawks and calls get the attention of anybody around. Crow, however, is soft-spoken, and the tone of his voice is low, like Johnny Cash, who debuted on the Grand Ole Opry last summer right around my birthday. Granny and I listened to him on the radio.

"I made it home just fine," I say, not mentioning how hell broke loose when I did.

"I'm glad," he says, with a smile that adds to the potential swooning. "I just passed Bee on the road," he adds.

"She brought banana bread," I say. "Would you like a slice?"

He says he would and then follows me inside.

As we walk together, I catch a whiff of Old Spice after-shave. I know the smell because Pearl bought a bottle at the drugstore in Rocky Bluff for her dad at Christmas with the money she'd saved from babysitting. That same trip she bought herself a lipstick called Cherries in the Snow, even though her mother doesn't let her wear lipstick, and it stays hidden in the bottom of her dresser drawer.

In the kitchen, Mama and Granny greet Crow, and Granny goes on and on about how handsome he looks in his uniform. She pours him a cup of coffee and then gets him a plate to put his banana bread on. When he joins us at the table, Mama asks him questions about the Army.

Every now and again, Crow glances at me like he's remembering us sitting alone in the dark next to the mountain stream just a few hours before. At the same time, I pretend I'm not disappointed that he'll never leave Katy's Ridge. Maybe Granny is right about Melody Monroe being bad news. Trouble started as soon as she came back to Katy's Ridge. I remember her staggering off into the darkness last night, and hope she made it home all right, too.

While Crow eats his second piece of banana bread, Granny excuses herself and goes into the living room. She brings back a gold picture frame Aunt Meg gave Granny from Woolworths, with a photograph inside of my Uncle Nathan holding me while wearing his Army uniform.

"Our Nathan didn't come back," Granny says, her voice shaking a little. "But I want you to promise me that you will."

Crow promises, and looks over at me like I'm one of the reasons he might make such a promise. A lump of new emotion catches in my throat. He glances at his watch and apologizes that he has to leave. He thanks Granny for the banana bread and coffee, and I walk him to the door just like Mama did Miss Blackstone.

"I enjoyed spending time with you last night," he says on the front porch, looking about as sleepy as I feel.

"I enjoyed it, too," I say.

"Is it okay if I write to you?" he asks. "I mean if you don't want me to, that's fine, too." He looks at his shoes, something he seems to do when at a loss.

"I'd like that," I say, and wonder if I might be persuaded to stay in Katy's Ridge after all.

He hesitates again.

"Can I kiss you?" he asks.

"That would be nice," I say, feeling about as awkward as a mule on roller skates.

When Crow leans in, I have to resist backing up. But then I follow his lead. He closes his eyes, and I do, too. His lips feel soft and warm at the same time. A tingle shoots through my body like a small electrical charge that's looking for a place to ground itself.

The kiss ends, and I thank him like he's just given me a gift. He thanks me back, and then we laugh. It seems I'm not the only one wearing roller skates. Then the events from the day before push their way into my thoughts and I almost scream my frustration at remembering Mama and Miss Blackstone's kiss, too.

"I guess I'd better go," he says. "My dad is waiting at the bottom of the hill to take me to the bus station."

We look at each other, and I feel like I'm in one of Aunt Meg's romance novels, where the two main characters are trying to memorize each other's faces before they part.

"Stay safe," I say, not wanting him to go.

He smiles again and gives me a little salute before taking off down the hill. After I lose sight of him, I touch my lips, remembering our kiss. But before I have time to go back into the house, a third visitor walks up the path.

CHAPTER TWENTY-FOUR

Wildflower

Lily calls me from the front door, her voice sounding desperate. I rush to the porch to see Melody Monroe weaving in the yard, sipping a familiar clear liquid from a ball jar. The past flares my nostrils as I remember the smell of corn liquor, and Melody's brother, Johnny, drinking from a similar jar.

After the morning I've had, I'm not sure I can take much more drama. It doesn't help that I've barely slept and have drunk enough coffee to keep a coal miner awake.

"She's drunk," Lily whispers, as if I haven't noticed.

Melody nods her head in an exaggerated way to confirm the situation. She can barely stand.

"I thought you were going to come visit me today," Melody says to Lily, her speech slurring.

I step to the front edge of the porch to discourage Melody from coming any closer.

"Were you supposed to visit her?" I ask Lily.

"I don't think so," Lily says.

Melody's shoes and clothes are still muddy, and I wonder if she has soap up at that old cabin.

"Why are you lying like that, girl?" Melody yells to Lily. "Of course you said you'd visit. You said it last night when we heard the whispers."

"Last night?" I say, looking at Lily.

"She was standing by the road," Lily says to me. "At the start of the path that goes to the cemetery. I didn't say anything about visiting her today."

"Chip off the old block," Melody says to Lily. "Your daddy was quite the liar, too."

My hackles raise. "I have a mind to slap you from here to Sunday," I call out to Melody.

She laughs as though that's been tried before. Yesterday, she was friendly. I don't understand why she's being so different now, except that the liquor has changed her.

Melody's hair hasn't been combed today, and even from twenty paces I can smell the alcohol. She is wearing a different dress, her arms and legs exposed on this late October day. Her thinness reminds me of the photographs in the newspapers when the Americans liberated the concentration camps in the last war. It is easy to imagine the skeleton underneath. The mother in me wonders if she's had anything to eat today. Should I offer her some of Bee's banana bread?

The screen door slams behind me, and Mama joins us with Daddy's shotgun again.

"What's with you people and shotguns?" Melody asks, attempting to focus on the current danger.

"You best be getting home," I say to Melody.

"You best be watching yourself," Melody says.

"Why are you here?" I ask.

"I came to help you," she says. "The rumor mill has started up and the story isn't good." Melody's words slip and slide like a car on icy mountain roads.

"I'm not worried about rumor mills," I say.

"Well, you should be," she says, with a drunken wink.

Mama and her gun take a step closer. "What's she saying, Louisa May? I can't hear."

"It's nothing, Mama," I call to her.

"That's probably smart," Melody says, keeping her voice low. "You wouldn't want your mama to hear about this. It would probably break her heart."

I narrow my eyes at her, wondering what she thinks she's protecting me from. "I'm not interested in the gossip on the party lines, Melody."

"Oh, you'll be interested in this," she says with a grin. "It's about your fondness for a certain teacher who lives here in Katy's Ridge."

I take a step back and glance at Mama on the porch, who asks again what's being said.

"You want me to speak up, Mrs. McAllister?" Melody raises her voice. "I was just telling your daughter here about—"

I charge toward Melody like a bull after a red cape. When I stop inches from her face, she looks surprised, like I've performed a magic trick and appeared out of thin air. Instead of being scared, she smiles at me.

"You will *not* destroy my family like your brother nearly did," I say through gritted teeth.

The smell of corn liquor makes my gut tighten. I want to run like Lily did the day before.

"Looks like you and that teacher have already destroyed your family without any help from me," she says, sounding almost lucid. "You think the dear people of Katy's Ridge will have anything to do with you when they find this out?" She pauses. The look in her eye is one of wickedness. "I never would have taken you for one of the devil's own," she whispers. "No wonder my brother couldn't keep his hands off you."

"Go home," I say, my jaw clenched nearly shut.

Not that I would want to go home either, considering where she's living right now. Not even corn liquor could help that place feel like a home.

"Does your girlfriend know how tough you are?" Melody smiles again. "Or maybe she likes you tough."

Her words knock the wind out of me, like when her brother tackled me to the ground. I try to get my bearings, and hope Mama's hearing doesn't all of a sudden get better.

I point a finger in her face. "How dare you come here and says these things."

She slaps at my fingers but misses. "You've got a lot of nerve acting all holier than thou." Her retort has a sneer in it and reminds me of Johnny. "That girl of yours looks just like her daddy. Now, who could that be?"

Lily takes a step forward like she's going to defend me, but I put up a hand to stop her. My secret sense tells me that Lily should get the hell away from Melody.

"Lily, I don't want you having anything to do with this woman," I say.

"We need to talk about what she told me yesterday," Lily says.

"I promise we will," I say.

I pivot back to Melody. "You need to leave," I tell her.

She takes another sip from the ball jar. "You know where I am if you have more questions," she says to Lily. "We can talk about you coming to Kentucky, too."

"She won't be going anywhere near Kentucky," I say.

She narrows her eyes at me. "I'd take those rumor mills seriously if I were you," she says, before turning to walk away.

Melody takes off down the hill again with an unsteady gait.

Meanwhile, Mama goes back in the house like she's had enough company for one day. I trust she hasn't heard what Melody said or she would be yelling at me about finding another place to live.

At the cemetery two days before, I felt that life was somehow on track, like a railway car with a clear destination. Safe. Secure. With no possibility of derailing. Yet does anything ever go according to human plans? Fourteen years after my life was forever changed, trouble has come looking for me again, and found me.

CHAPTER TWENTY-FIVE

Lily

"We need to talk, Lily, and I'm not taking no for an answer," Mama says, all solemn.

"Where we going this time?" I ask her. We both know that no serious talking can happen while Granny's around.

"The sawmill," she says. "Unless you've got a better idea."

I tell her I don't.

We've had a year's worth of big talks in less than a day. It turns out Mama isn't who I thought she was. Turns out I barely know her at all.

We follow the steady stream of visitors that have headed down the hill this morning. At the bottom, we get into Mama's pickup and pull into the road. In the opposite direction, Melody weaves down the middle of the road toward her house.

While driving, Mama doesn't speak. Instead, she chews her bottom lip, her forehead creased. I feel like I'm being punished for something, but as far as I can tell I'm not the one who did anything wrong. Once we get to the mill, Mama unlocks the front door and we go inside. The smell of lumber meets us at the doorway as it always does, and the floor is littered with sawdust that feels like a carpet of moss. Silas, who saws the trees into lumber, doesn't work on Saturdays so we have the place to ourselves.

We stand in the main room where all the lumber is cut. The giant rough-toothed saw stands in the center like a silent witness. I wonder if Mama is avoiding her office because of what I saw happen in there.

"What do you want to know?" she asks.

Something about her willingness to finally speak about it makes me quiet.

"Talk to me," she says, and rests a hand on the long table next to the saw.

I imagine she is alarmed about Melody's threats, but can only deal with one thing at a time.

"Were you ever going to tell me about Miss Blackstone?" I ask.

"We went over that last night," she says. "But if you need to talk about it again—"

"No," I say, remembering how emotional Mama got telling me about it. I don't think I could take her tears right now.

"What did Melody tell you?" she asks.

I pause long enough for her to ask me again.

"She told me that her brother, Johnny, was my father," I begin, "and that he was as mean as a snake."

Calling someone a snake is about as insulting as you can get in these parts. I've never had anything against snakes. They serve an earthly purpose just like everything else. They keep the rat population down and that's a good thing. But church people tie them to temptation and blame them for Eve eating apples in the Garden of Eden.

Meanwhile, Mama is silent and stares at the sawdust like any words she might speak have spilled out of her mouth and landed at her feet.

"Mama, are you okay?"

"What else did she say?" she asks, looking up at me.

"She said I looked just like him," I say.

"What else?"

"That's about it," I say. "But then Granny told me that Johnny Monroe hurt you bad and that you didn't have a choice."

Mama lowers herself to a nearby stool and the color leaves her face.

"Is it true?" I ask. "I don't want to hurt you, but I have to know. "

"It's not as simple as all that," she says, her voice soft, almost weak.

"What I want to know, is why you didn't think you could tell me?" I ask.

Mama doesn't look up.

"Didn't you think I deserved to know?" I ask.

She hesitates before lifting her head and looking me directly in the eyes. "Sometimes knowing the truth does more harm than good, Lily. Sometimes knowing the truth changes everything."

I remember seeing her and Miss Blackstone kiss, and agree that the truth can change everything.

"How come Granny knows?" I ask.

"About Johnny?"

I nod.

"Because she and Daniel found me that night," Mama says, her voice heavy with history.

"What about Aunt Jo?"

"Everybody in Katy's Ridge knows," she says, sadness in her voice.

"Everybody except me, you mean?"

If I could turn into an insect at this moment, I'd choose a bee. I want to sting her, even if it means I die as a result.

Mama takes a deep breath.

"If it matters, I was going to tell you once you got older," she says.

I scoff. "I'm trying not to hate you right now," I say, feeling snake-like.

She looks disappointed, but then softens like she doesn't blame me for hating her.

"I know what it's like to hate people," she says. "I can't say that it does much good. But sometimes it's what you need to do."

Her understanding ignites my frustration. I would hurt her, if she wasn't already doing such a good job of hurting herself.

"You lied to me," I say, but it comes out half-hearted. "You've lied to me for fourteen years."

"I kept the truth from you," she says, as though this is different. "But I had my reasons," she adds.

"Just like you have your reasons for kissing Miss Blackstone?"

She narrows her eyes at me, and I sip pleasure from the moment.

"So you're going to threaten me, like Melody?" she asks.

"What if I am?" I sound like a puffed up bully, but I don't even care. My whole life has been a lie.

"Do what you want," Mama says, as if she's tired of worrying about it. "Just remember that everything has a cost, and not always the cost you think."

I put a hand on my hip, daring myself to stand up to her.

"What did he do to you?" I ask Mama. But I'm not so sure I want to know anymore. Maybe Mama's right. Maybe the truth is best left buried sometimes.

She pauses for a long time, like she's considering the cost of this one thing. She stands and reaches for the large push broom nearby.

"I need to sweep," she says.

Like Granny, Mama sweeps when she needs to think. Sometimes she'll sweep the entire house when she's got something bothering her. Granny says we have the cleanest floors in Katy's Ridge, on account of all the thinking she and Mama do.

She begins to sweep the sawdust, creating small piles of powder that were once trees. I tap my foot, wishing I felt like singing or humming so I'd have something to do while I wait. Mama sweeps the piles of sawdust out the door, and then stops and looks over at me.

"To answer your question, Lily, sometimes a woman doesn't have a choice in life."

She sounds like Great Aunt Sadie. "What do you mean?" I ask, tapping my foot again.

"I was younger than you are now when I had you," she begins. "I imagine you've figured that out already, subtracting our ages. But I wasn't a woman at all. I was still a girl. A girl forced into being a woman way too soon."

Even though part of me wants to run, my shoes feel nailed to the floor. Does every family have these kinds of secrets? Or is it just mine?

"The crazy thing is, for the longest time I thought I deserved it," Mama begins again. "That day, my secret sense warned me that something bad was going to happen, but I didn't listen."

Mama has preached to me my whole life about how important it is to listen to your intuition. Great Aunt Sadie has said the same thing. Now I know why.

"When I was thirteen," she continues, "Johnny started bothering me and saying things to me that he shouldn't have said. He was older than me. Daddy had died by then, so I told your Uncle Daniel about it. He went to talk to Johnny and Johnny's father, who didn't seem to care."

Mama puts away the push broom and sits on the stool again.

"Melody Monroe was still living at the cabin then," she says, her eyes thoughtful. "She was a sad little thing. Her sister Ruby had just died who was the same age as me in school."

She pauses, like the story is a river that could meander off course if she isn't careful.

"I was up at the cemetery for the one-year anniversary of your Granddaddy's death, and Johnny followed me up there."

She stops and looks over at me. "Do you want me to keep going?"

I nod and stand straighter. Bravery is called for when it comes to hearing the truth. But I need to know where I come from. I need to know who my people are, and not just the McAllister side of the family.

"On the way back from the cemetery, Johnny attacked me," she says.

Even though I'd guessed what was coming, the words shock me. "He attacked you?" I ask.

"He chased me and then tackled me to the ground," she says.

Tears come to her eyes again, and I fight the guilt of needing to know.

"I fought back as hard as I could, but he was just too strong," she continues. "Then at some point I passed out."

Mama looks at me as though the war she's been fighting for years has been lost, and she has finally raised the white flag. I turn away, not wanting to see her surrender.

Secrets are like genies in bottles, I decide. Once they come out, you can't get them back in again. No matter how hard you try. Words can't be unspoken. Nor can I ever undo seeing Mama and Miss Blackstone kiss. But maybe learning a painful truth is a necessary thing, too. When I look back at Mama the surrender has passed and she seems lighter, like she's finally set down something heavy she was dragging around.

"When did you know you were carrying me?" I ask.

"Right away," she says. "I just kind of knew, deep down, that something good was going to come out of it."

Mama stands. When she opens her arms, it's like a magnet turns on and pulls me toward her, into her embrace.

CHAPTER TWENTY-SIX

Wildflower

As Lily and I release our embrace, Daniel opens the door to the mill.

"You two okay in here?" he asks. "Nell got worried. She came to the house. Said you just disappeared and she didn't know where you'd gone."

It is just like Mama to send Daniel looking for us. He takes off his hat and steps inside, pulling his bum leg over the threshold. He waits at the door until I motion him in.

"I just told Lily what happened with Johnny," I say to him.

He walks over to where we're standing, and puts an arm around Lily, asking how she is.

"Why didn't anybody tell me?" she asks us.

"We were trying to protect you," I say. "But maybe we were wrong to do that. If we were, I'm sorry."

"Now I wish I'd just left well enough alone," Lily says, although that wouldn't be like her at all.

"Anyone would have been curious," Daniel tells her.

My gratitude for Daniel at that moment is no surprise. If he hadn't found me in the forest that night, I might have frozen to death, and Lily and I wouldn't be here at all.

"Does everybody know except me?" she asks. "Do the kids at school know?"

"Probably not," Daniel says. "It's ancient history now."

But it wasn't ancient history after it happened. I remember how people looked at me and how many friends I lost. It was like I had a contagious disease that everybody was afraid to catch. Bee was the only non-family member to stay by my side. None of us were equipped to handle it.

The three of us stand in a small circle in the large room.

"Tell me about what happened when you found Mama that night," Lily says to Daniel.

Daniel and I exchange looks, as though questioning the wisdom of telling more. My instinct is to pull Lily close and cover her ears, shielding her from the rest of the story. But Daniel takes a seat on the stool next to the biggest saw, and we pull up two more. I take a deep breath, readying myself.

"When your granny and I found your mother she was beaten so badly we thought she was dead," Daniel says to Lily. He studies his hands like they hold his memories. "Nell and I exchanged a look that night that I'll never forget. We both thought we'd lost your mother." Daniel looks over at me, his eyes soft.

Hearing the story reminds me of the gold Mary. I didn't want to leave her that day. She was going to take me to Daddy. But it wasn't my time to go. I know that now.

"It took her weeks to recover," Daniel begins again. "Then at some point she discovered she was going to have you." He pauses, studying his hands again. "After you were born, Wildflower never looked back. We all helped the best we could, but your mama raised you with an astonishing amount of love and care." His voice cracks with emotion.

For a long time, we are silent. I can't imagine what it is like for Lily to hear some of the events surrounding the beginning of her life. At least she hasn't run away.

"We agreed as a family to keep what happened from you as long as we could," Daniel begins again. "Or at least until you wanted to know. If we failed you in that way, I'm very sorry. But your mother is a brave woman, Lily, and trust me when I say you are lucky to have her."

Again, it occurs to me how lucky we are to have Daniel here. He's like the footbridge helping us get across this rough part of the path.

"Lily, I know you've wanted to know for a long time now who your father was," I say. "But I just didn't know how to tell you." I apologize again and she lowers her head. "Wounds heal," I tell her. "And sometimes in the middle of a curse is a blessing. I got you out of it, after all, and you've been the brightest and best gift of my life." My voice wavers, and I bite my bottom lip to keep from crying again.

Lily's brow is furrowed in that way she gets when she's thinking hard about something, I can almost see her effort to make peace with it. Although, I know from personal experience, that peace takes a long time to come with things like this.

Outside, the wind picks up, as if announcing a new direction. The boards of the old sawmill creak.

"How do you not think of him when you see me?" Lily says finally.

Her question causes me to pause, and I choose my words carefully. "The night you were born I knew you were mine and mine alone," I begin. "I named you Lily because lilies are resurrection flowers. You see them on Easter because they promise to bring new life. Aunt Sadie says they are the flower most associated with Mary, Jesus' mother. She holds them in those paintings of the Annunciation from a long time ago."

For the first time I realize Lily isn't wearing the necklace I gave her. It was my way of giving her a piece of her story. But now isn't the time to ask her about it. She gets quiet again, and Daniel and I exchange another look. I'm not convinced that knowing the reality of the situation is the best thing.

I think about what Melody said in her drunken state. That people know about me and Bee.

What people? I wanted to ask her.

With the exception of yesterday, Bee and I had been so careful. It is hard to imagine how Melody might have found out.

"How did my father die?" Lily asks, as though one question remains unanswered.

Daniel looks at me, and I motion that I will tell her.

"A couple of weeks after it happened, Johnny tried to break into the house and your Aunt Amy shot him," I say.

"Aunt Amy shot him?" A disbelieving look crosses her face.

"He was wounded," I begin again, "but not badly. That day, your Uncle Daniel and Uncle Nathan and I went out looking for Johnny. We found him at the bottom of the ravine. He had evidently fallen off the old footbridge trying to get away."

"So he really did die before I was born?" Lily asks.

"He really did," I say. "He's buried up in the cemetery. I can show you where, if you want me to."

Lily pauses, as though trying to take everything in.

"All this time, I imagined my father was someone totally different than who he was," Lily says. "I made up this whole story about a stranger who came to Katy's Ridge and swept you off your feet. A soldier maybe, who went off to war, never to return." She looks at me, her expression wistful. "I imagined the tragedy was so great when you lost this amazing man that no one could bear to talk about it. Especially not you, Mama, because your heart was broken."

Lily's wistfulness falls to the floor like sawdust.

"I would have preferred that story, too," I say. "But life isn't a romance novel, Lily, no matter how much we wish it were. The truth is, life is really hard sometimes."

"I know that," she says lowering her eyes again.

The secret finally out, I expect us all to look different somehow, but everyone looks the same. But then a relief comes, after finally releasing what I've kept a tight grip on for so many years. I'm not sure whether to laugh or cry. What quickly follows is fear. Fear that my secret about Bee may yet cause the most damage to our lives.

CHAPTER TWENTY-SEVEN

Lily

With Granny feeding the chickens, I am finishing up the breakfast dishes at the kitchen sink when Mama comes in. It has been a week since she and Uncle Daniel told me about my father, and I am still getting used to not having a fantasy to rely on anymore. In addition, after a week of rain and gray days, a grouchiness has descended on me that I can't seem to shake. A grouchiness that seems to be aimed at Mama.

"Want to go to a movie in Rocky Bluff this afternoon?" she asks. "Your Aunt Jo and Aunt Meg want to see *The King and I.*"

The Rocky Bluff Theater only shows movies on Saturdays, and it doesn't usually get a movie so recently released. Not to mention it's a musical, which is rarer, still. But I haven't sung for over a week now, and I wonder if I'll ever feel like singing again. Besides, my current state of misery won't allow for anything that could be fun.

"No, thank you," I say. Is it my imagination or does my response make the room feel colder?

Other things feel more urgent. I need to talk to Melody again, who as far as I know is still in Katy's Ridge. The story of how my life started is like a nightmare crossing over into the daytime. My father was a monster. Yet, as Great Aunt Sadie says, even monsters aren't only one thing, so I need to know more.

At least with Mama at the movies, I won't have to sneak around.

"Oh, come on, sweetheart. Come into town with us." It's not like Mama to plead. "You know how much fun you have with Meg and Jo. We can stop at the Woolworth's after the show."

"No, thank you," I repeat, this time louder in case she's suddenly gone deaf.

I glimpse the disappointment in her eyes. It's not right to blame Mama for any of this, but that's exactly what I'm doing. If Johnny Monroe was so mean, she should have stayed away from him. She should have fought harder. Surely there was something she could have done to stop him.

I wish Crow were here to talk me out of my bad mood. I can't believe I used to complain about nothing ever happening in Katy's Ridge. Now I just want to get back to my boring, uneventful life.

I'm not the only one who has been moping around. Ever since Melody Monroe told Mama she knew about Bee, Mama has, too. As far as I know, she hasn't told Bee about it, probably because she doesn't want to upset her.

With Mama getting dressed to go to Rocky Bluff, I go over to telephone Pearl from Uncle Daniel's and she agrees to go talk to Melody with me. After I get back home, I wait on the porch for Pearl and see Aunt Jo and Aunt Meg traipsing up the hill smiling. It is a cool day and requires a sweater, but the sun is out and hits the south facing porch.

"You coming with us?" Aunt Meg calls to me.

"Not today," I say.

"But it's *The King and I*," Aunt Jo says. "Deborah Kerr and Yul Brynner."

She looks at me like Preacher does whenever he's rounding up sinners, full of hope and expectation.

"The singing is supposed to be incredible," Aunt Meg says. "All the Hollywood magazines say so."

I'm not sure I can bear to hear singing when a song hasn't graced my lips for days. It's like they've dried up after I found out about my father.

"I can't believe you're passing up a chance to see a musical," Aunt Jo says, her smile fading. "Are you not feeling well?"

"Save your breath," Mama says, coming out of the house. "I've already tried to convince her."

Mama joins them in the yard. At that moment, they look like the Red Bud sisters standing there, their relatedness unmistakable. All three women are about the same size and height, their hair and eye color in harmony, their features offering the only variety. Mama looks like a photograph I've seen of Granddaddy McAllister. Aunt Jo looks like a beautiful version of Granny and Aunt Meg looks like a mixture of both. Aunt Amy was the unluckiest in the family, getting the big version of Granny's nose, and the tiny version of Granddaddy's eyes.

Aunt Amy isn't the type to go to movies and is probably sewing today, getting dress orders ready for Thanksgiving and Christmas. She disappears every fall, which is her busiest season.

"Last chance?" Mama says.

I tell them to go on and hide my regrets. The truth is, I don't feel like I deserve to go to the movies right now. Bad blood flows through my veins. Blood, that until recently, I thought was perfectly fine and maybe even superior to everybody else in Katy's Ridge. Bigger places called me. I thought I was special. But it turns out I'm half-hoodlum. Destined to be unremarkable.

Shortly after Mama and her sisters leave, Granny comes out of the house carrying a basket of quilt pieces.

"If you need me, I'll be at Sadie's," she says, and takes off following the others.

I go inside. It is rare to have the house to myself. The only sound is the crackling of wood in the wood stove in the living room. While I wait for Pearl to arrive, I go into the bedroom Mama and I share and open the bottom dresser drawer. This is Mama's private space, where she keeps all her special things. Out of respect, I've never looked inside, but I wonder now if there's any information about my father in there.

I pull out a large cigar box and sit on the bed debating whether to open it. I imagine my father would have done more than open it, maybe even stealing it or tossing away the contents. I give myself permission to look inside. On top are a pair of booties I used to wear and a faded bib, hand-stitched, folded in a small square. A handful of photographs are scattered within. One is of Miss Blackstone in a small golden frame. Others are loose in the box. A man is in one. The name Victor is written on the back, with the date 1946. Another one is of a girl and Mama standing arm-in-arm. The name Mary Jane is written on the back of that one, and the date 1941.

Mama would never go through my things. She would be too honorable. But it turns out I'm not as decent as she is, especially when I want information. A small white Bible is tucked in the corner the box. Inside, the date she got baptized is written in the faded blue ink of a fountain pen. I thumb through its thin pages and find two yellowing newspaper clippings. One is the obituary of Joseph McAllister, my grandfather. It tells of an unfortunate accident at the local sawmill. It then lists the names of his wife and daughters left behind. *Louisa May, age 12,* is listed last.

In that moment, the poignancy of Mama's loss becomes real to me. I imagine it is much different to know who your father is for twelve years before losing him, instead of never knowing who he was in the first place.

The second clipping is also an obituary from the Rocky Bluff newspaper and is much smaller. It reads:

Johnny M. Monroe, age 17, fell to his death in Katy's Ridge. He is preceded in death by his mother, Mabel; his father, Arthur, as well as his sister Ruby Monroe, who died at age 12. He leaves behind one surviving sister, Melody, age 10, who resides in Louisville, Kentucky.

I stare at the words and hold the clipping for a long time. Long enough for my hand to begin to shake.

At least somebody put it in the newspaper, I tell myself, even if it is a tiny announcement. There is no photograph, and I wonder if one even exists. Mama told me once that when she was a girl, a man with a big camera would come to Katy's Ridge every year or two to take photographs for anybody who had the money to pay for them. From the looks of that cabin, I doubt the Monroes had any spare money hanging around for such a thing. I try to imagine someone who looks like me, but who is taller and almost a man.

"Hey! What are you doing?"

Pearl startles me so bad I let out a short scream.

"You scared me to death," I say. I put a hand to my racing heart, as though it might otherwise jump right out of my chest.

She mumbles an apology. "Are you going through your mama's private things?" She tilts her head like the truth, and nothing but the truth, is required.

"I found out who my father was," I say, as if this gives me permission to snoop.

"Just now?"

"No, last Saturday."

Pearl looks hurt. "Why am I just now finding out about it?"

It is a good question. Truth is, I don't feel as close to Pearl as I used to. It's like life has forced me to grow up, but she gets to stay a kid.

"A lot's been going on," I say, which is an understatement.

"Well, who is it?" Pearl asks.

"Not who I'd hoped," I say.

"You mean it's not Cary Grant?" She giggles.

"Not even close," I say.

At least she is one other person who didn't already know like almost everybody else. She sits on the bed next to me, giving it a bounce. Pearl knows I've been wanting to know his identity my entire life. "Tell me," she says.

Despite Pearl's admirable secret-keeping about Mama and Miss Blackstone, I don't want to risk anybody else finding out that Johnny Monroe is my father. Pearl waits for me to answer, exhibiting a patience that is unusual for her. I put Mama's secret box back in the bottom drawer and close it.

"You can't tell a soul," I say, not knowing a way to back out.

Pearl licks her lips as though secrets are a delicious treat she doesn't get that often. I make her do a double pinkie swear, and then tell her the one thing that causes my cheeks to burn with shame. Johnny Monroe is my father. Johnny Monroe forced himself on her and didn't give Mama a choice. That means I was never meant to exist.

CHAPTER TWENTY-EIGHT

Wildflower

Two of my three sisters are in my truck, our hips touching in the front seat. We are on our way to see a movie in Rocky Bluff. Initially, it was planned as a special treat for Lily, but she refused to come along. My heart isn't exactly in it now, but Jo and Meg are so excited I decide to go anyway.

Earlier that morning when I went over to Jo's to see if she was up for a movie, I telephoned Meg and Amy from Jo's house, and also Bee. I invited her to join us and make it look like a coincidence. For the last few days, I've avoided Bee, not having the heart to tell her what Melody said. Maybe it's nothing. A wild threat. But something tells me it isn't. Someone is feeding Melody information, and I can't put off much longer talking to Bee about it.

"How is Lily taking the news that Johnny's her father?" Meg asks.

Daniel must have told Jo and Jo told Meg and Amy about the talk we had at the mill. I imagine they've all formed an opinion about it. I crack my window suddenly needing air, and Jo holds her long hair with one hand to keep it from blowing in the wind.

"She's been very quiet about it all," I say. "She had this huge fantasy built up about who her father was."

"I wish she hadn't turned down going to see the musical," Meg says. "Musicals make anybody feel better."

"I think she's had about all she can stand of me for a while," I say. "I'm trying not to worry."

"I would be worried, too," Jo says. "When Daniel gets quiet like that I know he's remembering the war. And when he's remembering the war, he shuts himself in our bedroom and doesn't come out for a while. I hate it when he does that."

I've experienced the part of Daniel that gets quiet, too, but not that often.

"You know, I haven't heard Lily sing for days," I tell them. "It used to be I couldn't walk into the house without hearing her singing something."

Both sisters turn to look at me.

"That's not good," Meg says.

"I know," I say.

"It's hard to imagine Lily not singing," Jo says.

We ride a few miles in somber silence—the shocks squeaking with every bump in the road—as if the thought of Lily not singing is reason enough to be gloomy.

"Maybe she just needs time," Meg says. "Things will get back to normal soon enough."

"Lily's good enough to sing in a musical herself," Jo says. "She should go to Nashville or someplace where they pay people to sing like that."

"Or New York City," Meg says. "The King and I was a Broadway play before it was a movie. Yul Brynner starred in that one, too."

Meg reads movie magazines and is the dreamiest of my sisters. I doubt there's a practical bone in her body, except that she married Cecil.

"Yul Brynner is bald," Jo says. "I like a man with hair."

The mood lightens and the three of us laugh.

"Daniel has a nice head of hair," Meg says.

"I've threatened to leave him if he goes bald," Jo says with a smile, though I can't imagine her ever leaving Daniel for any reason.

"Well, it's too late for Cecil," Meg says, with a sigh.

I'm not sure what Meg sees in Cecil. I imagine she was just tired of being unmarried. At least I don't have to worry about Bee going bald, but I'm not about to say this to my sisters. Although sometimes I wish I could.

"We need to find Wildflower a man with a good head of hair," Jo says. "It's about time you settled down with someone, little sister."

They look at me as if their matchmaking project requires a response.

"You haven't called me Wildflower in years," I say to Jo. "Nobody has, except Daniel."

"Perhaps it's time we started calling you that again," she says.

In the pause that follows, I play around with the notion of telling my sisters about Bee. It's hard to imagine their reactions, other than pure shock.

"What about Crow Sector?" Meg says finally, as if she's been making a list in her mind of all the eligible men in Katy's Ridge.

"He's Lily's age," I say. "I used to babysit him."

"Yeah, too young," Jo says.

"Besides, Lily is the one with the crush on him," I say.

"Really?" Jo says.

"I thought you knew that," Meg says to Jo.

"I guess I didn't," Jo says.

We bounce along the main road out of Katy's Ridge. I know this road so well I could practically drive it without looking.

Outings with my older sisters are rare these days. Jo stays busy with the house and farm while Daniel works at the mill. And most of the time Meg is distracted with Cecil and her step-daughter, Janie, who—at best—is a strange girl.

"I can't imagine what it's like for Lily to find out about Johnny," Jo says.

"How do you make peace with Johnny Monroe being your father?" Meg says, her voice somber.

Meg and Jo both sat with me in the days that followed Johnny's attack. They know full well what he was capable of.

"When I went to see her, Melody promised she wouldn't tell Lily unless she asked."

"I guess Lily asked," Meg says. "She's always been full of questions."

"Reminds me of somebody else I know," Jo says.

Meg and Jo exchange a look that tells me I wasn't always the easiest of siblings.

"But why on earth would Melody show up now?" Jo says.

Evidently she found some old letters written to her aunt," I say. "They were about Johnny dying and also about Lily."

"Melody didn't even know Johnny was dead?" Jo asks.

"Not until recently," I say.

"How awful," Jo says, looking out her window.

"Who wrote the letters?" Meg asks.

"Doc Lester," I say.

She grimaces.

"It's a shame Lily knows," Jo says. "She's obviously hurt."

"I probably would have kept the secret forever if Lily had left it alone," I say. "But I was totally naïve to think I could keep it from her."

I wonder what else I've been immature about. I'm almost thirty years old and sometimes I feel like I haven't learned a thing. I remember Melody's threat to expose me and Bee and wonder if 'normal' is too much to ask for. This saga isn't over. And if I tell Bee, I fear she may leave Katy's Ridge again.

We go along the narrowest part of the road that hugs up against the mountain, and I grip the steering wheel tighter. We always stop talking along this stretch and hold our breath. On the other side is a sheer drop down to the river, the reason this section is called the bluff. Tree roots dangle where the road was cut into the mountain. Suspended like flailing legs reaching, to no avail, for solid ground.

I can relate to exposed roots. It feels like my private life is being cut away and revealed. Things I've preferred to keep buried.

"Time heals all wounds," Meg says, with a sigh.

I wonder if she's talking about Lily or if she's heard my private thoughts.

Fifteen years after Daddy's death I still think of him every day. Not in the painful longing way that it was at first. But at certain milestones, I miss him. Like when Lily was born and when she first sang at the church. Actually, every time she sings I wish he could hear her. I imagine he would be so proud. Like I am proud.

The road widens, and we all start talking again. The bluff is one of the reasons Katy's Ridge stays small. Not that many people want to make such a hazardous drive to get in and out of the area.

We park in front of the small theater in Rocky Bluff, and I look around for Bee's car. As planned, Bee stands in the small lobby holding a bag of popcorn, pretending not to wait for anyone. I let Jo and Meg go in ahead of me to discover her first and hear their greetings. It feels special to run into people we know in Rocky Bluff, even though this incidence is prearranged.

I greet Bee, dulling my smile so as not to appear too glad to see her. "Are you here alone?" I ask, like an actress playing a small part in a play.

"Join us," Meg says, grabbing her arm. Bee puts up a tiny fight just for show.

Melody's threat follows me into the darkened theater. I wonder if anybody knows. I give myself permission to not think about it while the movie is playing, and let the others go in first so I can sit next to Bee.

Our shoes touch as Deborah Kerr and Yul Brynner go from adversaries to two people who respect each other. When they sing *Shall We Dance?* our hands reach into the bag of popcorn in a move as orchestrated as the score that plays in the background. Our hands touch. Stolen moments. Stolen in dark places where prying eyes can't see. Yet eyes have seen. At least according to Melody Monroe.

Only once do we let our hands touch between our chairs. Skin against skin. The tingle of recognition that this is the hand of the person I love, even if our hands can never touch in public. For years I tried to see Victor as more than a friend. He didn't deserve to be strung along. But the more I wanted to love him, to commit to a life with him, the more it didn't happen.

If God and I were still on speaking terms, I would ask why life is so hard sometimes, for the God-fearing and heathen alike. As far as I can tell, no one escapes difficulties and some suffer more than most. Yet there are everyday miracles, too. I can't imagine a life without Lily or Bee or my family. Or June and Horatio, who welcome us into their home. In terms of work, after years of struggle, the sawmill finally has enough customers to sustain us. I never thought the mill would be part mine someday, and eventually all mine.

In the movie, the King and Anna are ending their dance. It is nice to get a respite from all that is going on. But then, a foreboding shivers through me that is so strong I gasp. Lily is in danger. I have to get home.

Bee looks at me, her eyes questioning. "I need you to give Jo and Meg a ride back to Katy's Ridge," I whisper to her. "Something isn't right."

"Are you sure?" she whispers back.

Actually, I'm not sure, but I can't take the chance. Not while Melody Monroe is still around. I rush out of the theater and back to Katy's Ridge, unsure of what I might find.

CHAPTER TWENTY-NINE

Lily

With the last few sunny days, the mud has hardened, making it easier to get to the Monroe cabin. This doesn't stop Pearl from complaining every few steps.

"Why are we doing this again?" she asks.

"Because I want to find out more about my father," I say.

"Don't you know enough?" she asks. "Sounds like he's not much to write home about."

"Nobody is all one thing," I say, repeating what Great Aunt Sadie said. "Even monsters have a bit of goodness inside, just like saints have a bit of badness."

"You say the strangest things," Pearl says. She leans over to wipe dirt from her shoes, before complaining again.

As much as I wish it weren't true, Melody Monroe is kin. I figure I owe her an explanation as to why I'm never going to see her again. But before that, I want to learn more about my ne'er-do-well father, Johnny Monroe. Mama wouldn't like that

I'm coming here. Something about it feels dangerous, even to me. I reach for the gold Mary around my neck for added protection and realize again that I've lost her. As far as I can figure, it must have been the night I walked to Crow's house in the dark.

When we get there, the door to the cabin is wide open.

"This place is creepy," Pearl says.

I don't tell her about the girl who died here, or I'll be seeing Pearl's backside as she hightails it home. I step up to the door and call out Melody's name. When she doesn't answer, I take a step inside and find her sleeping on an old mattress in the corner. A mason jar sits on the small kitchen table with clear liquid inside, along with a loaf of bread and a hunk of cheese. I remember the banana bread Miss Blackstone brought last Saturday morning and how elegant it was in comparison.

Melody snorts awake and jumps when she sees me standing there. "You know I could shoot you for trespassing, don't you?" She sits up and holds her head like it weighs a thousand pounds. "That is, if I had a gun," she adds.

Pearl's eyes widen like she's asking what I got us into.

"I need you to tell me more about my father," I say to her.

"Oh, so you believe me now?" she asks.

"Mama told me the story," I say.

"Did she?" Melody makes her way to the kitchen table. "What would that story be?" she asks. She spies the leftover liquor and puts it up in the cabinet, as though not willing to share.

"She was attacked and left for dead," I say, not naming any names.

Pearl looks at me. I can tell she's never heard this part of the story.

"That sounds like something Johnny would do," Melody says, matter-of-fact. "But Doc Lester said she asked for it."

"Well, Doc Lester is a liar and a horse's ass," I say.

Pearl giggles, and then stops herself when Melody turns to look at her. Pearl's been known to laugh at inappropriate times when she's nervous.

"Your daddy's that Indian, isn't he?" she says to Pearl.

Pearl nods.

"His name is Horatio Sector," I say.

"And your mama's white?"

Pearl nods again.

Melody gives Pearl the once-over, like she's trying to see the Indian in her.

"Something tells me you have something to ask me, little-miss-full-of-questions." Melody turns her heavy head toward me.

"I want to hear more about what he was like," I say.

"You mean Johnny?" She plops down in the chair and it wobbles even though she doesn't weigh much at all. "Well, like I said, he was mean as a snake."

A stray piece of sunlight breaks through the small window and touches the top of the table.

"What was he like besides being mean?" I ask.

Melody scoffs and puts her hand on the piece of sunlight, as if to claim it as her own. She pushes the spare chair out with her bare foot so I can join her, and then rubs her eyes to clear the sleep out of them. Pearl is left standing, but she doesn't seem to care. My guess is she's happy to stand if it means she will get a head start running if we need to get out of here.

The cabin smells sour from cigarettes and rotting wood.

"I want to know what he was like besides being a monster," I say.

Melody grunts a short laugh. Then she looks up at the ceiling, as if her memories are all stored in the single light bulb that lights the room. She sits long enough without speaking that I wonder if she's fallen back to sleep with her eyes open. But then she leans forward.

"Before our mother died, Johnny was a different boy," she begins. "Our life was a lot better then. But after our mother died, our father started drinking more and more. He was a horrible drunk," she says. "It was our mother who kept him civilized, and without her he didn't stand a chance."

I've seen Melody do a lot of drinking in the short time she's been here and wonder if it's a family trait. She pulls off a chunk of bread and offers some to me and Pearl. We decline.

"Johnny was older than me by four years, and my sister, Ruby, was two years older."

She stops long enough to cut a slice of cheese with a rusty knife and eats it with the bread. She doesn't offer us any cheese. The cups from our tea the week before still sit on the end of the table. The one I used overflows with the stubbed out ends of cigarettes. I try not to gag.

"I still miss Ruby," she begins again. "Hung herself out in that old oak out there."

Melody points with the knife to a tree in the distance.

Pearl's eyes get about as wide as the silver dollar she gets in her Christmas stocking every year. I hope she doesn't take off running and leave me here.

"How old was your sister?" I ask.

"Almost thirteen," Melody says. "But I could understand why she did it. If I'd had the nerve, I would have joined her."

Melody's eyes grow dark, as though visiting the past requires dim lighting.

"But why would she do such a thing?" I ask.

"When you're being messed with, it's hard not to feel trapped," she says. It sounds like she's given this some thought.

Melody stands and goes to the cupboard to get the liquor she put away earlier. Instead of drinking out of the jar, she pours some in one of the teacups and drinks it.

Pearl inches toward the door. I make a motion with my hand to stay put. It's obvious she doesn't want to be here, but I may never get this chance again.

Melody stares at the old bed in the middle of the room like it's a crystal ball showing her the past. "I think Daddy knew about Johnny, and that's why he sent me to Aunt Reenie's." She pauses and takes another sip. "I guess there was enough decency left in him that he didn't want what happened to Ruby to happen to me."

"Why did you come back to Katy's Ridge if it holds so many bad memories?" I ask.

Melody takes another sip and sits straighter, as though the liquid is giving her courage.

"I found out a couple of years ago that I can't have children," she says. "So when I read Doc Lester's letters to my aunt, it gave me hope that the family wouldn't die out." She finishes off what's in the teacup.

I haven't given a whole lot of thought to family bloodlines and didn't realize it was so important to some people.

"You have Monroe blood in you," Melody begins again, confirming my thought. "My parents came over from northern Scotland," she continues, staring into the empty teacup. "They headed south because the land was cheaper. They ran into somebody in Virginia who told them about this little place called Katy's Ridge that was a gem. Hard to think of this place as a gem," she says, looking around the room.

I'd heard others who'd settled in Katy's Ridge tell similar stories. Granddaddy and Great Aunt Sadie came over from Ireland, too, and Granny came over from Germany with her sister. Everybody's family is from somewhere else, except maybe Horatio Sector. Pearl told me the Cherokee are from North Carolina and Tennessee, and that her father's grandparents went to Oklahoma by way of something called the Trail of Tears.

"What were your parents like?" I ask, wanting to fill in the missing picture of my unknown grandparents.

"Would you believe my mother laughed all the time?" Melody says, looking straight at me. "That's what I remember about her most. Her laughter. And then after she died it was like all laughter died with her."

Melody's smile fades and sadness takes its place. Her sorrow appears as tangible as the design on the teacup. The design and the sorrow weathered, but not really gone.

"We were all devastated," Melody continues. "But it hurt Johnny the most. As the oldest, he never got over it. He was a mama's boy before he got mean. 'Sweetest little boy in the world,' Mama used to call him."

It's a long journey from *sweetest little boy in the world* to *mean as a snake*. I imagine it's a sad journey, too. Mama likes to say that everybody's got reasons for being the way they are. Even Mama and Miss Blackstone have their reasons for loving each other. It doesn't matter whether I understand it or not. I want to ask Melody how she knows about them, but don't want to distract her from talking about her family. *Our* family.

"After our mother died, Johnny couldn't even get to school on time anymore, and Daddy took switches to him," Melody continues. "Of course, that just made matters worse."

Melody looks at Pearl standing near the door and asks if she'd like to sit down, as though all of a sudden remembering her manners. Pearl declines. It is the quietest I've ever known her. I don't think either of us expected Melody to tell all this. Most grownups won't even talk to people our age. But she seems younger than most adults.

"Before our mother died, Johnny won the third grade spelling bee," Melody begins again. "He was also a good reader. Way better than Ruby and me. And he was good with numbers, too. But none of that seemed to matter to him anymore after our mother died."

Melody walks over to the door and Pearl steps aside. Melody stares out into the forest, the sun sprinkled through the trees and smiles. Then she twirls once, as though hearing a distant tune and dancing with a ghost. A ghost she's missed.

"Lily won the spelling bee in third grade, too," Pearl says to Melody.

"She did? You did?" She turns to me. "That's Johnny's influence, I bet." She looks almost pleased.

A sadness visits me that feels older than this cabin. I remember the whispers again. If I could ask my father a question, I would ask him how someone who used to be so smart could drop out in the sixth grade and turn mean. But I already know the answer. If Mama died, I would be heartbroken, too, and I'm not sure I'd ever get over it. At this moment, I'm not sure how I'll ever leave Katy's Ridge without her.

"Johnny really changed," Melody says, as though intent on finishing her story. "He took out every bit of anger he had about Mama dying and tormented me and Ruby. I remember asking him once where that sweet little boy went, and he slapped me hard in the face like he was slapping that memory right out of my head. I think that little boy died when Mama died."

I stand next to my chair, feeling almost dizzy from all I've heard. Pearl's eyes plead with me to go.

"We've got to get home," I tell Melody. "Thanks for telling me all this."

"Wait," she says. "You've got to come with me to Kentucky. It's just a few hours by bus."

"Now?" I say.

"Good a time as any," she answers. "You don't belong here," she whispers, and I think of the whispers at the footbridge. "Louisville is a big city. There's a lot more going on."

A Greyhound bus stops at the Texaco station every day in Rocky Bluff. More than once, I've fantasized about hopping onboard and going anywhere north of here or south or east or west.

"I doubt Mama would go for that," I say.

"Don't tell her," Melody says. "Just come with me." She extends a hand like she might offer me a poison apple.

"We need to go," Pearl says to me.

"We can leave for Louisville right after I pay my respects to Ruby and Johnny," Melody says. "This place gets under my skin. I can't stomach it for much longer."

I wonder if this is why the moonshine is never far away from her.

"So what do you say?" she asks, as if not willing to let it go.

"I can't do that to Mama," I say.

"Sure you can," she says. "We could be in Louisville by tomorrow morning." She reaches for me again.

"Lily, we need to go," Pearl says, her voice strong.

"Sorry," I say to Melody.

She lets out a long sigh, as though Mama's just won at a game they've been playing.

"Suit yourself," she says. "Come give your Aunt Melody a hug." She stands and opens her skinny arms.

Pearl gives me a wary look, but I decide that one hug can't hurt anything. Melody's embrace is weak, though the smell of alcohol and cigarettes is much stronger. Melody must not have had much practice. She holds me longer than I expect, and I have to push her away, which isn't hard because she's so thin. She finally takes a step back.

"Doc Lester says you can sing. Is that true?" she asks me.

"She sings like an angel," Pearl says. "She's the best singer in Tennessee."

Despite the sudden chill in the cabin, I feel my face warm.

"Well, just so you know, Johnny couldn't sing a lick," she says to me. "So you must have gotten that from the McAllister side of the family."

Pearl stands at the door, tapping her foot. Mama would be glad she's trying to get me out of there. But it appears Melody has more to say. In a way, it's as though this might be the last time she sees me, and she wants to make sure she says certain things.

"I hope you can forgive Johnny for what he did to your mother," she begins again. "I wish that it hadn't happened, but life is just full of things we all wish had never happened."

Melody is smarter than I thought she was at first. Just because someone has a hard life doesn't mean they're stupid. Everybody is unlucky in one way or another. Johnny being my father wasn't the luckiest thing, but having Mama as a mother has made up for it.

All of a sudden a creepiness descends, and I want to be home. At fourteen, I'd like to think I'm past needing a mother, but right now I do. Something about the way Melody is acting scares me. I head for the door again, but Melody grabs my arm.

"If you won't go to Kentucky with me, come to the cemetery. I want to introduce you to your grandparents and Ruby and Johnny."

The last place I want to go with Melody Monroe is the cemetery. The moment feels so ominous, I almost expect to hear the organ music they play on the radio mysteries that Granny listens to in the kitchen.

"I need to get home," I say, looking down at her hand on my arm.

"If we go to the cemetery, I bet we'll hear the whispers again," she continues, her fingers digging in a little more. "Don't you want to know what they're saying?"

A shudder climbs my spine. My fledgling secret sense tells me to get out of there, but I'm so surprised it finally showed up, I forget to take action.

"Let's go," Pearl says, grabbing my other arm. Melody finally releases her grip and we rush down the porch steps and run through the forest, as though Melody is chasing us.

When we finally stop at the road, we lean over to catch our breath. As I straighten up, I get that creepy feeling again like I've just walked over somebody's grave. The whispers voice their agreement.

CHAPTER THIRTY

Wildflower

It was Lily who noticed the body at the bottom of the ravine, similar to where I had seen Johnny's body that day many years ago. She had been inconsolable at first, never having seen a dead body. Who wouldn't be? Melody Monroe was dressed in the same clothes she'd worn when she arrived. She'd likely been drinking, the authorities said, and had somehow fallen from the footbridge trying to see the ravine below. But I wondered if she had chosen to jump.

Lily went on and on about how Melody had wanted her to come with her to the cemetery that day, and also about the whispers. About how Melody had heard them, too, and thought they were Johnny trying to talk to Lily from the grave. Perhaps the whispers called Melody home with the rest of the family. For whatever reason, Lily says she hasn't heard them since Melody's body was retrieved.

Three days later Lily, Aunt Sadie and Bee and I attend Melody's service. Mama refuses to go after hearing about Melody trying to get Lily to go to Louisville. The only other person there, besides Preacher Evans, is Doc Lester. It is a small gathering for a funeral. Perhaps only Johnny's was smaller.

I wonder how many will attend my burial rites when the time comes. Daddy's funeral filled the church to overflowing, and I get teary just thinking about it. Sitting in the usual McAllister pew, waiting for the service to begin, I finally understand Aunt Sadie's reasoning. Everybody should have someone to witness the end of their life. No matter how many devils or angels sat on their shoulders during their lifetime.

The ceremony begins and Preacher says his usual things about heavenly rewards and pearly gates. He does little to hide his dislike of Aunt Sadie and me, for not being regular churchgoers, or his continuing desire to get Lily to sing in order to fill his offering plate. I keep thinking about the time Bee saw him in downtown Nashville picking up a lady of the evening, and wonder if anybody is what they seem.

Doc Lester, in the pew opposite us, keeps an eye on me. His letters to Melody's aunt are why we're all here. The ceremony begins and Preacher asks if anyone wants to say something. I doubt he remembers much about Melody Monroe. All of us are quiet. Somehow, there is too much tragedy to make room for words.

Any other time I would expect Lily to sing. Perhaps *Amazing Grace*, the song Miss Mildred played at Ruby's funeral, fifteen years before. The song Lily sang two weeks ago for the anniversary, minutes before Melody Monroe walked up the hill to our house. Had it only been two weeks ago? Somehow it seems longer. I nudge Lily and whisper the suggestion that she sing something, but her lips form a tight line and she refuses.

It is already dark when Bee puts two plates and silverware on her small white kitchen table for us, supper still cooking on the stove.

"It's so tragic about Melody," she says. "I wish I'd said something at the funeral."

"We were all struck speechless," I say. "Some things just don't make sense."

Melody died in the same manner Johnny had, landing only a foot or two away. So close they could have held hands if they'd been there together. I still haven't told Bee about Melody's threat, and hope that Melody's knowledge of the two of us died with her. Yet something tells me it isn't over, and that Bee needs to know.

We stand in Bee's small kitchen, the curtains pulled closed even though there aren't any neighbors for miles. We are used to this. We are used to hiding.

"I need to tell you something," I say.

"Okay," she says, not looking up.

I always fear that Bee will take off again. She can get a job teaching practically anywhere, and has made it clear that the only reason she's still in Katy's Ridge is me.

I hesitate, and Bee turns to look at me. "Before she died, Melody visited the house again and said some things that concern me," I begin. I don't tell her that it was actually several days before that, before we went to the movie. The day I rushed home from the theater and found Lily and Pearl in the bedroom talking. At first I thought I'd rushed home for nothing, until I later learned that Lily and Pearl had been with Melody the same time I got my premonition. In fact, Melody had tried to make Lily go to the cemetery with her that afternoon. The next morning Melody was found dead.

"What did Melody say?" Bee asks.

I pause. Bee touches my hand. "Just spit it out, Lou," she says.

This nickname is only ours, though I call her *Bee,* as does the rest of the world, except for her parents who still call her Becky. What I'm about to tell her won't go over well, but she needs to know. No matter how much my bravery wanes.

Bee leans against the counter. I forget how beautiful she is sometimes. At least beautiful to me. I wonder if there are other women like me and Bee. Just because I've never seen any, doesn't mean they don't exist. Planets exist that I've never seen. Millions of them. Yet, when I look up at the sky, it's hard not to feel alone.

"You're driving me crazy," she says. "Tell me what Melody said that has you all riled." Bee folds her arms at her chest, waiting. I stare at the hands of the gold wristwatch her parents bought her last Christmas, the hands pointing straight up and down to 6 o'clock.

"Melody asked if anybody else knew about me and you," I say.

Bee releases her arms, her eyes flashing a sudden terror, "She asked what? Tell me exactly what she said."

A timer goes off on top of the stove, as if to add further alarm. She turns off a burner, all the while shaking her head like she can't believe what she's just heard. I am too far in to stop now. She turns around again to face me. I wonder briefly if I should hide her suitcase.

"Melody said she knew about us," I begin again, "and that everybody else might find out if she had anything to do with it. Something about the rumor mill starting up."

Worry digs a trench along Bee's brow. "But how would Melody know these things?" She sits at the kitchen table. I sit across from her, and reach for a hand that she doesn't offer. From the smell of supper cooking, I also have other concerns. Bee isn't that great a cook.

"Maybe she was just guessing." Bee looks up at me, a hopeful tone to her voice.

"That's a pretty accurate guess," I say.

She frowns again. "We've been so careful," she says. "Well, except with Lily."

"That was an accident," I say. "Lily never comes to the mill that time of day. She was upset. She had been over at Melody's."

"I can't believe all the trouble that woman has caused," Bee says.

Perhaps it is a good thing that the last of the Monroe family is dead, except for the part that lives in Lily. After Melody was found and I tried to get in touch with her aunt in Kentucky, I learned that the old woman had been dead for years. Melody evidently lived over a bar she worked at until she was fired a few months before for drinking away their profits. No one I talked to was surprised about her death.

"You don't think Lily told her, do you?" Bee's cheeks redden.

"I honestly don't," I say. Not that I haven't given it a thought myself. More than one teenager has complained about their parents to the outside world. "The timing doesn't match up anyway," I continue. "She hadn't seen us yet. Lily saw Melody the morning before she saw us."

Bee stirs another pot on the stove, as if stirring up her concern. My stomach growls, reminding me how hungry I am. At the same time, I don't feel like eating. I'm not sure I can take much more trouble.

"Maybe everything will go back to normal now that Melody is gone," I say. "Let's hope all this trouble died with her." But Bee doesn't look convinced.

"What if people find out?" Bee says. "Lou, I could lose my job. You could lose your customers."

She pours me a glass of tea without ice and no lemon.

"Could be nothing," I say. "Could be she just wanted to scare us."

"Could be she wanted to ruin us, too," Bee says. "Where was she getting this? That's what I want to know."

"I'm just so tired of hiding," I say, taking a sip of tea that could use sugar. "Every time I visit you it's like something out of a radio mystery," I continue. "I stop at the end of your road to make sure nobody's looking and then accelerate to get out of sight quickly, and then duck into your driveway. Not that anyone is even around. If Katy's Ridge had sidewalks, they'd be rolled up by 5 o'clock at night."

I want to laugh at the situation, but can't even muster a smile.

"I'm tired of hiding, too," Bee says. "I've forgotten what normal is like. If I ever knew. I guess if we were normal, we would have married someone years ago and never looked back. At least you had an offer."

When Victor and I dated, it never occurred to me to keep it a secret. In fact, I wanted everyone to see me. It was my proof that I didn't have feelings for Bee. Of course, this wasn't at all fair to Victor.

"Maybe you should have married him," Bee says, as if she's read my thoughts. "Then I would have stayed in Nashville and never would have come back to Katy's Ridge."

"We're not criminals," I say.

"Aren't we?" She motions for me to sit and goes back into the kitchen with our plates, serving us from the stove.

The meatloaf is burned and the color of tire rubber. The mashed potatoes, piled high on the side, have visible lumps. The peas, from a can, have a tiny dab of margarine on the top. While I adore Bee, I am not that fond of her cooking.

She joins me at the table and unfolds a napkin, placing it across her lap. Her family lives in Rocky Bluff and even has a housekeeper. In this way, she is much more sophisticated than me.

When I make a bold cut into the meatloaf, the burnt crust crackles and steam escapes. I move the margarine with the tip of my knife to encourage it to melt. It isn't encouraged. I hide it underneath the peas to avoid eating it. I make sounds like I enjoy the food, even though it is the worst meatloaf I've ever tasted.

She chews the meatloaf and makes a face. "Oh my, this is awful," she says, offering an apologetic look. She retrieves a bottle of ketchup from the refrigerator. We both pour on an ample amount. I chew a lump of mashed potato and wish Bee had a dog. A hungry dog, under the table. I pour on more ketchup.

"Do you think the Sectors told?" Bee asks.

"Never," I say.

"Then who told Melody?" she asks.

"That's the big mystery," I say.

We sit in silence for several seconds.

"Sorry about supper," Bee says.

"It's delicious," I say, convinced a lie isn't always a sin. According to firsts and lasts, if all the cooks were lined up in heaven, Bee would be at the head of the line.

In spite of my need for levity, my secret sense stops me mid-chew.

"What is it?" Bee says.

"I think somebody's here," I whisper.

Bee starts to stand, but I motion for her to stay seated. Butter knife in hand, I creep toward the front door. The porch light is on, and I pull back the curtains to get a look. Another face looks back at me. I scream, and then fling the door open.

"What are you doing here?" I ask.

On his knees, Doc Lester looks up and his weasel eyes accuse me. He is in a perfect position to see through the tiny opening in the front door curtain. He smells like someone who hasn't bathed for a while, his graying hair dirty and slicked back. I can understand now why he's always lived alone. With the two doctors in Rocky Bluff who actually have medical degrees, his kind of quack doctoring is no longer needed.

"I should be asking what *you* are doing here," he says. It takes him a while to stand, as if he's been on his knees for a long time. He is a head taller than me, yet I am not intimidated. He's aged significantly in the last few years.

Bee enters the hallway.

"He was spying on us," I tell her.

"You two are going to burn in the fires of hell," Doc Lester tells us, his eyes wide.

"For eating supper together?" I say, to cool the hellfire.

"That's not all you're doing," he says. His look is sour, as if he's taken a bite of Bee's meatloaf.

"You need to leave," I tell him.

He takes a step back to unleash more hatefulness.

"God will smite you down for this, Wildflower McAllister. I've known you were no-good for years now."

"Keep your smites to yourself," I say, grateful that he isn't a physical danger.

"You won't be saying that when everybody in Katy's Ridge knows about you two." He raises an eyebrow, as if excited by the exchange.

Bee appears frozen in place. Up until a few minutes ago, the biggest problem of the evening was getting supper down.

"You're trespassing," Bee says, finding her voice. "This is my property. You're breaking the law."

"Didn't see no *No Trespassing* signs up anywhere." He sticks his tongue in the side of his cheek like he's pleased to get the better of her.

"What do you want?" I say to him.

The other eyebrow raises, a drop of saliva dots the edge of his lip.

My throat tightens. I always thought Doc Lester was lazy, so it makes no sense that he would go to all this trouble to spy on us out in the middle of nowhere unless he wanted something.

"You want to know what I want?" He pauses. "Let me watch," he says finally, lowering his voice, a crooked smile on his face.

Bee steps forward and shoves him off her steps. "You're disgusting," she says. "Get out of here!" I've never heard such fury in her voice.

Doc Lester laughs and his voice fades when I close the door and bolt it. It is only then that Bee sinks to her knees and begins to cry in deep, gulping sobs.

CHAPTER THIRTY-ONE

Lily

The whispers vanished after I found Melody at the bottom of the ravine that morning. I wondered if my father was somehow satisfied to have his sister finally with him. Or if he'd simply given up on getting through to me. After it happened, Mama barely left my side for three days and took off time from work to talk whenever I needed to talk. I'm not sure how a person makes peace with where they come from. It's not like we have any say in the matter.

While one mystery is finally solved, another has sprung in its place. I have no idea who I am anymore. It's like all my dreams died away with the whispers. I haven't felt like singing for days, and for the first time I've begun to question if leaving Katy's Ridge is my fate. Maybe I am meant to stay right here and marry Crow and have babies and sing in the small choir at the Baptist church. Maybe I've been fooling myself all this time that I'm meant for bigger things.

As a result of the ice storm, school has been called off for the day. Granny has a big fire going in the old wood stove in the living room, and I'm catching up on school work I missed while I attended Melody's funeral. Tiny ice pellets hit the tin roof with a ping that sounds like notes on Granddaddy's banjo that sits in the living room in the same place it was sitting the day he died. Mama dusts it every now and again, and I try to tune it when I have the patience, but it's like all the banjo's songs have dried up like mine.

A light knock on the door startles me. Uncle Daniel takes a wobbly step inside. Tiny ice pellets stick to his hat and coat and he takes them off and hangs them on the pegs next to the door.

"What is it?" I ask. "Is Mama okay?"

Against Granny's better judgment, Mama went into work this morning to do a few things, since she'd spent so much time watching out for me.

"She's okay," he says, "but she sent me to tell you something."

"Why didn't she come and tell me herself?" I ask him.

"She's fielding telephone calls at the sawmill," he says. He looks around like he's looking for Granny. I point to the kitchen. Granny spends most of her time in there with the oven door open to keep things toasty warm.

"Is there a place we can talk in private?" Daniel whispers, keeping an eye on the kitchen.

I lead him to the bedroom I share with Mama and then close the door. Uncle Daniel and I haven't really talked since I ran to get him when I found Melody that morning. I was on my way up to the cemetery to try to find my father's grave when I found an empty jar of moonshine sitting on the railing of the footbridge and cigarette butts twisted into the wood. It was Uncle Daniel who called the sheriff in Rocky Bluff to report Melody's death.

"Tell me what's going on," I say, all of a sudden scared that Mama is in danger.

He sits on the bed next to me, one hand on the cane he always uses.

"Word's got out about her and Bee," he says. "She wanted me to warn you."

His words jolt me to standing. "But who told?" I can only imagine how Mama might feel about this. At Melody's funeral two days ago she looked weary and older than I've ever seen her.

"She thinks it was Doc Lester," Daniel says, rubbing his bad leg like it's acting up on him. "A bunch of people are calling and canceling their accounts. We're losing customers like an artery has burst," he continues. "Wildflower's trying to talk them out of taking their business elsewhere. She's offering discounts and all sorts of bargains, but they're just hanging up on her. Not to mention the names they're calling her. My God, Lily, it's like another war." He rubs his leg again.

"Is she okay?" I ask.

"Not really," he says. "This will probably be the end of the sawmill. Your mama will lose all the money she's put into it. She'll lose her livelihood."

Uncle Daniel drops his head as if a prayer is called for, but maybe he's thinking about wringing necks, too.

"What about you?" I ask, knowing Mama pays him for keeping the books and that he and Jo count on that money.

"We'll be fine," he says. "We've got the farm, and I can always pick up something in Rocky Bluff if I have to. It's your mama I'm worried about, and Bee," he continues. "Mack Avery turned Bee away at the door when she went in to get papers to grade. Told her to pack her bags. To get out of town if she knew what was good for her."

"This all happened this morning?" I ask.

He nods.

"How can people be so mean?" I say.

"Honest to God, Lily, I have no idea. These are supposedly Christian people. At least most of them."

I wonder if I'll ever be asked to sing at the church again, and then feel selfish to think of myself. Truth is, my singing career may be over before it got started.

"Did you know about Mama and Miss Blackstone?" I ask.

"I didn't," he says. "But in a way, I wasn't surprised. Your mama has a lot of love to give, and she would need someone special."

I should have known Uncle Daniel would never abandon Mama, even about something he may not understand.

"Jo's having a hard time with it," he says. "So are Meg and Amy."

I wonder if all my cousins are overhearing what has happened. We made a game sometimes of snooping to hear what the grownups were talking about, and I imagine this is no exception.

"It's more about it being such a surprise," Daniel continues. "Your mother kept this huge secret from her entire family. I hate that she felt like she couldn't confide in anybody."

I remember the talk Mama and I had at the river where she was so honest about her feelings. "I think it's because she's ashamed, Uncle Daniel."

He looks at me like this idea never occurred to him. "Your mama shouldn't be ashamed of anything," he says. "She's the bravest person I've ever known."

"I don't think she feels brave about this," I say.

We exchange looks, and I can see how much he loves her and also how he's scared for her.

"Downright shame," he says.

"What can I do?" I ask. "Should I go over there, Uncle Daniel?"

"Actually, she said she needs you here. She wants you to make sure your granny doesn't hear about it before she can make it home and tell her herself," he says.

"Granny's not going to take this well," I say.

"I don't imagine she will," he says. "But Nell has surprised me before."

He turns and looks at me like he's wondering if it's okay to talk about my no-good father.

"It's okay," I say to him. "I'm getting used to knowing."

"You were brave to want to know the truth," he says. "You're just like your mama in the courage department."

"I don't think I could ever do what she's doing now, Uncle Daniel. How do you talk people into not hating you?"

Until recently, I never realized how strong Mama is. But now I'm realizing how much she's been through, and how she's always been there for me no matter what.

"How long have you known?" Uncle Daniel asks.

"Not long," I say, not mentioning the kiss.

"Did anybody else know before all this happened?"

"The Sectors know," I say. "Mama and Miss Blackstone go over there sometimes."

"Should have known the Sectors would lead the way on how to be decent human beings," he says.

I remember how Crow wants to stay in Katy's Ridge forever. Would he still be interested in me if I didn't sing anymore? He's always said how much he loves my singing.

"Your mama will come home as soon as the phone stops ringing," Uncle Daniel says, pulling me back into the current crisis. "There can't be that many customers left." He rubs his eyes like he's feeling weary, too.

"Maybe you should go get Great Aunt Sadie and bring her over here," I say. "Tell her what's going on. She'll want to support Mama. Granny will listen to her faster than she listens to anybody else. If she's speaking reason, it may go over better."

"Good idea," he says, and stands. "If your mama gets back here before I do, tell her to hold off on telling Nell. Tell her Sadie's on her way."

"I will," I say. "Until then, I'll go spend time with Granny and try to soften her up."

"Good luck," he says, and we walk to the door. "We need to keep an eye on this weather, too," he adds. "Looks like this storm may be a big one."

Before he leaves, he gives me a hug. Because of his height, a hug with Uncle Daniel means a big stretch, even when he meets me halfway.

"Who was that? I heard voices," Granny says, coming out of the kitchen.

"It was Uncle Daniel. He says bad weather might be coming in."

"I wondered about that," she says. "My arthritis is acting up."

I follow her back into the kitchen and offer to help with supper. I imagine Granny as the Thanksgiving turkey that I am supposed to butter up. She can be hard on Mama sometimes, and I can't imagine how this latest news will be taken any different.

Thirty minutes later, Great Aunt Sadie calls from the front porch needing help with getting off her boots. I find her sitting on the porch swing waiting for me to give them a pull. Yesterday the weather was sunny and almost warm. Yet today, the cold wind hits us from every direction.

"How's it going in there?" she asks, as I pull the first boot off revealing a red wool sock.

Great Aunt Sadie is wearing her old fedora and a scarf around her neck and her big coat. Sticking out of one pocket is a bottle of her blackberry spirits. She looks worried, which isn't like her.

"You thinking about Mama?" I ask.

She nods. "Some people get more than their fair share of suffering, and your mama hasn't done one thing to deserve a lick of it."

"I'm glad you're here," I say, tugging at the other boot. After it slides free, I wrap my arms around myself to capture warmth.

"I didn't see your mama's truck. She isn't home yet?"

"Not yet," I say.

"And Nell has no idea?"

"She's too calm to know anything," I say. "Right now she's mainly worried about Mama making it home safe."

"It's not quite freezing yet, but it will be soon. If she comes home within the next thirty minutes or so, I think she'll be okay."

She leaves her winter things just inside the door and we go into the kitchen. Like old friends sometimes do, Granny and Great Aunt Sadie forego greetings, and Granny serves her a cup of coffee she's heated up on the stove.

"How's the weather?" Granny asks.

"It's gearing up for something big," she tells her. Then she pours blackberry spirits in her coffee and offers the same to Granny.

"What's the occasion?" Granny asks her.

"No occasion at all," she says, glancing in my direction.

The three of us sit in the kitchen, the clock over the stove clicking off the seconds as the storm brews and we wait for Mama's return.

CHAPTER THIRTY-TWO

Wildflower

A slushy ice has accumulated on my windshield by the time I leave the mill. The temperature is hovering around freezing. Now if I can just make it home and up the hill before it freezes. It is already dusk. Our hill is almost impossible to climb in ice. Winter has caught me by surprise.

My business is ruined. The only accounts that weren't closed are the Sectors and Sweeney's store. Sweeney's does little business now that the big grocery store in Rocky Bluff opened, and the Sectors use even less lumber. When I anticipated the worst of what might happen if news of Bee and I got out, it wasn't this bad. The biggest surprise was the coldness with which people closed their accounts. They told me that I should be ashamed and that I was going to hell, and that was before the name-calling started. This from people I'd grown up with. People my family had helped through hard times. People who practiced the golden rule, at least on Sundays.

Tears blur into the mess of old windshield wipers brushing away slushy ice. I feel tired down to my bones, but promised Bee I would come by. I pull in front of her house, momentarily grateful that I no longer have to hide my truck behind the biggest hedge. A handmade *No Trespassing* sign is sitting by the front door.

"I was worried about you," she says, meeting me at the door.

To my surprise, Bee appears almost calm. Instead of her usual school clothes, she wears a pair of denim pants and a blouse with a bumblebee stitched onto the collar. It has been a day of surprises. A winter storm is coming, not even predicted in the Farmer's Almanac. I've lost the sawmill. And now Bee, at a time when I imagined she'd be sobbing, is unruffled.

"I'm exhausted," I say.

"How bad is it?" she asks.

"I'm officially out of business."

"Well, I'm officially out of a job," she counters. "It only took Mack Avery until noon to bring all my things from the school. He stood here in the doorway until I gave him the key to the building. I'm not to talk to any students or parents and never step foot on the school grounds again or he's threatened to have me arrested."

"Why don't you look upset?" I ask.

"I cried a river after Mack left here, but now I'm angry."

"I haven't reached anger yet," I say.

We move from the doorway and she takes my coat and hangs it on the coat rack. Bee leads us into the living room, not even closing the drapes. I never realized how much it bothered me that whenever we were alone we were concealing ourselves. The thought of not hiding behind thick curtains feels liberating, but also exposed, like two deer in a large meadow with hunters nearby.

"I've still got to go home and tell Mama," I say. "It's one of the few times I've been glad we don't have a telephone. She won't know yet, unless someone's come to the house. Lily's waiting there for me, and Daniel called the mill to tell me he went to pick up Aunt Sadie and took her to the house. At least I'll have reinforcements."

"How do you think she'll react?" she asks.

"I don't even want to think about it, Bee. But the first thing I'm doing when I get home is hiding her shotgun."

I attempt a laugh. We sit on the couch, and Bee holds my hand in hers. "What do we do now?" she asks.

A mixture of rain and ice begins to hit the picture window.

"I'm not sure," I say. "But I can't stay long. I've got to get home. If it's all right with you, I'll come by as soon as I can get down the hill again and we'll talk it through."

I squeeze her hand to reassure her.

"It must have been Doc Lester who told," she says.

"Who else?" I say.

My legs feel heavy as I go to the door and put on my coat again, so soon after I took it off.

"Good luck telling your mother," Bee says, buttoning the top button of my coat.

"She won't understand this," I say. "Next time you see me I may be looking for a place to live."

"You can always stay here," she says.

"And risk someone burning the place down?" I ask. My mood doesn't allow for a happy ending.

We say our goodbyes and a blast of cold air cuts through my coat as I make my way to the truck. A misty sleet has begun to fall. Chains still in the bed of the truck, I drive slow and pull off onto the side of the road instead of on the slight incline where I usually park. The slush is hardening to a light crunch. Two sets of footprints go up the hill before me, probably Daniel and Aunt Sadie. I hate to think how Daniel's leg must have hurt him as he helped her up the hill. The wind rips across the mountain and the ice is in solid pellets now. I'm glad I thought to put Daddy's old rain slicker over my winter coat. The ice hits it with dull pops.

I make my way home holding onto the branches of trees and bushes to keep me from sliding back down. The last fifteen years have, in some ways, felt like an uphill climb. Lily has helped me have no regrets, the reward of having her in my life has been so great. On my way up the steepest part of the hill, I wonder if telling Mama about Bee will break us apart forever.

When I get in sight of the house, every light is on. I re-member the night when people came to pay their respects af-ter Daddy died. The whole community of Katy's Ridge showed up. Some of the same loving and caring people who called me today and told me they were never doing business with me again because I was now loathsome and disgusting.

On the front porch, I stomp the caked ice from my boots and call on whatever courage I have left for the next obstacle. I leave my boots next to Aunt Sadie's, relieved that she will be with me as I face Mama.

Warm air greets me as I open the door. I am lucky to make it home. Aunt Sadie will probably be spending the night until this storm moves through.

Voices come from the kitchen and then laughter. The laughter is probably Lily's doing. She knows how to tame Mama's lion side. I go into the bedroom and change out of my work clothes. When I catch a quick glance in the mirror, dark circles are underneath my eyes. How is it possible that I look ten years older than I did this morning?

I sigh, wishing I could run away instead of tell Mama the truth. Then I go to her bedroom and take the shotgun from behind her door and slide it under my bed. Not that Mama would actually use it, but why take chances. I take a deep breath, wishing Daddy were here.

It's twice as warm in the kitchen as it is in the rest of the house. Three people I love sit at the kitchen table, dirty supper dishes pushed to the side. Mama stands as I enter, as if her relief at seeing me safe and sound has pulled her tall.

"You made it," she says.

"I made it," I repeat.

"I've got your supper warming in the oven," she says.

Of all the suppers we've had together in this kitchen, I wonder if this will be the last one.

"I'm actually not hungry, Mama," I say.

"Since when are you not hungry?" Mama asks. She hands me a plate full of food anyway.

"Did you have trouble getting up the hill?" Aunt Sadie says. She beams courage in my direction. Tears threaten to come.

Lily stands and puts her arms around my neck. I want to thank her for not hating me and make every effort not to weep. Not every child would be so accepting. It occurs to me that as long as my family doesn't desert me, I can take whatever the rest of the world says.

"Sit down," Mama says. "You want a cup of coffee?"

I nod. It's late, but I am tired enough to sleep tonight even after a dozen cups of coffee.

"Tell us about your day," Mama says.

At that moment, I want to keep her unaware. I can't bear her being disappointed in me like everybody else in Katy's Ridge.

"I have something I need to tell you," I say to her, wishing the strong coffee could give me more backbone.

Mama's face turns from sunlight to dark clouds. "What is it?"

I take a bite of the pork chop on my plate to fortify me, followed by a bite each of mashed potatoes and collard greens. Mama's country cooking could strengthen anyone.

"Something's happened that you need to know about," I say.

"Something bad?" she asks, her eyebrows raised.

"Something bad," I repeat, thinking the only worse news I might deliver would be another death in the family. Although, it's entirely possible that I will be dead to Mama after this, which is kind of the same thing.

Mama's lips tighten. She does not cater to bad news.

Aunt Sadie offers her more blackberry spirits, and Mama brushes the offer away, all the while keeping her eyes on me.

"Nell, it's important to remember that nobody's hurt and nobody's dead," Aunt Sadie says, like she's been reading my thoughts.

"You know what's coming then?" she asks Aunt Sadie, her voice low.

"I do," Aunt Sadie says.

"You know what's coming, too?" Mama turns to Lily.

Lily nods.

"It seems a conspiracy's afoot," Mama says, her look the opposite of pleased. She turns back to me. "Best to pull the bandage off real quick then," she tells me.

I hesitate. The speech I'd practiced on the way up the hill disappears like the dove of a county fair magician.

"Mama—" I falter again.

"You'd best be saying something quick, Louisa May." Her voice is louder and her eyes don't leave mine.

I start talking, unrehearsed, and tell her everything: that Bee and I have been more than friends for years now and that we've been keeping it a secret all this time.

Mama's expression doesn't change.

"Trouble is, the word's got out and everybody in Katy's Ridge knows," I say. "And today Bee got fired from teaching and nearly everybody we had business with at the sawmill has canceled their accounts."

I pause long enough to hope the shotgun isn't loaded that's under my bed that Mama might find if she takes a notion to. "I'm very sorry if you're ashamed of me," I continue, "but I didn't set out to hurt you or anybody else. Not at all."

The clock over the stove is the only sound in the room, as if clicking down the seconds before Mama hits the roof.

Outside, the wind soars down the mountain behind the house and rattles the door and windows. Ice pierces the tin roof. Mama's expression still hasn't changed. Aunt Sadie and Lily seem as puzzled as I am by her silence.

"Are you okay, Nell?" Aunt Sadie asks.

Mama doesn't answer and looks like she's giving serious thought to how to react. Either that or she's having a stroke and unable to tell us.

Lily looks at me, one brow raised with an unasked question.

I give a slight, one shoulder shrug. I expected yelling, maybe even weeping, not silence.

"Mama, did you hear me?" I ask.

Her gray eyes fill with tears. My shoulders drop with the knowledge I've broken my mother's heart.

I tell her how sorry I am, and lower my head.

"It's not the end of the world," Aunt Sadie says to her. "Wildflower's just being the person God meant her to be."

"That's right, Granny," Lily says. "We want Mama to be happy, don't we?"

Tears cling to my eyelids like the ice clinging to the trees outside.

Mama wipes her tears and turns to me with the same fierce, loving look she wore in Daniel and Jo's barn before Lily was born. A look I've wondered if I'd ever see again.

"Louisa May, I knew you two were in love as soon as she came back from Nashville and started teaching in Katy's Ridge again."

I exhale, wondering if I heard her right. Aunt Sadie and I exchange a look that reminds me of when I was in labor with Lily. I remember that last push Aunt Sadie encouraged me to make after the long, twenty-hour ordeal. At the end of all that pain, Lily came into the world with a sudden ease.

"You knew all along?" I ask Mama.

She nods. "Of course it worried me at first. Worried me a lot. I prayed about it every day here in this kitchen, petting that boney cat until I thought his hair might fall out. But I couldn't throw you out, not after all you'd been through. I'm more loyal to my kin than that," she continues. "Then over the years as I watched the two of you together, I didn't see what harm happiness could do. Not to you or to anybody else."

"Why didn't you tell me?" I ask, thinking of all the grief this might have saved me.

"Well, it wasn't really any of my business until you decided to tell me about it," she says. "That day Bee brought over the banana bread, I thought you two might finally tell me then. But off you go, sneaking around and kissing each other at the front door. I know I'm going a little deaf, but do you think I'm blind, too?"

She laughs a short laugh before her expression turns serious again.

"As for you losing all your business, and Bee getting fired from being a school teacher, that disappoints me. I wish you'd been more careful. But country people despise anybody or anything different. When we moved here, your daddy said we'd best be careful who we trusted, that they could turn on a dime. He was right about a lot of things, my Joseph."

"But what will I do to make a living?" I ask her. "What will Bee do?"

"You are smart girls. You'll do what you have to do," Mama says. "Maybe you'll leave Katy's Ridge and find someplace new."

"But won't it be the same everywhere?" Lily asks.

Until now, I haven't realized how quiet she's been.

"What you're always looking for are the pockets of good people," Aunt Sadie says. "There are good people everywhere. There are good people here, too, just not enough to keep the mill open."

Mama swipes a wayward tear and straightens her apron. "This isn't something that can be solved in an evening," she says to me. "Do you want me to heat up your supper again?"

All of a sudden, I am ravenous and tell her so. Mama gets up to warm the food again. I am relieved and exhausted at the same time and unsure of what to do next. Rest is required.

As Mama readies the food, I walk over to the stove where she stands. "I underestimated you," I tell her. She laughs a short laugh.

"About time you realized who you're dealing with," she says.

We embrace for several seconds, longer that we've ever hugged each other before. Mama smells of wood smoke and supper cooking and Jergen's lotion. She smells like herself. Like Mama. If forced to move away, I will miss this smell. I will miss living so close to my family—to my sisters and Daniel and my nieces and nephews. I will miss Aunt Sadie most of all, and the memories here that have Daddy in them. I will even miss visiting that old graveyard. What I won't miss is how frightened people are with their small ways. I won't miss that at all.

It dawns on me, am I really considering leaving Katy's Ridge?

CHAPTER THIRTY-THREE

Lily

The ice storm keeps us at home for two days until it feels like I might go crazy with boredom. Pearl shows up at the house with a message from June to Mama that the roads are mostly clear. Granny makes us hot chocolate and we sit in the living room and talk in whispers. Pearl tells me about the latest boy she's decided she has a crush on—which feels almost as boring as being stuck in the house for two days—and I tell her about Granny surprising us all by not throwing a fit about Mama and Bee.

Mama has been quiet during our time at home, as though doing major thinking. No more has been said about what she might do after the sawmill closes for good.

Right as Pearl leaves, Uncle Daniel comes up the hill to take Great Aunt Sadie back to her house now that the roads are clear. Mama and Uncle Daniel talk in hushed tones before he leaves.

"I need to talk to Bee," Mama says, a few minutes later. "You want to come?"

Thrilled by the thought of getting out of the house, I agree.

Patches of ice remain in the shade and on the north sides of hills, but the path and the road are clear. At the road, we see several cars over at Uncle Daniel's.

"Looks like somebody's called a meeting I don't know about," Mama says.

It is unusual for her sisters to get together without inviting Mama, but part of the reason may be that they all have telephones and Granny doesn't.

"We need to go over there," Mama says to me. "I haven't talked to them since all hell broke loose. You okay with that?"

I tell her I am.

When we go over to Aunt Jo's, we find Aunt Meg and Aunt Amy there, too, along with all of my cousins. You'd think Aunt Jo was having Thanksgiving at her house this year. The room falls silent when we come through the back door. Within seconds, the cousins and me are shooed out of the house, but I refuse to go. Luckily, nobody forces me to.

Nat is ushered out by Bolt and gives me a look that asks what's going on. Meanwhile, Lizzy takes a second to make sure she smirks at me. It is only Janie who appears to know what's going on and for once the dull sheen on her face has color to it.

I realize how little I've seen my cousins in the last few weeks. The last time being at the anniversary of Granddaddy's death. That was the day Melody Monroe showed up and my whole life changed. All of a sudden, I had an aunt I never knew existed, and a mama with a secret she hoped no one ever found out about. Like country folks, who Granny says can turn on a dime, my life turned on a dime. One day it was nothing new, the next it was full of unexpected trouble. The biggest surprise, however, is playing out in front of me as my aunts and uncles gang up on Mama.

"You disgraced us," Uncle Cecil says to Mama, his voice raised. "Now we're all in danger of losing our jobs."

I can't imagine how Mama could disgrace anybody.

"Did you not think about how this might affect us?" he says.

In Jo and Daniel's living room, Mama stands in the middle of all of them, while I stand next to the wall that leads to the kitchen. She looks tiny compared to everyone else, like the runt of a litter. I wonder why I never noticed that before. Uncle Cecil, especially, towers over her. He's never been one of my favorite people, and now he's proving why.

"I can understand why you might be upset," Mama says. "But I didn't plan for any of this."

"Well, you must have known it might get out," Aunt Amy says, the first of her sisters to speak. The others chime in their agreement.

Aunt Jo isn't looking at Mama and has her arms folded across her chest like she's trying to hold herself together and not say anything. Uncle Daniel isn't back from taking Great Aunt Sadie home, or I imagine he would step up in defense of Mama. Perhaps that's why they've started without him.

Aunt Meg looks away, as though she's feeling guilty. Uncle Cecil is leading the dissension and the angrier he gets, the redder his strawberry birth mark. Then everybody starts talking at once with Mama just standing there watching them like she's having a bad dream. A minute or so later Uncle Daniel walks into the living room and asks what's going on. He steps in next to Mama and tells everybody to quiet down.

"Is this how you treat family?" Uncle Daniel asks the others, raising his voice, too.

"What about how she's treated us?" Aunt Jo says.

Uncle Daniel shoots her a look I've never seen him give her, like she should be ashamed. "Wildflower is family," he begins again. "And I, for one, don't turn on my family. If our family turns on us, who do we have?"

I think of what Granny said, along the same lines, when she found out about Mama and Miss Blackstone.

Uncle Cecil scoffs. "This is ridiculous," he says.

"What if we all disagreed with something you did, Cecil?" Uncle Daniel says.

"Well, I'd never do anything to put this family in danger," he says.

At that moment, I want to slap Russia right off his face.

"Just so you know," Daniel continues, "Nell has known all along and she sees nothing wrong with it."

The reaction is of stirring bees in a hive. It takes a few minutes for everybody to settle down again. Meanwhile, Mama stands in the middle of the living room like the wary queen, though I don't think anybody recognizes her nobility besides me.

"It's just caught us all unawares," Aunt Jo says to Mama. "It's hard to stand by somebody when you're the last to know something. Makes me feel like I've been shut out. I can't believe you told Mama before you told us."

I wonder how Aunt Jo knows this and then realize Pearl must have gone straight across the road to tell everybody what I shared with her this morning.

Everybody looks at Mama, including me, waiting on her to defend herself about telling Granny. Pearl's going to need to defend herself, too, next time I see her. Her secret-telling is a part of this hornet's nest.

"If the Sectors knew all along, why not tell us, too?" Aunt Meg asks.

The hive gets stirred again.

"Settle down," Uncle Daniel yells over the buzz.

Everybody does.

"Wildflower needs to think about what loyalty means," Aunt Jo says. "She let us get blindsided by all this."

"Everybody in Katy's Ridge knew before I did," Aunt Amy says. "One of my customers in Rocky Bluff asked me if the rumors were true and I had to say 'What rumors?'" She looks straight at Mama. They have never been the closest of siblings and at that moment the gap widens. "I've never been so embarrassed in my life," Aunt Amy concludes.

Meanwhile, Lizzy spies through the front window and gives me a look of total glee that Mama is in trouble. When I turn back to look, the color has left Mama's face. She needs rescuing fast, and even Uncle Daniel has been unable to control how everyone is acting. Maybe if I sang one of Granddaddy's favorite songs, like *Down in the Valley*, that would get everyone's attention. Mama says my singing calms anyone who listens, and calmness is what is needed. But when I open my mouth there's no song there. I momentarily panic. I've never had music abandon me like this, and somehow this feels more alarming than what's happening between Mama and our family.

"We can talk about this later, whenever you want," Mama announces. "But right now I have somewhere I need to be." Then she motions for me to follow her and we leave Uncle Daniel's house. She has a speed to her step that she seldom has. I even have to run to catch up. I don't have to ask where we're going.

Within minutes, Mama knocks on Miss Blackstone's door. She opens it with a cautious smile. I imagine we are unexpected, in an expected kind of way, in that we were bound to

show up eventually. We take off our coats and Miss Blackstone leads us into the living room where packing boxes are
stacked.

"You going somewhere?" Mama asks her.

"Got to find work," she says, in a matter-of-fact way.

"Were you going to tell me?" Mama asks, her eyes wild
and full of instant tears.

They sit on a light green sofa together, and I sit in an arm-
chair to the side with soft cushions that are the same light
green. Though I'm sitting still, Mama's tears make me want to
squirm out the door. She tells Miss Blackstone what just happened at Uncle Daniel and Aunt Jo's. When she hears the
story, the tenderness on Miss Blackstone's face makes me look
away. But I am relieved that Mama has someone to rely on
besides me.

A clock ticks on the fireplace mantle. A table with a lamp
sits nearby with a few neatly stacked books. For some reason,
I imagined Miss Blackstone read textbooks, not poetry and
novels. Sometimes, I wish Miss Blackstone was still my
teacher. It's because of her that I graduated elementary school
a year early. My high school English teacher doesn't take an
interest in me the way she did. But now I wonder if Miss
Blackstone's interest was because of Mama and not me.

The north facing road that stretches between Katy's Ridge
and Rocky Bluff stays icy longer than the main roads, so I
won't be expected to return to school for another day or two.

I am a sophomore this year and wonder if the gossip will reach the high school by the time I return.

"We'll figure this out," Miss Blackstone tells Mama, when her tears finally slow to a stop.

"Lily, can you give us a minute?" Miss Blackstone asks.

I stand and look around. I have no idea where to go or what to do to give them a minute.

"Maybe you could put the kettle on the stove so we can have some hot tea," she says. "You can close the kitchen door if you want."

When I call her Miss Blackstone, she says to call her Bee, but I don't see that happening any time soon, if at all. I walk into the kitchen and find the empty tea kettle already sitting on the stove. I fill it with water and turn on the electric stove eye with a simple click. Granny's old one uses gas and we have to light it with matches. I wish Granny could see this one. It looks brand new. Not that she sees any use in new things when the old ones still work.

The voices from the living room are muffled, but Mama still sounds upset. I busy myself with looking through the cabinets for teacups and saucers and set out three sets. I remember Melody Monroe offering me tea in the tiny cabin. A civilized thing to do in such poor surroundings. I find a box of Lipton tea bags and drop a tea bag into each cup.

After a while the tea kettle rattles and then sings and I turn it off, realizing the voices in the living room are now quiet.

Moments later, the kitchen door opens and Mama and Miss Blackstone come inside.

"We need to talk to you," Mama says. Her tears have passed, but her eyes are still red.

Miss Blackstone pours hot water in the teacups and covers each with a saucer. She tells me I did a good job putting the kettle on, and I am surprised by how much this means to me. It is strange to touch her things and see her and Mama together now that I know about them. But it is a strangeness that I am willing to get used to. Miss Blackstone brings a chair from her bedroom to put at the end of the table that only seats two people.

"Join us," she says.

We doctor our tea with sugar and milk, me imitating Miss Blackstone's motions. Then it is Mama who starts talking.

"How would you feel about moving to Nashville?" she asks me.

I stop stirring my tea. Have I misheard? I look at them and wonder if this is what it's like to be thunderstruck. How is it that just when I decide to stay in Katy's Ridge and possibly settle down with Crow, I am presented with the one thing I've dreamed about for years?

When I don't answer, Mama repeats her question, and I wonder if I've lost my speaking voice, as well as my singing. Nashville is an hour and a half away, almost in the center of the state. It's the capital of Tennessee. Compared to the tiny hamlet of Katy's Ridge, it's the entire Roman Empire.

"I lived in Nashville for a couple of years and already know some people there," Miss Blackstone says.

"That's where the Grand Ole Opry is, too," Mama says, in case I've lost my mind and don't remember.

Granny listens to the Opry every Saturday night. I listen, too, whenever there are female singers on like Kitty Wells or Mother Maybelle Carter and the Carter Sisters. Granny says I sing as well as they do, but grandmothers are supposed to say things like that.

"Lily, are you okay?" Mama asks, her expression serious.

"I don't know what to say," I answer, which is the truth.

A look passes between Mama and Miss Blackstone. "I thought you'd be overjoyed," Mama says. "I've known you wanted to leave Katy's Ridge ever since you started keeping a road atlas under the mattress."

Miss Blackstone laughs and asks, "Is that true?"

Mama says it is. But I don't feel like joining in their laughter. How do I tell Mama that all my dreams have died and been buried along with the knowledge that I am the daughter of a snake? Someone who didn't give her a choice. How do I tell her that if the world were a better place, I wouldn't even be here? No wonder I haven't felt like singing for weeks. For all I know I may have lost my voice forever. Someone like me doesn't belong in front of an audience, singing all over the world. I deserve much smaller things. I deserve to stay here with all the ghosts.

Mama tries to act excited about the possible move, but I can tell this is hard for her. She probably thought she'd be staying in Katy's Ridge the rest of her life. I was the one who was going to fly the nest as soon as I figured out how to grow wings.

"Can I think about it?" I say. It surprises me that I've not already packed my suitcase. It evidently surprises Mama, too.

"Of course," Mama says.

They exchange another look. Miss Blackstone's forehead crinkles like it does whenever she gets worried. I wonder if Mama's told her that she won't go anywhere unless I agree.

"There's a university in Nashville, too," she says to me. "You are more than smart enough to attend Vanderbilt. You could major in music there."

Just hearing the word *music* is like hearing the name of someone I used to love who has now died. It would make more sense to wear black and sit in the cemetery. Maybe I will start having an anniversary this time every year, too. I think of Granny and Great Aunt Sadie and all the aunts and uncles and cousins we would leave behind if we moved to Nashville. But after what happened today, where my aunts and Uncle Cecil ganged up on Mama, I'm not so sure I'd miss them.

CHAPTER THIRTY-FOUR

Wildflower
Six Months Later

We stand outside a large church in downtown Nashville. Desperate to find a soloist when their usual one got the flu, Lily has been asked to sing. A woman Bee works with lined it up for her, taking Bee's word for it that Lily was an amazing singer. It is a fancy church. Rumor has it that people in the music industry go here. It is across town from where we're living, in a rich area. My old truck looks out of place in the parking lot, and I hope they don't tow it off.

"Are you nervous?" I ask Lily, feeling my own butterflies bumping against each other in my stomach.

"More nervous than I've ever been in my life," Lily says. "This isn't Katy's Ridge," she adds with a swallow.

"No it isn't," I say. "But this is good, Lil. This is meant to be."

She looks at me like I'm about to throw her into a lion's den. She hasn't sung in front of anyone in over six months. Bee and I have worried over this for at least that long. Our hope is that this solo will help Lily remember who she is and what she has to offer the world. It is a huge risk to take, but we fear that the longer she goes without singing, the easier it will be for her to forget.

We enter the immense foyer. Worshipers straighten themselves and tidy their children before walking into the sanctuary and finding seats. Being Easter, the church is packed with people. Family after family—the men and boys in suits and ties on this hot spring day, and the girls and women in store-bought dresses, hats and gloves—file past us. I look down at my simple dress, no hat or gloves. Although Bee did go out behind our small apartment building this morning and find a wildflower that she pinned to my dress.

Lily is to enter with the minister and the choir who create a procession down the center aisle. I've never been in a church building this big in my entire life. Our church in Katy's Ridge could practically fit inside this single entryway.

"What if nothing comes out?" she says, her eyes wide.

This is our fear, of course. The thing Bee and I have discussed many times. We've agreed that if we need to, we'll simply walk up front to wherever Lily is standing and each take her by the hand and walk out of the church, heads high.

"You'll be fine," I say, reassuring her. "You've done this hundreds of times. Just pretend you're standing on the front porch of Mama's house, singing to your family."

I straighten the small bow on the front of her dress. A dress Amy made special for the occasion, now that we're finally speaking to each other again. The fabric matches Lily's rosy cheeks and she looks grown up, a proper young woman. She's wearing the gold medallion I gave her that she found one afternoon while we were packing. A side pocket on her dress reveals a letter tucked inside.

"Is that from Crow?" I ask.

She forgets her nerves and smiles. "He gets military leave again in a few months and he wants to stop in Nashville before going home." Her pleasure contains hints of sadness.

All of us have been homesick to one degree or another. I, for one, never dreamed how difficult it might be to leave Katy's Ridge. For months now I've missed everything about it. Not only Mama and Aunt Sadie and my sisters and Daniel, but also the way the mountains burst with spring every year. The light green of new leaves and blossoms walking up the hillside like an old woman sowing seeds. I miss the quietness there, the bustle of squirrels instead of traffic. I miss visiting Daddy's grave and sitting underneath the old willow tree and telling him about my life. I miss how the wind sounds when it plays in the trees. I even miss old Pumpkin, who Mama told us in her last letter, is of failing health. I don't know what she'll do when Pumpkin dies, now that she's living in that old house alone. Yet Aunt Sadie has been sticking close and they are working on a new quilt.

Crow's letters to Lily arrive faithfully once a week, and I'm convinced they've helped Lily with the move. Pearl sends letters, too, but infrequent ones. Their friendship has waned, and I wonder if the people we grow up with ever stay best friends for life.

"Where's Bee?" Lily asks.

"She's saving me a seat near the front," I say.

Lily and Bee have become good friends over the last six months. Bee got a job at the high school Lily attends and they ride in together. My job is quite different from the sawmill and has taken some time to get used to. As a secretary in the admissions office at Vanderbilt University, I have to dress up every day. No more boots and overalls. It took weeks to get used to wearing even short heels. But at least it's close enough that I can walk to work when the weather is good.

I have not made peace with churches. Even ones as large and beautiful as this. Nor have I made peace with God or God's people. It has been hard to forget the names I was called when people found out about me and Bee, evidence of their less than Christ-like natures.

The choir gathers wearing purple choir robes—thirty people at least—along with a choir director and a young organist who proceeds down the side aisle alone so he can play as the choir enters. Lily is singing during the offertory, when the collection plates are passed.

Why do all churches smell alike? Is it the hymnals? A universal cleaning product only sold to churches, mixed in with old lady perfume dabbed on a little too freely?

Lily grabs my arm, her fear renewed. "Mama, I can't do this," she whispers.

Her grip makes me wince. I take Lily's hands in mine and look into her eyes. "Remember that first time you sang in church in Katy's Ridge when you were nine years old?"

She nods.

"Remember how easy it was to sing nearly every Sunday after that?"

She nods again.

"Well, you're on the same path, just a little farther along. Someday, *this* place will feel small."

"Are you trying to scare me more?" she asks.

"You're going to be fine," I tell her.

She pauses, like she wants to believe me, but isn't quite sure. "I miss it, you know. I miss Katy's Ridge. I never thought I would." Her eyes mist.

"I miss it, too, honey," I say. "You can't live somewhere your whole life and not miss it."

"I'm so glad Granny and Great Aunt Sadie are coming for Easter supper," Lily says. "I wish the others could come, too."

"They'll visit another time," I say.

Daniel and Jo are to bring Aunt Sadie and Mama up from Katy's Ridge this afternoon. They will see our small two-bedroom apartment for the first time. Evidently Meg and Amy weren't up for the trip, though they were invited. There's still mending to do with my sisters. Amy made Lily's dress, but things have been strained for months. Meg has been distant, too, which isn't like her. She says it is Cecil who is having a hard time with me and Bee and that he doesn't want Janie exposed to the likes of us. To me, odd Janie could only benefit from knowing that people can be different.

"I wish they were all coming to hear me sing," Lily says. "Like they used to at home." She bites her lip.

"I wish they were, too," I say, "but Mama wanted to go to Easter service in Katy's Ridge, so she could stare down the people who said hateful things to me."

Lily smiles. Mama writes as faithfully as Crow and her letters are full of her advice. A small price to pay after she surprised me with her acceptance of Bee and me. Aunt Sadie told me once that Daddy would have never married Mama if he hadn't seen something special in her. It has taken me years to see that specialness.

The organist begins playing the introduction to the first hymn and the congregation stands. Lily shoots me a look of sheer terror. My butterflies lurch on her behalf. She looks toward the door and I wonder for a second if she's going to take off running. But then she looks at me with a determination I haven't seen from her in a while.

"I'll be fine," she tells me. She stands straighter and clears her throat. She hums a few notes, the first I've heard out of her mouth in months.

"I guess I'd better go to my seat," I say. "You okay?"

She nods, and I believe her.

As the first stanza is sung, I walk down the side aisle looking for Bee's familiar yellow hat, a bumble bee stitched on the side. I find her on the second row and scoot in next to her, taking my half of the hymnal. She points to the verse, but I have no interest in singing. She leans close to my ear.

"Lily okay?"

I give a hopeful shrug.

It is hot for April and all the windows in the church are open to let in the breeze. Programs are used as paper fans and are already going limp. Strangers surround us. Other women note what we're wearing. I imagine they think Bee and I are two single friends going to church together, trying to attract the eyes of a man. People see what they want to see.

After we finish the hymn, there are several scripture readings and then the sermon begins. My mind wanders. The lesson rambles like a stream down a mountain, gravity pulling it toward a certain conclusion. From an open window, I view a squirrel playing in a pruned dogwood tree in the courtyard, along with a male and female cardinal, the red vivid against the white dogwood blossoms. Tennessee is the most beautiful place on earth when the dogwoods bloom in April. I remember the gnarled dogwood—wild, instead of tamed like this one—that marks the beginning of the trail to the old cemetery.

As the warm breeze scoots through the window next to me, I close my eyes and picture the weeping willow in the graveyard dropping leaves onto Daddy's grave. I send him greetings—Air Mail—floating on my thoughts. I imagine the church service going on down the hill from his final resting place. So much history is there. My history.

In my imagination, Mama sits in her usual pew, wearing one of her better old dresses, with the hat she wears on special Sundays. A purple ribbon around the brim in honor of Easter. No matter how many times Amy has offered to make Mama brand new dresses for holidays, she insists on wearing the old ones. I remember the faded dress Melody wore the day she showed up in Katy's Ridge. She was wearing the same dress the day she died. I imagine her at peace in the old cemetery, talking with her family, maybe even conversing with Daddy from time to time.

I picture Daniel and Jo sitting next to Mama, Bolt and Nat in the pew behind, along with Lizzy looking grumpy as usual, and Janie blending into the beige wood of the pew. Next to Jo will be Amy, and then Meg and Cecil, and then the rest of the pew will be empty, where Lily and I might normally sit. An ache rises from deep inside my chest. A broken place that hasn't healed, from having to leave the mountain home I know and love.

I want to squeeze Bee's hand and get her support, but we would never risk it in public. In proper society, even friends don't touch unless there is good reason. I don't understand this world we live in, or the suffering that goes on in the midst of family, friends and strangers alike, with no one acknowledging the pain. It seems we are beasts of burden with blinders on, urged ahead by an unseen driver. I refuse to believe that God is the one who is driving us. This wouldn't make any sense.

During the prayer following the sermon, I take a deep breath and Bee glances at me, her eyes asking if I'm okay. I don't know how to tell her that at that moment I am so homesick I might burst into tears that flood the sanctuary. Her shoe touches mine, a secret signal that she's here for me. It is Easter, and I am in need of a resurrection. A coming back to life in this new place. Perhaps God can spare one not only for Jesus but for me, too. For all of us who are tired of having blinders on.

The sermon has ended and the offering begins, Lily's time to sing. I am so nervous for her, I have to remind myself to breathe. She rises from her seat next to the choir and steps up to the front. A piano begins to play, and I think of Miss Mildred at the Katy's Ridge Church, approaching eighty and still playing. Her bad notes have increased over the years and now she is losing her eyesight, so sometimes the congregation can't even recognize the hymn. But that is not the case in this church. It sounds like an angel is playing, each note perfect.

Lily wipes her hands on her dress. She will be fifteen this summer. It is hard to believe I have a child this old. Sometimes I still feel fifteen myself, instead of twenty-eight, and sometimes I feel fifty.

When she was hours old, I held Lily in my arms and fell in love with this helpless creature that had come through me. Now that she is in front of this crowd, without knowing if her voice will betray her or not, I feel like I might faint from fear. The hardest thing any parent does is watch their child step out into life, not knowing if they will experience painful stumbles or great accomplishments. I don't know how she'll react if she does poorly. The move from Katy's Ridge has made her more cautious. Occasionally she asks a question about Johnny, and I realize that she's still grappling with the knowledge of how she came into this world.

The intro plays, and I wonder if my heart can take it. Will her voice be there? Will the song insist on being sung? It is a song I haven't heard her sing before. It is a gospel song. *His Eye is on the Sparrow.*

When Lily begins to sing her voice is soft at first and shakes as if announcing her nerves. *Why should I be discouraged?* the song begins, but she quickly gains control. By the refrain of the first verse, her voice is steady and strong and soars toward the rafters. More than one person gasps.

Bee and I exchange smiles. Our gamble, of whether or not to let Lily sing, has worked. As the melody builds, Lily's tone becomes as clear as a mountain stream that flows through the Appalachians. Her nervousness falls away and she looks out over the congregation as if to sing the song to every single person.

Goosebumps rise on my arms and Bee pulls a handker-chief from her purse and wipes her eyes. We've been through a lot together in the last few months. It started last fall with the anniversary of Daddy's death and the arrival of Melody Monroe. Up until then, I never dreamed I'd leave Katy's Ridge or that the sawmill would be boarded up and closed once and for all. Easter is about Jesus lying in the tomb, waiting for three days, before being restored to life. In a way, this transi-tion has been about waiting. Waiting to feel at home again.

All of a sudden, the sun pours through the window, mak-ing the walls look gilded. I wonder if the gold Mary has de-cided to join us. Tears blur the scene. Fourteen years ago she came to me. A gold woman in the trees, surrounded by light, reaching to take my hand, Daddy standing next to her. That day, I thought I was going to die and that she and Daddy had come to take me to where they were. I felt at peace to be go-ing, and then sad when I realized it wasn't my time.

As Lily continues to sing, I become aware of how motion-less everyone is. Enraptured. They haven't taken their eyes from her. Even their makeshift fans have stopped beating the breeze. Lily comes to the last verse leading to the final chorus. Whatever nerves she had before, are completely gone. I have never heard her sing better. I imagine Daddy in the graveyard, listening to his granddaughter on this Easter morning.

The song soars to its conclusion:

I sing because I'm happy, the song says. *I sing because I'm free. His eye is on the sparrow....*

In a moment of what I can only call grace, my heartache releases. I take my first deep breath in years. Maybe ever. A cool breeze makes its way into the warm church, as though arriving special delivery from Katy's Ridge. My chest expands, and I clasp Bee's hand.

At that moment, I feel free. Free to release Lily into her own life where her music will always be with her. Free from the past that has often kept me prisoner. Free to start over somewhere fresh. A new life delivered on the wings of Lily's song.

Thank you for reading!

Dear Reader,

I hope you enjoyed *Lily's Song*. As I say in the acknowledgments, I wrote it for all those readers who loved *The Secret Sense of Wildflower* and asked to hear more of the story.

Since it had been years since I'd worked on *The Secret Sense of Wildflower* (fourteen years since I wrote the first draft; four years since it was published), I had to read it again and take notes on characters, dates and details in order to write *Lily's Song*. But then once I sat to write it, the story started playing out in my imagination very naturally, as if I'd never left Katy's Ridge. I felt like I knew Lily personally, even though I'd never imagined her before. She was Wildflower's daughter, after all, and I had loved Wildflower for years, as well as her family. So it felt, in a way, like a family reunion, where I got to catch up with everybody I hadn't seen for a while.

With *Lily's Song*, I tried to create the best story I could offer you. I also wanted it to encourage you to sing your own song, in whatever way that might mean. It doesn't matter where you come from or what's in your past, we all have something good to give the world.

As an author, I love to hear from readers. To me, as the story travels from writer to reader and then back again, it is like completing a circle. You are the reason I write. So feel free to tell me what you liked, what you loved, even what you wish I'd done differently.

You can write me at susan@susangabriel.com or message me on my Facebook author page: www.facebook.com/Susan GabrielAuthor.

Finally, I want to ask a favor. If you are so inclined, please consider leaving a review of *Lily's Song* on Amazon, Goodreads, Nook, iTunes, Kobo or elsewhere. Reviews help other readers take a chance on a book or an author they may not be familiar with. A review doesn't have to be long or "literary." Just two or three heartfelt sentences is enough.

Thanks so much for reading *Lily's Song* and for spending time with me.

In gratitude,
Susan Gabriel

P.S. I'm now working on Book Three of the Wildflower series (Books One and Two—*The Secret Sense of Wildflower* and *Lily's Song*—are already out). I will also be writing a sequel to my comic novel, *Temple Secrets*. If you would like to be notified about these and other future books, please sign up for my newsletter at https://www.susangabriel.com/new-books/

Acknowledgments

A special thank you to the treasured readers who told me through emails or reviews that they loved *The Secret Sense of Wildflower* and were sorry when the book ended. They wanted to hear more of Wildflower's story and more about the McAllister family and Katy's Ridge. I listened, and thought of them often as I wrote *Lily's Song*.

Also, my heartfelt thanks to my entrusted first readers who proofread, corrected my grammar, fact checked and offered the occasional story suggestion. They brought different strengths and sensibilities to the task and were each a gem. In alphabetical order they are: Anne Alexander, Susan Burnside, Deb Klingender, Krista Lunsford, Linda S. Moore and Tarra Thomas. They were an insightful and powerful team. I am very grateful for their input.

Also my gratitude to the members of my early review team, Gabriel's Angels. I thank them for their honest reviews, support for my writing and help getting the word out about my new books.

Finally, to Wildflower and Lily. Though they are fictional, they feel as real to me as family members. I thank them for allowing me to write their story. It has been an honor.

P.S.

Insights, Interview & Book Club Discussion Questions

About the author
– Meet Susan Gabriel

About the book

Frequently Asked Questions
– Answered by the author, Susan Gabriel

Book Club Discussion Questions

Other Books by Susan Gabriel

About the author

Susan Gabriel is an acclaimed southern writer who lives in the mountains of Western North Carolina. Her novels, *The Secret Sense of Wildflower* (a Kirkus Reviews Best Book of 2012) and *Temple Secrets* (2015) are Amazon and Nook #1 bestsellers.

She is also the author of *Trueluck Summer, Grace, Grits and Ghosts: Southern Short Stories* and other novels. Find out more about Susan and her books at SusanGabriel.com.

Frequently Asked Questions

Answered by the author

1. Have you always wanted to write?

Actually, as a little girl I wanted to be Sally Field in *The Flying Nun*. I thought catching a wind current with the help of my nun hat and flying around the countryside would be the ultimate of coolness. A few years later I thought making people laugh would be better than flying, so I would sneak down to the den to watch Joan Rivers on *The Johnny Carson Show*, the volume so low on the television that I had to put my ear against the speaker to hear.

Then I got a little more realistic and set my sights on becoming a professional golfer. Needless to say, my golfing career never got off the ground, either, not even with a good tailwind. I did, however, write funny things in high school that made my friends laugh, yet it never occurred to me to be a writer.

Never the one to dream of having a traditional career, I majored in music in college and became a professional flutist for a time, but that was never enough to live on. After that, I got sensible and taught elementary school (special needs kids) before traipsing off to graduate school to become a psycho-therapist. A career I was drawn to, in part, I think, in order to understand the quirky southern characters in my gene pool. It was in graduate school that I excelled in writing case studies—think of it as character development—and the writer in me woke up from a deep sleep. I was in my late 30s when that happened. So I have always considered myself a late bloomer.

2. Where do you write? Do you have a writing schedule?

My best writing seems to occur when I am in the company of dogs. My two beautiful mutts and I tend to follow the seasons, seeking out sun in winter and the shade in summer. With this is mind, I have different places around the house where I sit and write. In the summer, I sometimes write outside on my back porch. Right now, it's February and cold here in the mountains of North Carolina, so I am writing from the family room, the sunniest part of the house. I also have a home office.

I write on a laptop, unless I am revising a manuscript, then I print it out and make changes by hand. Something about holding the pages makes a story seem more real to me.

My most creative time to write is in the mornings, from around 9 o'clock to 12:30. In the afternoons I go about the "business" of writing. I answer emails from readers and other writers, post on my Facebook author page, type in revisions or write a blog post. I work five days a week and take the weekends off. Writing is my livelihood, so I have never suffered from writer's block. I also consider writing my calling. It helps me get up in the morning to know that I have readers awaiting my next story.

3. Are your novels autobiographical?

I think everything we write is autobiographical in one way or another. As a writer, the things I notice are things that are unique to me. Anyone who has read more than one of my novels knows I have a style and a way of seeing the world that can be recognized. The landscapes I write about, the places I set my stories, are all places I've been. The emotions expressed by my characters are all emotions I've had myself. While the story and characters are imagined, they are as real as fiction can be, so there are always elements of me in my books.

I told another southern writer in an email recently:

Most of my fiction that takes place in the South is about strong women. Courageous women. Women who are lost and then find their way home again. Perhaps I keep writing my own story, trying to create a map in my fiction that might show me and others a way to get free. A kind of Underground Railroad of fiction, except the route is to the south instead of the north.

4. What are your favorite things about being a writer?

My most favorite thing about being a writer is the actual writing, the using of my creativity and imagination every day.

After two decades of doing this thing that I love, it's still hard for me to believe that I create stories for a living. It sounds like somebody else's life, not mine. But I am very grateful for the opportunity, and grateful that enough readers like what I'm doing and buy my books that I can keep moving through the seasons.

The creative process is fascinating to me. Even on the days I'm not writing, I carry around in my mind whatever story I'm working on. Characters walk around in my imagination and sometimes I'll even hear them talking and see the story playing out and have to take notes so it doesn't get away. Sometimes the characters even show up in my dreams at night. When I talk about this process during a writing class or when I visit a book club that is reading one of my books, I usually make a joke about how writing is one of the only careers where you can hear voices and the people in white coats don't come looking for you!

My second favorite thing about writing is hearing from readers. It is incredibly rewarding to get an email or see a review from a reader who expresses how much a story has meant to them. It really makes the struggle of getting books out into the world worth it.

5. Why do you often write about secrets in your books?

I write about things that intrigue me, and secrets intrigue me. Death intrigues me, too, as well as spirits and ghosts, and mysteries of any kind. Like the alchemists of old, I am constantly trying to transform base metals (ordinary life) into gold (an extraordinary story or experience for the reader).

We all have secrets, whether we realize it or not. We keep a lot of secrets from ourselves. Sometimes the biggest secret we keep from ourselves is our greatness, our creativity, or how worthy we are.

Decades ago, when I read *The Secret Garden* by Frances Hodgson Burnett, I loved the concept of having a secret place to go to where you could get away from all the scary and hard things of life. A place with nature all around, which after much hard work transforms into something beautiful. I just love that metaphor. Not all secrets are positive, of course, some can destroy us. But I think secrets, if dealt with respectfully, can be transformative.

Also, in terms of storytelling, secrets create tension, as they do in real life. Tension and conflict is what keeps readers turning the pages. I love it when readers tell me they read a book straight through the night and couldn't put it down. I'm sorry that those readers lost sleep, but it tells me that I've written a compelling story.

6. Where do you get your ideas?

At this point, my imagination is primed to tell stories, so I'm very lucky. In fact, I feel like I have characters waiting in a long line down my street to get their stories told. Mainly, I try to not get overwhelmed by all the ideas I have and the backlog of novels I have at different stages of completion. This is what happens if you write five days a week for over a decade.

I love stories in general, and I read a lot of fiction. I also watch a lot of films. I don't use outlines for my books. I am what is called in the biz an intuitive writer. I may have a sense of what I want to write about, but I rarely know where I'm going. Basically, a story plays out in my imagination like I'm watching a movie, and I write down what I see. I'm very visual, and it's very in the moment. I think that's why I enjoy writing in first person, present tense. It's like I get to be an actor, embodying the characters and telling their stories. In a way, I guess I finally got to be Sally Field, after all, catching the latest current in my imagination. Crazy fun!

––––––––––

Do you have any questions that you'd like to ask me about my writing process or about any of my stories? If so, feel free to email me and your question may be included in the Frequently Asked Questions of my next book.

Book Club Discussion Questions

1. If you were Wildflower, would you have kept from Lily the secret of who her father was, or would you have done something different? Explain.

2. How well do you think Lily handles the truth? What might you have done in her shoes?

3. What role do you think secrets play in families and small communities? Do they affect how people communicate and interact with each other? Do you think they are avoidable?

4. In the book, Wildflower says, "Christians can be some of the worst people there are for judgment." Do you think there is any truth to this? Why might she feel this way?

5. What do you think Melody Monroe was ultimately searching for when she returned to Katy's Ridge?

6. What things surprised you in the novel?

7. Did Wildflower's secret make sense in the novel? Why do you think so many people didn't understand?

8. Who were your favorite characters in the McAllister family? Have you known families like this one?

9. Why do you think Lily lost her voice in those months after she found out the truth of who her father was?

10. Discuss the role of redemption in the story.

Other books by Susan Gabriel

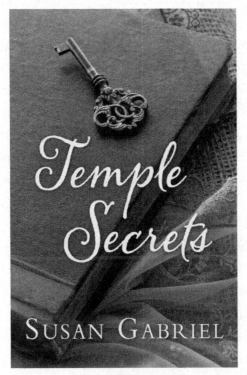

Temple Secrets
A novel

Fans of *The Help* and *Midnight in the Garden of Good and Evil* will delight in this comic novel of family secrets by acclaimed writer, Susan Gabriel.

Every family has secrets, but the elite Temple family of Savannah has more than most. To maintain their influence, they've also been documenting the indiscretions of other prestigious southern families, dating as far back as the Civil War. When someone begins leaking these tantalizing tidbits to the newspaper, the entire city of Savannah, Georgia is rocking with secrets.

The current keeper of the secrets and matriarch of the Temple clan is Iris, a woman of unpredictable gastrointestinal illnesses and an extra streak of meanness that even the ghosts in the Temple mansion avoid. When Iris unexpectedly dies, the consequences are far flung and significant, not only to her family—who get in line to inherit the historic family mansion—but to Savannah itself.

At the heart of the story is Old Sally, an expert in Gullah folk magic, who some suspect cast a voodoo curse on Iris. At 100 years of age, Old Sally keeps a wise eye over the whole boisterous business of secrets and the settling of Iris's estate.

In the Temple family, nothing is as it seems, and everyone has a secret.

Available in paperback, ebook and audiobook.

Praise for *Temple Secrets*

"Temple Secrets is a page-turner of a story that goes deeper than most on the subjects of equality, courage and dignity. There were five or six characters to love and a few to loathe. Gabriel draws Queenie, Violet, Spud and Rose precisely, with a narrative dexterity that is amazingly and perfectly sparse while achieving an impact of fullness and depth. Their interactions with the outside world and one another are priceless moments of hilarious asides, well-aimed snipes and a plethora of sarcasms. What happens when the inevitable inequities come about amongst the Haves, the Have Nots and the Damn-Right-I-Will-Have? When some people have far too much time, wealth and power and not enough humanness and courage? Oh, the answers Gabriel provides are as delicious as Violet's peach turnovers, and twice as addicting! I highly recommend this novel." – T.T. Thomas

"Susan Gabriel shines once again in this fascinating tale of a family's struggle to break free from their past. Filled with secrets, betrayals, and tragedy, the author weaves an intricate storyline that will keep you hooked." – R. Krug

"I loved this book! I literally couldn't put it down. The characters are fabulous and the story line has plenty of twists and turns making it a great read. I was born and raised in the south so I have an affinity for stories that are steeped in the southern culture. Temple Secrets nails it. All I needed was a glass of sweet tea to go with it." – Carol Clay

"The setting is rich and sensuous, and the secrets kept me reading with avid interest until most of them were revealed. I read the book in just a few days because I really didn't want to put it down. It is filled with characters who are funny, tragic, unpredictable and nuanced, and I must admit that I really came to know and love some of them by the end of the story." – Nancy Richards

"I was glued from the first moment that I began reading. The book accurately portrays many of the attitudes of the Old South including the intricate secrets and "skeletons in the closet" that people often wish to deny. Each character is fascinating and I loved watching each one evolve as the story unfolded. This was one of those books that I did not want to finish as it was so much fun to be involved in the action." – Lisa Patty

"I just finished reading Temple Secrets today and I truly hated for it to end! Susan Gabriel writes with such warmth and humor, and this book is certainly no exception. I loved getting to know the characters and the story was full of humor and suspense." – Carolyn Tenn

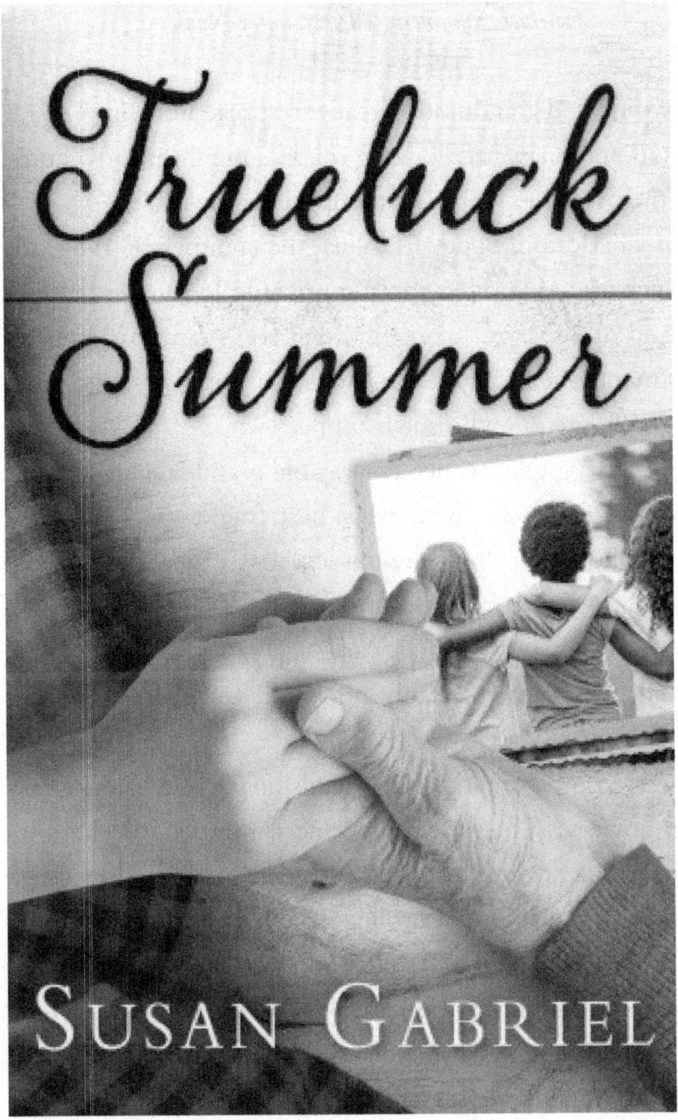
Trueluck Summer
Susan Gabriel

Trueluck Summer: A Lowcountry Novel

A widowed grandmother ready to spread her wings. A 12-year-old granddaughter looking for a summertime adventure. Together, they are going to attempt the impossible.

In Charleston, South Carolina, the summer of 1964, Ida Trueluck moves into her son's house after losing her beloved husband of 40 years. Living with her son's family is quite an adjustment—her daughter-in-law is a bit uptight—and she's trying to figure out who she is on her own.

Her saving grace is her 12-year-old granddaughter Trudy. Smart and feisty, Trudy and her best friend Vel—short for Velvet, who wears all pink and is a Nancy Drew wannabee—are trying to figure out what to do on their summer vacation. When a black boy named Paris saves Trudy from being crushed by a runaway Sunbeam Bread truck, they become friends.

Navigating a multi-racial friendship in 1964 is no easy thing, however. The racism they encounter inspires them on an audacious adventure: to take down the Confederate flag that flies atop the South Carolina State House. And they can't do it without the help of Trudy's grandmother, Ida.

If you like funny, heart-warming southern stories, you'll love the unforgettable characters in this captivating novel about the courage friends and family inspire in each other and the risks and rewards of trying to make the world a better place.

"A quietly powerful story, at times harrowing,
but ultimately a joy to read."

- Kirkus Reviews, starred review
(for books of remarkable merit)

Named to Kirkus Reviews' Best Books of 2012.

Set in 1940s Appalachia, *The Secret Sense of Wildflower* tells the story of Louisa May "Wildflower" McAllister whose life has been shaped around the recent death of her beloved father in a sawmill accident. While her mother hardens in her grief, Wildflower and her three sisters must cope with their loss themselves, as well as with the demands of daily survival. Despite these hardships, Wildflower has a resilience that is forged with humor, a love of the land, and an endless supply of questions to God. When Johnny Monroe, the town's teenage ne'er-do-well, sets his sights on Wildflower, she must draw on the strength of her relations, both living and dead, to deal with his threat.

With prose as lush and colorful as the American South, *The Secret Sense of Wildflower* is a powerful and poignant southern novel, brimming with energy and angst, humor and hope.

Praise for *The Secret Sense of Wildflower*

"Louisa May immerses us in her world with astute observations and wonderfully turned phrases, with nary a cliché to be found. She could be an adolescent Scout Finch, had Scout's father died unexpectedly and her life taken a bad turn...By necessity, Louisa May grows up quickly, but by her secret sense, she also understands forgiveness. A quietly powerful story, at times harrowing but ultimately a joy to read."
– Kirkus Reviews

"A soulful narrative to keep the reader emotionally charged and invested. *The Secret Sense of Wildflower* is eloquent and moving tale chock-filled with themes of inner strength, family and love." – Maya Fleischmann, indiereader.com

"I've never read a story as dramatically understated that sings so powerfully and honestly about the sense of life that stands in tribute to bravery as Susan Gabriel's, *The Secret Sense of Wildflower*...When fiction sings, we must applaud."
– T. T. Thomas, author of *A Delicate Refusal*

"The story is powerful, very powerful. Excellent visuals, good drama. I raced to get to the conclusion...but didn't really want to read the last few pages because then it would be over! I look forward to Gabriel's next offering." – Nancy Purcell, Author

"Just finished this with tears streaming down my face. Beautifully written with memorable characters who show resilience in the face of tragedy. I couldn't put this down and will seek Susan Gabriel's other works. This is truly one of the best books I've read in a very long time." – A.C.

"An interesting story enhanced by great writing, this book was a page turner. It captures life in the Tennessee mountains truthfully but not harshly. I would recommend this book to anyone who enjoys historical fiction." – E. Jones

"I don't even know how to tell you what I love about this book —— the incredible narrator? The heartbreaking and inspiring storyline? The messages about hope, wisdom, family and strength? All of those!! Everything about it!" – K. Peck

"Lovely, soul stirring novel. I absolutely could not put it down! Beautifully descriptive, evocative story told in the voice of Wildflower, a young girl of the mountains, set in a wild yet beautiful 1940's mountain town, holds you captive from the start. I had to wait to write my review, as I was crying too hard to see!" – V.C.

"This writer is fantastic. The story is authentic and gripping. Her voice through the child, Wildflower, is captivating. This story would make a great movie.   I love stories that portray life changing tragedy and pain coupled with power of the human spirit to survive and continue to love and forgive. Bravo! Susan. Please write more and more." –Judi D.

"This is a wonderful story that will make you laugh, cry, and cheer." –T.B. Markinson

"I was pretty blown away by how good this book is. I didn't read it with any expectations, hadn't heard anything about it really, so when I read it, I realized from page one that it is a well written, powerful book." – Quixotic Magpie

"If you liked Little Women or if you love historical fiction and coming-of-age novels, this is the book for you. Definitely add The Secret Sense of Wildflower to your TBR pile; you won't regret it." – PandaReads

"Bottom line: A great story about a strong character!" – Meg, A Bookish Affair

Also by Susan Gabriel

Fiction

The Secret Sense of Wildflower
(a Kirkus Reviews Best Book of 2012)

Temple Secrets

Trueluck Summer

Grace, Grits & Ghosts: Southern Short Stories

Seeking Sara Summers

Circle of the Ancestors

Quentin & the Cave Boy

Nonfiction

Fearless Writing for Women:
Extreme Encouragement & Writing Inspiration

Available at all booksellers
in print, ebook and audio formats.

CPSIA information can be obtained
at www.ICGtesting.com
Printed in the USA
BVOW03s0930270717

R8062600001B/R80626PG489703BVX1B/1/P